"Eleanor Sullivan has constructed a medical mystery that rings with authenticity, and a spunky, likable, interesting nurse-protagonist to do her crime-solving for her. May we see much more of Monika Everhardt!

However, this is NOT a book you want to read before going in for a hospital stay. . . . but if you must go to a hospital, my advice is to stay the heck away from St. Teresa's!"

Aaron Elkins

"Eleanor Sullivan is one author who writes what she knows, using her career in nursing as a backdrop for her mysteries. So it's no wonder that DEADLY DIVERSION crackles with authenticity. Death in the ICU may be part of the job for her protagonist, Monika Everhardt, but it's a different case entirely when the diagnosis is murder."

Susan McBride, author of BLUE BLOOD

DEADLY DIVERSION

Eleanor Sullivan

Published by

P.O. Box 3358
Frederick, Maryland 21705-3358

First Edition

ISBN 1-59133-076-9

Designed by HILLIARD HARRIS

Cover Illustration © S. A. Reilly
Release date: September 1, 2004
Manufactured/Printed in the United States of America
2004

To Karen W., who always believed.

Acknowledgements

Many people contributed to this book, generously sharing their time, knowledge, and expertise. I am truly grateful for their assistance.

Elaine Level, RN, BSN, a highly-skilled intensive care nurse, explained complicated procedures understandably and offered creative story ideas. Susan Klingerman, RN, added specific nursing details. Leonard Naeger, PhD, from the St. Louis College of Pharmacy, provided the germ of the story and clarified technical details. Roger Jackman, MD, freely shared his medical knowledge. Fran Buehler told me details known only to native South St. Louisans. Charlene Hill at the Joint Commission on Accreditation of Healthcare Organizations, Liz Cardwell at the Missouri State Board of Nursing, John Schmidt at United American Nurses, and Leonard Perez at the National Labor Relations Board all contributed specialized information. Commander Jack Titone, Homicide Division (retired), Sergeant Dick Buehler, both with the St. Louis City Police Department, and Officer Jeff Chellis of the Creve Coeur Police Department helped with many details of investigation. Along with Officer Chellis, Corporal Jeff Myer and Officer Kent Barry of Town and Country Police Department offered the Citizens Police Academy course and gave me an opportunity to experience real-life police work. If there are any errors of fact in spite of the contributions of these experts, the fault is mine.

My supporters in Sisters in Crime include Shirley Kennett, Eileen Dreyer, Susan McBride, Nancy Pickard, Carolyn Hart, Lee Harris, and Mary Dolan. I thank you all.

Colleen Daly again edited my work with patience and fortitude. Stephanie and Shawn Reilly at Hilliard & Harris continue to be enthusiastic and professional in publishing and promoting my work. Finally, a special thank you to LeClair Bissell, MD, for the title.

Eleanor Sullivan

Three may keep a secret, if two of them are dead.
Benjamin Franklin

Three may keep a secret, if two of them are dead.
Benjamin Franklin

Prologue

THE LOUD SPEAKER WOKE HIM. It was happening again, another one was trying to die. They'd left the curtain open because it was night time and they thought all the patients were asleep. But not him. With the first sound, his training had kicked in, propelling him awake, alert.

After a few minutes he knew something was wrong. The nurse was competent, that he could tell from the swift, sure movements. But it was all going down too quickly. Much, much too quickly. Each task required specific steps in exactly the correct order. Otherwise, the mission could go wrong and someone could get hurt or die. He'd learned that long ago.

He knew who the patient was because the family had been in and out for the past few days and he had recognized them. But he'd kept quiet, concealing his presence.

Now he lay quietly and watched. He was good at that. And listened. He was good at that, too.

Chapter 1

Wednesday, 08 August, 0645 Hours

"GUARDINO'S GONE." Bart said, giving me a quick glance.

"Gone? Where?"

"Dead," Bart replied, continuing to write in the chart in front of him.

I sat down hard, rattling the chair back. "What happened?"

Bart shrugged. An experienced critical care nurse, Bart had moved to St. Louis to study anesthesia in graduate school and had started work at St. Teresa's Hospital six months ago. He'd wanted to work nights so he could go to school during the day. Few nurses wanted the night shift so I was glad to give it to him.

"Where's his chart?"

"Why?" Bart asked, turning to face me.

"I want to know what happened."

"As soon as I finish." Bart shifted his attention back to the chart.

"Where's the body?" I asked, looking around for a gurney from the morgue.

"I sent it on down," he said, writing as he spoke. "I wanted to get it out of here before everyone arrived."

"So what happened?"

"Here. See for yourself." He closed up the chart and tossed it onto the counter in front of me. It landed with a clatter.

"The chart's supposed to go with him," I said, opening it up.

I had started out at St. Teresa's straight out of nursing school more than twenty years earlier, working on medical-surgical floors until I'd been able to get my clinical legs under me, then I'd transferred to intensive care where the rush of adrenaline fed my need for excitement. Head nurse—now called patient care manager—for the last five years, I found the job becoming more and more difficult as managed care squeezed ever-increasing dollars out of our budget, and the nursing shortage meant each shift was a gamble.

"I'll take it down when I leave." Bart stretched his arms above his head, muscles rippling under his green scrub suit top. He closed the fat textbook that lay on the counter and stacked a yellow legal pad covered with notes on top of it.

"No surprise, I guess," I said.

Mr. Guardino had come in three days before, unconscious from a stroke. Since he'd arrived his body had been shutting down, one organ system after another, in spite of our best efforts to keep him alive.

"My god!"

"What?" Bart asked, wadding up some scraps of paper. He tossed them toward the trash can under the counter. They fell short.

"You didn't intubate him? Or shock him?"

"He was a B code, wasn't he?" Bart asked, referring to the A, B, C system of coding we'd recently adopted to designate what should be done in case of a cardiac or respiratory arrest.

"No! The family was emphatic—full resuscitation. He was an A."

An A code required that everything medically possible be done to resuscitate the patient. B codes, generally used for patients unlikely to survive, specified limited resuscitation efforts; and with a C code, previously designated as a "do not resuscitate" order, no resuscitation would be attempted.

"It wouldn't have helped anyway," Bart said. "He couldn't have been revived, no matter what the code was."

Determination of the appropriate code was based on the patient's condition and likelihood of recovery as well as his or her previously-stated wishes and the family's desires at the time. It wasn't a perfect system, by any means. Such life-and-death decisions are difficult even if they are discussed ahead of time, but under the stress of a critical illness families and staff alike find themselves torn between wanting to keep the person alive and accepting the futility of trying. And seldom do all those involved agree.

I wiped my hand across my face. "You didn't know that. I've seen them come back from. . . . Anyway, it was your job to know which code to use and to follow it."

"Do you know how much care he required?" Bart asked, going on without waiting for my reply. "The constant juggling act it took to keep all those drips going? Keep his pressure up, they say, we've got to save what viable brain he has, they say, but not too high, they say, or he might stroke out." He flung his arms outward and heaved a sigh.

"I know all that—"

"You don't know the half of it, Monika. Do you know how many meds he was on? Antibiotics, muscle relaxants, a beta blocker—that was for the heart damage from the defibrillator they used in the ER to restart his heart—and more." He rubbed the stubble on his chin. "And me here in charge alone on nights. It's all we can do to keep up with the ones who are recovering. as understaffed as we are." Bart stood and reached for his lab coat draped across the counter. "I did the best I could. No one can ask for more than that." He swung the lab coat over his shoulder and started toward the door.

"I've got to write you up for this." I reached for the incident report forms in the drawer.

He turned toward me, and I caught a flicker of anger. Just as quickly it was gone.

I stared at the form. Damn. This was the last thing I wanted to do—write up a competent nurse of whom I had far too few.

"Listen," he said, coming back. "Are you really going to screw things up for me over some old man who was dying anyway?"

"Policy, Bart. And the law. It's not your decision." I looked back down at the form in front of me.

He dropped his book on the counter and leaned over me on the desk, fingers splayed. Wisps of blond hair curled on the backs of his hands. "I need this paycheck 'til I finish grad school," he said, "and you're not going to mess me up!"

Two nurses on the day shift came through the door.

"You keep quiet," Bart said, then he picked up his book and papers and left the unit.

Ruby banged through the swinging doors carrying an insulated lunch bag. "What's he in such a hurry for?" she asked, tossing a bulky red-white-and-blue cardigan over one chair and arranging herself in another. A ward clerk since before I had come to St. T's, Ruby kept tabs on everything. And everyone. "Whose is that?" she asked, pointing to the chart in front of me.

"Guardino's. He's dead." I took in a deep breath and let it out slowly, looking up at the ceiling.

"Hey, you ain't that upset over him, are you?"

I shook my head as much to clear it as to tell her no.

"What's it doing up here? And where's the body?" Ruby asked, glancing toward Guardino's room.

"Bart was going to take it down—"

"Here. Gimme," Ruby said. "I'll take it down to the morgue."

I handed her the chart. "Just don't go visiting all your friends on the way."

"Hey, I ain't got no friends in the morgue." She chuckled. "No, sir, I don't want nothing to do with the dead ones," she added, clutching the chart to her chest. "I know some folks. That's how I find out stuff. And you don't seem to mind knowing what I find out, neither," she added with a flip of her top-knot as she marched out the door.

Mr. Guardino had not had any hopes of recovery; that much was clear. Undoubtedly we had just been keeping him alive until his heart stopped and he couldn't be revived, or until the family agreed to let him die. His death had been imminent, regardless of what code was assigned to him; Bart was right about that.

I'd have to report Bart to my boss, chief nurse Judyth Lancelot, and see what she wanted to do. Although I only saw him briefly in the morning at change of shift, Bart hadn't seemed to have any problems adjusting to our unit. With the hospital's accreditation on warning, I doubted Judyth would want to fire him over this incident. We had received strong recommendations to improve in several areas, but our top mandate was to increase the number of nursing staff. We were dangerously understaffed, and with the current shortage of nurses in the St. Louis area and our less-than-competitive salaries, we were struggling to find new hires.

"Safety is the issue here," one surveyor had said during her accreditation visit. I had to agree. And the team was due back any day, a surprise visit intended to catch us doing the right thing. On top of that, a small group of nurses was threatening to unionize if staffing didn't improve.

A new nurses' aide, who had just started on Monday, came out of a patient's room. "Where are the blankets?" she asked me, popping gum.

"There should be some in the room. If not, there's more in the storage closet out in the hall."

"He's already got three but he wants another one," she said, turning toward the door.

"Wait. Who needs a blanket?" I asked.

"He does." She waved toward the room she'd just left. "Says he's, like, cold."

Jessie came out of the med room. "Who's cold?" she asked, setting her tray of syringes and medicine cups on the counter. A small frown creased her forehead and her good eye looked at me, the other into the distance.

"Kleinfeldt."

"Oh, my god, he's got blood hanging." She hurried toward the room. "Call the blood bank," she yelled over her shoulder.

Serena, currently a student at a local nursing school, came up to the desk. "What's happening?" she asked me with alarm in her voice. Serena had worked as a student assistant in ICU part-time during the school year and now was working full time for us through the summer.

Waiting on the phone for the blood bank to answer, I quizzed her. "Tell me, what's his complaining of being cold mean?"

Serena ran her fingers through her spiked hair, a brilliant red this week. "Uh . . . reaction! He's having a reaction to the blood."

Jessie came out of the patient's room carrying a nearly full bag of blood and holding the tubing up so it wouldn't drip. "Yet another mistake," she said, keeping her voice low. The blood bank was short-staffed, too.

"What happens now?" Serena asked me.

"It depends on the mistake. They might have made an error in typing or cross-matching his blood, or maybe they issued the wrong product."

"You mean packed red blood cells instead of whole blood?" Serena asked.

"Exactly. They'll send someone up to draw another blood to type and cross match again and recheck the order. I hope they get it right this time."

Jessie came back and I asked her to do the code-cart check.

"Didn't you and Bart do it?"

"He got away before we did," I replied.

"Oh?"

I shook my head and she went to do it. Jessie was one of several experienced nurses in the intensive care unit I could count on to do a good job no matter how busy we were.

Part of the change-of-shift routine required that the charge nurse going off and the one coming on check that the code cart was stocked with supplies, that the defibrillator was charging and delivering a charge, and report to pharmacy if the medication drawer needed restocking. Bart and I had also neglected to sign off on the narcotics, which were supposed to be counted and recorded at the change of each shift. These were serious infractions of the rules, but I had too much to do now to think about it.

I had just finished checking the day's roster of staff against patients' conditions to see how much care they required when the doors swung open, crashing against a linen cart that had been left there.

DEADLY DIVERSION

"Who killed my pop?" screamed Mr. Guardino's son.

Chapter 2

Wednesday, 08 August, 0750 Hours

Joe rushed toward his father's room and grabbed the curtain screening the bed, jerking it loose from the rod. "Where is he?" Joe screamed, flinging the torn curtain aside. "What have you done with Pop?"

Guardino's older son, Charlie, tried to put an arm around his brother's shoulders, but Joe shook him off. "He was real sick, Joe. We all knew it."

"He moved his finger yesterday. I saw it, he did!" Joe said, choking on a sob. A hefty young man about thirty, Joe had been in nearly constant attendance at his father's bedside the past week. "He was getting better until they. . . ." He waved his arm toward us. ". . . didn't take care of him. He was just an old man to them. But he was my pop," he wailed. "And they're gonna pay."

Joe lunged toward Serena, who stumbled trying to get out of his way, and he swung around, hitting his brother in the face. Blood spurted from Charlie's nose as he reached for Joe's arm, but Joe shook him off.

Charlie held his hand to his nose as I motioned for Jessie to help Charlie, waved Serena behind the desk out of the way, and nodded to a lab tech, who was already calling security. I hurried around the desk toward Joe.

He whirled around at my approach. "You! You killed him!" he screamed, lunging for me.

I backed up quickly. "Joe! Get a hold of yourself! You're in a hospital!" I yelled, keeping my eye on him as he jerked his head back and forth, looking for another target.

"Joe," Charlie said, his voice muffled by the blood-soaked towel someone had tossed him. "Stop it." He pulled the towel away. "Calm down," Charlie sputtered, coughing on the blood that splashed down his chin. Jessie reached out to help him but Charlie waved her off, flinging the bloody towel at his brother.

The towel hit Joe's face and a streak of red splashed across his cheek. Jaws clamped and arms held away from his sides in a body-builder pose, Joe balanced on his feet, clenching and unclenching his fists. Then he threw back his head and began to roar from someplace deep in his chest.

Two security guards banged through the doors behind me. One grabbed Charlie, pinning his arms behind him. Blood spurted from Charlie's nose again, and the other guard jumped back from it. He yelled into his radio that they needed backup.

Tim, coming in the door from the stat lab, dropped his tray of specimens on the counter and joined the second guard and me just as Joe advanced toward us. Joe's right arm shot out, hitting Tim in the face. Tim doubled over as Joe's other arm swung wildly. The guard and I both ducked but I raised my head a moment too soon. Joe swung back around and connected solidly with the side of my head. I staggered back and slammed up against a door frame.

Suddenly there were more guards behind us and out of the corner of my eye I caught the blue uniform of a city police officer. Joe raised his arms and emitted one last animal-sounding bellow as guards and police surrounded him. His head hit the floor with a crack, and handcuffs clicked shut on his wrists. He was jerked to a standing position.

His eyes unfocused, he stumbled toward the doors, held upright between the guards. His brother was telling him to keep quiet as they were led out. Joe didn't seem in any shape to talk anyway.

My knees felt rubbery but I turned to check on Tim as he leaned against the linen cart. Sweat stood out on his forehead, and the color had drained from his face, leaving a saucer-sized red blotch on his cheek ending just above his eyebrow.

"You're going to ER and get that X-rayed," I told him.

He mumbled something about patients.

"Now."

I told Serena to go with him.

I ran my hand through my hair and yelped as I touched a knot on my scalp.

"You better get an X-ray, too," Jessie said, tucking a strand of gray hair back into her bun.

"Nah. It's nothing," I assured her. She shrugged and passed me the bottle of ibuprophren we kept on the desk for the not-infrequent headaches, backaches and other assorted aches that plague overworked and overstressed nurses.

I shook my head, intending to tell her I didn't need it, but pain shot through my skull, convincing me otherwise. I dumped out a couple of tablets and went out to the drinking fountain in the hall.

Jake Lord stepped off the elevator as I raised up. Jake was our staff physician, intensivists they're called now, doctors who specialize in intensive care. One of the first African-American physicians on our staff, Jake sometimes suffered from patients' and staff's distrust but overcame their prejudices with competent, compassionate care.

I told him about what had happened with the Guardino sons and then, my voice lowered, I explained about Bart doing a limited resuscitation on the man.

He shook his head. "No matter how bad it is, some family member always thinks the patient's going to recover, and then they blame us when he doesn't."

"Maybe we ought to do a post," I suggested. "To make sure the cause of death really was a stroke."

"Probably a good idea," Lord agreed.

"Will you talk to the family? I will if you don't want to."

"I'll call them. They can't attack me over the phone," he added, holding the door for me. "What are you going to do about Bart?" he asked.

"Report him to Judyth. Then, I don't know. We sure can't afford to lose any more nurses right now."

EVERYONE WAS CALMER than I expected. Ruby, back from the morgue, was complaining about how unsafe it was to work here and telling everyone we should get hazard-duty pay. Her son had recently joined the Army and she had started using military expressions. She'd have a soon-to-be-exaggerated story to tell her cronies throughout the hospital, the subculture of people who support the work of any large institution and who know more about what is happening than those who are supposedly in charge.

I needed to report Bart's behavior to my boss, but first I needed to see to our patients, see if any had been upset by the disturbance. Most of them were either comatose or so sick that they were unaware of what had happened. I reassured the few who were conscious that everything was all right now. Fortunately it had been too early for visitors.

"Good, you're here," Huey Castle said, taking a breath through the cannula that pumped oxygen to his scarred lungs. Huey had just returned from X-ray and had missed the fight. He gave me his winning smile—yellow, jagged teeth staining his grin. He took another shallow breath and slid his face into a frown. "It hurts, Monika. Bad." He scrunched up his face. "It's a ten."

Pain had become the fifth vital sign—along with blood pressure, temperature, pulse, and respiration—we were now required to check routinely. Patients are asked to rate their pain on a scale from one to ten with ten being the worst they could imagine and one, the least. Huey's pain was always a ten.

"Yeah, yeah." I checked his IV and O_2. Both running fine. "You're full of it, you know, Huey. You've been conning people for so long you wouldn't know the truth if it hit you."

Huey was a 56-year-old Vietnam veteran whose stomach cancer had spread. A victim of emphysema as well, he had been hospitalized for more than two weeks following an episode when he'd complained of not being able to breathe. The ambulance brought him to us—we were the closest—and then he'd been too sick to move to the VA hospital. This wasn't his first time with us, but it would be his last.

"I've gone straight," he said, waving the curved hook he used in place of an arm in my direction.

"Why don't you put that thing on?" I asked him. "Instead of just playing with it."

He smiled again, pain apparently forgotten. "They like it," he said, nodding toward the door. "I like to scare 'em with it. Pull it out like this."

I stepped back as he stuck the pincers in my face.

"That thing's dangerous, Huey. Put it on or put it away."

"Okay, okay. You don't have to get sore." He put the prosthesis on his bedside table. He waved his left hand in the air; rings flashing on every finger. "Now I'm the one-arm bandit," he said, repeating the same joke he'd been telling everyone since he arrived. Huey loved the casinos, he'd told us, especially the slot machines.

I pulled the blood pressure cuff out of its holder on the wall and slipped it around his arm.

"Hey," he said, watching my face. "I hear Guardino's dead."

I pumped up the pressure and slowly let it out, watching the numbers slide by. "You did, eh?" Huey's pressure was 160 over 90. High but not too high. His complaint of severe pain was probably exaggerated.

"You can tell me, Monika, I knowed him from the old days."

"You knew him?"

"Just from the neighborhood. St. Ambrose parish."

The Italian neighborhood in South St. Louis.

"How about some more drugs?" he asked.

"I want to talk to you about something."

"Then I get some drugs?"

"I need to ask you about what you want us to do if you aren't able to decide," I said, ignoring his question.

"What'd ya mean, 'aren't able to decide?' Why couldn't I decide? And what kind of things?" His eyes narrowed. "What'd ya want to do to me anyway? Use my body for research?" He laughed. "It's some body, ain't it?"

Huey's body was shriveled, the skin hung in uneven bunches on his upper torso, a tattoo of a naked woman rippled his upper arm when he moved, and he had the deathly pallor of a patient whose cancer had metastasized.

I pulled up a chair and sat down next to him. People need to be led into this gently, but I had hurried, thinking about all I had to do. I took a breath and started again. "If you're unconscious, we need to know how much effort you want us to make to bring you back to consciousness."

He frowned. "I want everything. What'd ya think? You should let me die?"

"Huey, your prognosis is pretty bleak. Most people in your situation just don't want to be kept alive if they're unconscious, hooked up to machines. . . ." I motioned toward the equipment surrounding the head of his bed.

He didn't say anything so I went on. "There are several choices. You can tell me exactly what you want us to do. You can decide if you want to be resuscitated even if there's little hope of getting better. You can decide if you want to be fed through a tube. Or fluids in the IV. It's your choice, Huey, but you need to make it now while you can think rationally about it."

I released the advance directive form from the clipboard I had placed on his bedside table and handed it to him. "Just read it over and let me know if you have any questions. Take your time and think about it. We don't want to rush you. I just want you to think clearly about it."

He shoved the paper back to me. "They asked me about this when I got here. I told them I don't need to think about anything." He shifted on the bed, one knee bobbed up and down under the sheet. "You just keep me alive. You make sure that if I stop breathing," he said, wiping his hand across his forehead, "that you revive me. I'm not ready to die!"

"Okay, okay. I understand. You'll be resuscitated, don't worry." I clamped the form back on my board.

"I told Mavis . . . if you don't. . . ." He struggled for a breath.

"We will, Huey, I promise we will." I gave his nearly-full IV bag a last glance and tucked his sheet around him.

"Or she should sue you," he said.

I waved off his threat and was nearly out the door when he added, "Not like Guardino."

I turned back. "What do you mean?"

"Let's put it this way." He took another breath. "That family ain't the kind to sue."

Chapter 3

WEDNESDAY, 08 AUGUST, 0920 HOURS

BACK FROM X-RAY, Tim stood at the counter reading a chart. The side of his face puffed out over the cheekbone, and a bruise was just beginning to darken under his eye. A cowlick at his hairline had pushed up a tuft of damp brown hair. Tim held himself steady, using slow, careful movements as if he were afraid he might jar something loose.

"No fractures?" I asked him.

"Just sore." He reached up and touched his face gingerly. "Nothing broken."

"Are you sure you're okay? Maybe you should take a sick day."

"And leave you here as short as we are? How's he doing?" he asked, glancing toward Huey's room.

"I don't get it, Tim. Jessie gave him 25 milligrams of morphine IV push and he says it didn't help. We should be worrying about being able to arouse him with that much in him. No matter how much we give him, he still complains. And with the accreditation folks coming back soon, we can't have a patient saying his pain is as bad as it can get."

"Why?" Serena asked, joining us at the counter. Her flame-colored hair stood up, giving her a permanently surprised expression in spite of her earnestness.

"Because our goal is to have everyone at level four or below," I told her. "They look to see if we're making our goal and mark us off anytime we're not close to it."

"And Huey'd be quick to tell them, too," Tim added.

I turned to Serena. "The more he gets, the more trouble he'll have breathing." I flipped through his chart. "I see his liver enzymes are up."

"His liver's shot," Tim said. "You notice his skin?" he asked Serena. "That his eyeballs are yellow?"

Serena had pulled a small pad out of the pocket of her scrub top and, pen clicked into place, she asked, "Jaundice?"

Tim nodded. "He's probably been a drinker, then with all the drugs he's had . . . he wanted to know if he could smoke pot."

Serena giggled. "He wants to get high?"

"I'm sure he does," Tim answered. "But he said he'd heard about people getting it for cancer."

"Why not? It can't hurt now, can it?" Serena asked.

"Besides the fact that it's against the law?" I asked her.

"I thought that changed for medical reasons." Serena twirled a ruby stud in her ear.

"That's in California. Marijuana is still illegal—for any use, including medical—in Missouri," I said as Ruby joined us. "And how would he get it? He can't go anywhere."

"Someone could bring it to him," Serena suggested.

"But he still couldn't smoke it," I told her.

"Why?" Serena asked. "Because of his lungs?"

"That, too, but it's the lighting up of the joint with all the oxygen in here—" Tim began.

"Kaboom," Ruby said, chuckling. "He wouldn't have to worry about pain no more."

"Neither would any of the rest of us," Tim added.

Jake came out of Mr. Kleinfeldt's room, and I caught him up on my conversation with Huey.

"What's his CO_2?" Jake asked, grabbing a chair and scooting up to the desk.

"It's not that high." I pulled Huey's chart out of the rack and flipped through to the lab printout to find out how much carbon dioxide they'd found in Huey's latest blood test. "Forty-five," I read.

"O_2?" Jake asked.

"Seventy-five." I shut the chart, confirming that Huey's oxygenation was compromised, as expected. When carbon dioxide in the blood goes up, oxygen levels go down. "But I still don't think you should intubate. You do and that'll be the end of talking to him."

"Okay. I'll hold off for now, but keep an eye on those labs." He swung around to face me. "Maybe I haven't been clear enough about his prognosis. Do you think he knows he's terminal? Really knows it?" he said.

I knew what Jake meant. Many times patients or their family members seemed to understand when we told them that their condition was terminal, but then went right ahead and made plans for months ahead, as if they expected to be here then.

"I don't know," I told him. "I'm pretty sure he's still in denial." I chewed my lip. "He keeps insisting that we do everything for him no matter how bad he is. I'll talk to Huey's wife if I get a chance," I offered. "How long does he have, do you think?"

Jake shook his head. "You never know. Sometimes these things go on for a while, especially with a guy who really wants to live, and it sounds like he does. Other times, they go like that." He snapped his fingers. "You know how it is."

Indeed I did.

Death kept it's own timetable.

"YOU WANTED TO SEE ME?" Judyth asked, her fingers tapping impatiently on the files in front of her. Judyth Lancelot was St. Teresa's chief nurse, my boss. She wore a business suit in red, her signature color, with fingernails to match.

"Guardino died this morning."

"I saw the report. Terminal, wasn't he?" Her voice was clipped, business-like.

"Did you hear about his sons?"

"Security called me. They want to know if we're pressing charges."

"Are we?"

She shrugged slightly. "The man's father had just died."

"That doesn't give him a reason to attack the staff!"

"Aren't you exaggerating a bit, Monika? As I understand it, he was distraught and just lashed out at everyone. He didn't really assault anyone, at least not intentionally, and nobody got hurt, did they?"

"Tim did."

"Oh?"

"He got punched in the face."

She sighed. "It wasn't anything serious, though."

"Judyth, a nurse gets hit and you just blow it off?"

"Of course not, Monika. We don't want anyone getting hurt, but I have to worry about the legal aspects. Tim's going to be all right, isn't he?"

"His face is swollen. Probably a black eye is all," I admitted reluctantly.

"Is that it, then?"

"No. I need to tell you about Bart Mickelson. He works nights and he should have called a full code on Guardino but he didn't. He only did a partial, a B code."

I handed her the incident report.

"Wasn't the patient terminal?" She scanned the report and looked up.

"Per the family's wishes we issued an A code. Full resuscitation," I said.

"Shouldn't he have been a C? Didn't Lord arrange that?" Her mouth twisted with distaste. "I told him to get all the terminals down to C."

"That's not the point. The man was a full code and Bart didn't implement it."

"We're thinking about going back to the old system," she said. "These A, B, C codes are too confusing. It was better when they're either a full code or no code. That way no one gets mixed up." She gave me a small smile. "Like you said, he was terminal. Even if they could have resuscitated him—which I doubt—the man didn't have long to live."

"Judyth, it's against the law. Bart could lose his nursing license. And you and I, our licenses are on the line, too. We've got to report him."

She shook her head slowly. "Not now, Monika. We've got to get through this next accreditation visit and get the union off our backs."

"Judyth, it's murder."

"No, Monika, it's not. An error in judgment, maybe, but not murder. I think you're overreacting a bit, aren't you? It's not like he didn't try to resuscitate him at all."

"No, but—"

"Sure you didn't get hit instead of Tim?"

"As a matter of fact, I did get hurt." I touched the lump on the back of my head where I'd hit the wall. "What do you think the family's going to do if they hear about this?"

She leaned forward, squinting through smoke-tinted lenses. "You just keep quiet. The man was nearly dead anyway."

"So you don't want to do anything? No discipline, no consequences?"

"That would be the worst thing to do. It would make us sound like we knew he did something wrong."

"He did! And he threatened me, too."

"Who?" She frowned. "The man's son?"

"No. Bart."

"What'd he do?"

"He just acted threatening," I admitted.

"Sounds like you're overreacting again. Maybe he was just rude. He was upset over what happened and let his anger spill out on you."

"He was more than rude. For godsakes, Judyth, aren't you going to do anything? What is it? The nursing shortage? Or our accreditation? You think you can't get rid of any more nurses till after the accreditors come back? Or are you afraid of the Guardinos, afraid they'll sue?"

"We're handling the shortage," she replied. She glanced at her watch.

"What about the state board?"

"What about them?" Judyth frowned.

"This is a reportable incident, a license violation."

She pressed her hands down on the desk and levered herself up to her full six feet. "You don't call anyone," she said with emphasis. "You don't talk to anyone about this." She handed the incident report back to me. "You just get up there . . ." she nodded toward the ceiling. "and take care of the people you've got."

I was dismissed.

"JESSIE'S IN WITH HUEY RIGHT NOW," I told Father Rudolf, who had come in right after lunch. "She should be out in a minute."

Rudolf glanced at his watch. "I just need to tell him I've set up the meeting he wanted."

"Meeting?"

"Uh, just someone he needs to talk to."

"A lawyer?"

"I can't talk about this, Monika."

"I just need to know if it's going to compromise his condition."

Father Rudolf smiled. "If anything it's going to help. He's going to feel a lot better afterward."

"THAT MAN WHO JUST LEFT," I asked Ruby later, coming onto the unit from my office. "What was he doing up here?"

Ruby had the phone cradled on her shoulder and she didn't look up. "A visitor, that's all."

"Who was he visiting?" I said, my voice rising.

"What you getting so bothered about, girl? He just in talking to Huey."

"Is he a relative?"

"I ain't got time to shoo people out. They want in, they in."

Although hospital policy restricted visitors to ICU to immediate family only, we'd been bending the rules lately, trying to keep patients and visitors alike happy. We needed the business.

"Who?" Serena asked, walking up.

"That guy in with Huey," Ruby told her. "Probably one of his Army buddies. Miss Nosy here wants a report on everyone coming and going. I ain't got time fer all your questions." She dropped the phone in its cradle with a thump.

"You know him?" Serena asked me.

"Is Huey okay?" I asked her, without answering.

"He kinda gives me the creeps. With that arm and all."

"Just check on him."

She gave me a puzzled look as she turned toward his room.

Dog, that's what he was called when I'd known him. I never knew his real name. His droopy jowls and sad eyes made him look as if his face had been made out of rubber that had been released from its mold too soon, causing his face to sag. No telling his age. He had the same rolling walk I remembered, too. He was a runner for the some of the bookies in town. I felt my face getting warm as I remembered the times when he'd picked up my money wrapped inside a slip of paper shielding my choice of numbers for that week. Since the lottery had become legal, though, the numbers' business had dropped off. I thought they had gone out of business. Maybe Dog was the person Father Rudolf said Huey wanted to see.

But it hadn't made him feel better. When Serena came out of his room she said Huey was upset and in more pain. Serena checked his chart and told Jessie that Huey could have another shot. "That should help," Serena said.

"WE LOST ONE TODAY," I told BJ when she joined me at Dolph's Restaurant later.

BJ had been my best friend since childhood. We had grown up together in the Dutchtown neighborhood of South St. Louis, long home to the city's German immigrants. Both our families descended from those earlier settlers, and the Southside remained a close-knit community. Most people, though, had moved farther south and west as inner city decay had encroached into the area. Dolph's bordered Dutchtown where it met up with the Holly Hills neighborhood, where I had moved.

Tall, blond, and blue eyed, BJ looked typically German, and although I had fair skin and blue eyes, my short stature and the coal-black mass of unruly curls that I kept cut close to my head hid my ancestry.

Now BJ was a St. Louis city cop.

She laid her cap on the seat beside her and rubbed the crinkled red line on her forehead that the cap had left. Sweat stained the armholes of her blue uniform. She bloused out her shirt and fanned herself with it.

"Sick?"

"'A course they're sick. Why else would they be in ICU?"

"Just making a joke." She held up her hand before I could open my mouth. "A sick one," she added with a grin. She smoothed strands of damp blond hair, tucking them expertly into the French braid on the back of her head.

A waitress plopped glasses of water in front of us, saying she'd be right back.

"The man's son got in a rage and just went crazy, swinging his arms and screaming at everyone. Tim got a punch in the eye, he slammed me against the door. It took four security guards and a St. Louis police officer to get him down."

"Who was it?"

"I can't tell you, BJ. Patient names are confidential. You know that."

"I mean who was the cop?"

"I don't know. And my boss said we're not pressing charges."

She fanned herself with the menu and looked around.

Dolph's was filling up fast with the older crowd here for the early-bird dinner special.

BJ nodded to two cops seated in the smoking section separated from us by a half wall. "Nothing funny about the death, was there?" she asked, turning back to me.

"Maybe."

"What do you mean, maybe?"

"One of the nurses. . . ."

"She did something wrong?"

"He. No, but he might as well have. He didn't do a full code."

The waitress returned and asked if we needed more time. We didn't. BJ ordered her usual—the Favorite Grilled Cheese—and I decided on the breakfast Grand Slam for my dinner.

"What do you mean 'he didn't do a full code'?" BJ asked when the waitress had gone.

I explained about the three levels of resuscitation.

"Why didn't he do it all?"

"Mistake, he said. The guy was terminal," I admitted, "but his family wanted us to do anything and everything we could to keep him alive."

"Wasn't there anyone else there? Didn't the other nurses step in and do something?"

I sighed. "Unfortunately, I didn't have anyone else on staff who wasn't already working this morning, so my boss had called the agency for two temps. They don't know the patients and would just do whatever Bart told them to do."

"Wasn't there a doctor around?"

"Only a brand-new resident who'd started last month. Bart probably told him what to do."

"What'll happen? Will somebody investigate? Will he be fired?"

I snorted. "My boss is worried about our accreditation. We don't have enough nurses as it is, and firing one more would make it worse. And Joint Commission is due back any day."

"What's that? Some kind of medical group that specializes in bones?"

I laughed. "No, the Joint Commission on Accreditation of Healthcare Organizations. JCAHO, or Joint Commission, Jayco for short."

"I guess that's bad," she offered.

"If we lose our accreditation, we're out of business. No more government funding, no more Medicare, no more St. Teresa's."

"What about the family? You think they might cause trouble?"

"Not if they don't know. And I've been ordered not to tell them."

"So, it's probably going to be okay."

"There's still the state board."

"What about them?"

"It's a practice violation. Bart could lose his license if it came to that. And I've been ordered not to say anything."

"Sounds like it's his problem, not yours. And the hospital's."

"BJ, I could be in trouble for not reporting this. The law says that any nurse who knows about a violation is required to report it. My license is on the line, too."

"You saw it?"

"Of course not, I would've coded the guy. Bart told me about it when I came in this morning."

"Then you're off the hook, aren't you? With your license, that is."

"The letter of the law, maybe, but not the intent. It for sure violates nursing's code of ethics."

"How often does a nurse get in trouble for not reporting something someone else didn't do?"

"Not much," I admitted. "I've never heard of it. Probably never," I said finally.

"You reported it up the line. You followed orders. Sounds like if anyone's in trouble with the board it would be your superior." BJ knew about following orders and chain of command. "Make sure you document what you've done."

"Good point. My boss gave me back the incident report. I'll file it along with a note about my meeting with her. Just in case something happens in the future."

The waitress returned with our food, and we busied ourselves with preparations. I smeared my pancakes with butter and drizzled syrup over them and added salt and pepper to my eggs, sunny-side up. I stabbed the yolks, twisting my fork around in the gooey centers before popping a dripping bite into my mouth.

BJ wrapped her hands around the grilled sandwich stuffed with tomato, bacon, and cheese. "The family must have been expecting it even if they didn't admit it." She bit into the crunchy wheat toast and cheese oozed out over the side and onto her hand. She put her sandwich on the plate and licked her fingers. "They'll bury him, and that'll be the end of it," she said, wiping her hands on a napkin. "Come on, eat those pancakes before they get cold. You can save the world on a full stomach."

Chapter 4

Thursday, 09 August, 0640 Hours

Coming into the hospital the next morning, I saw Tim hand a flyer to a nurse as she passed him. He turned toward me, his lopsided smile sliding into a neutral expression, his swollen black eye and bruised cheek distorting his face.

"I know you don't believe in this," he began, "but we've got to do something to get administration to listen to us." He smiled crookedly at a passing nurse. She took a flyer and moved on.

At this early hour the lobby was nearly deserted. Even the volunteers who staff the information desk hadn't arrived yet. One elderly man dozed in a chair opposite the wall of portraits of past hospital administrators, their cheery faces smiling at who knows what.

"You see the paper this morning?" He turned to me.

"CEO salaries?"

"Can you believe that? They're making hundreds of thousands," he said, loud enough to be heard across the lobby. "On the backs of nurses," he added, watching an administrator walk by without looking at us. "That's why we've got to get some leverage."

"Tim, I do believe in unions," I said after a few more nurses had taken flyers and the lobby was momentarily empty. "My dad was a union member all his life. And my grandfather."

His lip curled, twisting his face into a grimace. "But not for nurses, is that it?"

"Tim, I can't vote for a union. I'm part of administration. I'm not eligible."

"So would you if you could?"

Two nurses came up and took flyers. They stood there reading.

Tim was waiting for my answer.

"I'll see you upstairs," I said.

Tim nodded, his expression grim.

Bart was standing in the hall in front of ICU when I got off the elevator. His blond curly hair stood up as if he'd been running his hands through it, and his scrubs were stained with splatters of blood and fluids. "Can I see you?" he asked. A smile crinkled around his clear-blue eyes.

I nodded and opened the door to my office. I motioned to the small chair beside my desk, but he kept standing, bouncing up and down on the balls of his feet.

"I'm sorry about yesterday," he said, glancing around. His eyes flicked back to me. "I didn't mean to talk to you that way. It's just that–" He ran his hand through his hair and shook his head. His words spilled out in a rush. "It's getting to me, working all night, school all day, I just lost it yesterday. We are just so damn busy." He stopped and flashed me another quick smile. "Sorry, darn busy. Too many patients, too sick, not enough help. . ." His voice trailed off.

"Still—"

"It will never happen again, Monika, I promise."

I didn't know how to respond so I sat down.

"Please, don't report me. It would ruin everything I've worked for, and you know yourself he was about to die. We all did. Bringing him back—or trying to—I doubt we could have—"

"That wasn't for you to decide, Bart," I said before he could justify his actions any more. "It's the ethical thing to do and, more than that, it's the law. You know that." When he hesitated, I asked, "Don't you?"

"Yes, yes, yes, but—"

"There are no buts!"

He backed up, palms raised in surrender. "You're right, you're right. And it won't happen again, I promise you."

"I can understand what you mean," I said with a sigh. "We bring them back to nothing and the family's kept in limbo and then they die anyway. It goes on way too long for so many."

"We're so busy, I know I miss some things."

"We all do these days. By the way, did you do the counts this morning?"

"Yes," he said with a quick smile. "Jessie and I checked all the narcotics and everything's okay. None are missing."

"Good."

"Please, Monika, don't report me. I've learned my lesson. I'll code them all, immediately, no matter what code's been ordered. I promise." Another smile.

"Okay, but—"

"Thank you, thank you, thank you," he said, folding his hands prayer-like in front of his chest. "You don't know what this means to me," he added, bowing as he backed up.

"But if I'm asked, I have to tell the truth."

"You won't be sorry," he added, turning quickly. "I promise, I promise."

"I hope not," I said to his retreating back.

I WAS CHARTING at the nurses' station when I heard Ruby's chair squeaking. Her back was to me, and at first I thought she was crying.

Just then Huey's girlfriend, Noni, passed the desk, heading toward Huey's room.

"Stop!" I ordered.

She turned around, surprise on her face. "Me?"

"Yes."

She stood at the counter with a small frown on her face. "Anything wrong? Not Huey?" She fingered the top of a small, brown, paper lunch bag.

"He's fine," I reassured her. "We're . . . that is, the nurse is in there now. You'll have to wait." Thank goodness the curtain was drawn across his cubicle.

Noni was a small, contained young woman with straight black hair that swung loosely around her face. Her brown eyes had just a hint of a slant that gave her an exotic look, reflecting a mix of Far Eastern and, I suspected, Spanish heritage.

"Uh, it's going to be a while. Why don't you go get a cup of coffee and come back a little later?"

"Can't I just interrupt a minute?" She turned toward his room.

"No, no." My words stopped her. "They're in the middle of a, uh, procedure. They can't stop now. Just give us fifteen minutes. Can you do that?" I hoped I looked earnest.

She checked her watch. "I'd better go on to work." Huey had told us she worked at the Ambassador, the gambling boat on the Mississippi.

Before the doors had swung shut behind her, Ruby was bent over the desk laughing. "My god, girl, you conned her right outta here."

"Whew. That was close."

"She was barreling right on in there." Ruby pointed to Huey's room. "I gotta hand it to you, you're good!"

We both laughed, picturing Huey's wife and girlfriend meeting over his bed.

Serena came out of another patient's room. Ruby told her what was so funny. "I can't see anyone wanting him," Serena said, with the characteristic bias of a twenty year old. "It's not like he's good looking or anything."

"You wrong there, girl," Ruby said as Jessie joined us. "That guy's a lover."

"Uh huh," Jessie added with skepticism in her voice.

"He the king," Ruby said, giggling. "King. Get it? His name—Castle."

Jessie waved a dismissal.

Ruby's dark skin flushed. "Some folks can't take a joke," she said, flouncing off.

I sent Serena in to ask Huey's wife to come see me in my office and moved away to see what another visitor wanted.

"I NEED TO talk with you about what we should do about Huey," I said as Huey's wife, Mavis, settled herself on the chair in my office. Mavis was a lanky, almost skinny woman dressed in jeans, T-shirt and scuffed tennis shoes. Her dirty-blond hair, streaked with gray, hung below her shoulders, and her uneven bangs looked as if they'd been chopped off in a hurry.

"What about him?" she asked in a smoke-roughened voice. She played with the smooth, gold wedding band, her nicotine-stained fingers turning it round and round.

"What has Dr. Lord told you?"

"About what?" She fumbled in her purse and pulled out a package of Marlboro Lights.

"No smoking in here." I smiled to take the edge off my managerial tone. "Too much oxygen."

She fingered the cigarette, stroking it absently.

"Has Dr. Lord talked to you?"

She frowned. "About what?"

"About his prognosis."

"What's that?"

"It's serious."

"What's a prognosis? That what's wrong with him?"

"Sorry. I should have explained. I'm talking about what you can expect to happen."

"He's dying. I know that." Her voice was matter of fact. "He's had a good run of it." She smiled, revealing a missing molar. "Made the most of it, I'd say."

"In these cases, it's a good idea to think about what all you want done."

"You mean about a funeral or something?"

"Oh, no. Although that's not a bad idea. I'm talking about what steps you'd like us to take if he gets worse."

"Did you talk to Huey about this?"

I hesitated. "I don't think he's faced it yet."

"Probably not. He does love life." She smiled faintly.

"If he can't tell us, we'll need you to."

"What do I have to decide?"

"Just how much you want done to keep him going."

"I don't want him to have pain. I want him to go out smiling."

"Here are some things to think about." I handed her the list of possible treatments.

"Feeding tube?" she asked.

"That's a tube we put down into the stomach when someone can't eat for themselves."

"That'd be good, wouldn't it?"

"It would if he were going to get better. But if he were already unconscious and not going to come out of it, it would just prolongs the process."

"You're saying he'd just go on living, but not really be alive."

"That's right. And it's true for IV fluids as well."

She frowned. "So you're saying without these things he'd starve to death."

"Theoretically."

"I don't care about theoretically, whatever that is. I don't want my Huey starvin' to death." She stood and the paper slid to the floor. She stomped out, leaving a footprint on it.

"That went well," I said out loud.

Chapter 5

Thursday, 09 August, 0955 Hours

THE MEETING WAS held in the classroom used for orientation of new staff and in-service education for the rest of us, chairs arranged classroom style with a table facing the audience. We were a few minutes away from a mandatory meeting for administrators.

Judyth stood in front of the table flipping through some notes. She wore a double-breasted pants suit in black, white silk blouse underneath, and a ceramic red rose on her lapel.

Behind Judyth hung a poster stuck up on the wall with thumbtacks. "BE A NURSE," it proclaimed, showing a diverse group of smiling people dressed in clean scrubs, the obligatory male and woman of color included. A strip along the bottom had been torn off. Presumably it contained a phone number or website for more information.

Wanda, a fellow head nurse, joined me at the back of the room, scooting in the door just as Judyth looked up. "You want to make a quick getaway, too, I see." Wanda nodded toward the door on our left.

"These are about as much fun as a trip to the dentist."

"And twice as long."

Judyth tapped her pen on the table in front of her. "Two things on today's agenda," she began. "First, accreditation."

A hand shot up in front, but the speaker didn't wait to be acknowledged. "What about staff? When are we going to get some more nurses?"

A few others murmured their agreement.

"I'll get to that. Now to our accreditation." She cleared her throat. "We've had six months to correct the weaknesses the surveyors found on their last visit, the most serious being to adhere to our staffing plan, a Type I recommendation. As you know. The six months are up as of yesterday, so we can expect another visit by surveyors any time."

A hand went up in front. "How are we doing on staffing? Don't we have to have a certain number to pass accreditation?"

"Joint Commission doesn't tell us how many staff to have," she explained. "Just to have a plan and to adhere to that plan."

A few murmurs.

Judyth raised her hand for quiet. "Of course the plan needs to be realistic for safe practice." She ignored several hands that shot up. "And we're not up to full staffing yet. But we're making progress, and that's what they want to see when they get here."

"When?" asked a nurse in the front row.

"We don't know," Judyth answered. "It will be an unannounced visit. They'll just show up one day. So be prepared. Someone will probably just walk up to a nurses' station and identify themselves. If we're lucky, they'll come first to the administrative suite, and we can take them around like we did for the initial visit. This time, though, they'll be here to see if we fixed the problems.

"We were also cited for our failure to fully implement a sentinel-event policy. I'm sure you remember that." She looked around at the few nods, and went on to remind us. "That's when something goes wrong and a patient is hurt. We have to have policies in place to make sure it doesn't happen again."

"As long as you use incident reports to discipline nurses for this, you're not going to get people reporting," said someone in the middle of the room.

"We're working on that," Judyth said quickly. You just make sure," she stopped momentarily, "that every event gets reported. In addition, I've been making rounds." She motioned to her secretary, who was sitting in the front row, to hand her a file. She opened the folder and checked the sheet on top. "Here are some of the things I've observed. On one unit I found dirty instruments piled on a laundry cart. On another, several staff were showing each other baby clothes they had made while several call lights were lit up." She looked out over the audience, quiet now, to a spot high up on the back wall. "Finally, loud conversations, shouting back and forth with no regard, in fact, little notice that patients or visitors were around."

Someone coughed.

I asked, "Are these nurses you're talking about or some of the . . . uh, support staff?"

"You can't tell who's a nurse and who's not since you made us quit wearing RN on our name tags," came a voice from across the room.

"That's 'cause we're interchangeable," added someone else, eliciting snickers from the audience.

Judyth shrugged. "It doesn't matter. You're responsible for their performance. And their behavior, whether they're RNs or nurses aides."

Wanda asked, "Will you back us up if they come crying to you? Saying we're picking on them?"

"This is your job. If you can't handle management, let me know." She leaned back against the table. "Now, about hiring more nurses," she said. "I'm pleased to tell you administration has approved a bonus program for you. If you recruit someone who comes to work here, you get a bonus of $500."

Murmured approval.

"How do we get them to come here," Lucille, the head nurse in orthopedics, asked, looked at her friend next to her and then back at Judyth, "with our salaries?"

Judyth smiled slowly. "We've raised the starting pay."

"To what?" Lucille asked.

"To 19.50 an hour."

"Hey, that's more than I make now," someone said.

Judyth crossed her arms and frowned. "We can talk about that. Individual cases can be, uh, considered."

"What kind of double talk is that?" Wanda said in a stage whisper.

The time allotted for the meeting was up. People started gathering themselves to leave.

"One more thing." Judyth waited until the room quieted back down. "I want to talk to you about the people trying to get the nurses to organize. Not our nurses; they're outsiders."

More murmuring.

"Now there are strict rules about where they can hand out literature, where they can talk to the nurses. They cannot do any lobbying on the units or while the nurses are working. Is that clear? Good. Now be sure all of your staff know about this. If you see any violations, call me right away. And you all understand, don't you, that you are not eligible to vote for or against a union?"

A few heads nodded.

"That's all," she added.

"CAN YOU PICTURE her as a nurse?" Wanda asked while we were filling our plates at the salad bar.

We were early enough to beat the lunchtime crowd to the cafeteria. Only a few of the surgery staff, whose hours began and ended before the rest of us had trickled in, and were sitting at scattered tables.

"Judyth in scrubs? They'd probably be designer ones!" I said, topping my lettuce and spinach leaves with broccoli flowerets, shredded carrots, and sliced cucumbers.

"Judyth messy? No way," Wanda said, adding chopped eggs, a heaping of grated cheese, and a handful of Chinese noodles to her salad.

"You know where she used to work, don't you?" I shook vinegar and oil on my veggies.

Wanda nodded. "Isolation. Gowned, gloved, and masked. No contact with patients. She never touched them."

"It fits."

"With all these salads I'm eating I don't know why I don't lose weight," Wanda said, ladling a second helping of ranch dressing onto her salad.

We were settling ourselves at a table by the window when Wanda said, "Judyth sure knows how to get everyone on her side, doesn't she?"

A man outside was picking weeds out of a bed riotous with red geraniums, yellow marigolds, and purple petunias. It was a luxuriant display of blooms, unlike my garden at home.

"How do you mean?" I asked.

"Right at the time the union tries to organize us, she comes up with this hare-brained scheme to raise starting salaries and make nurses who already work here mad. They'll either vote for the union or leave," Wanda said, slathering a roll with butter. "There're plenty of jobs in nursing now. Nurses can call the shots."

I giggled.

"What's so funny? Oh, I get it. Nurses call the shots. Ha. Ha."

"I know, nothing's funny right now."

"But we need a bit of comic relief, don't we?" Wanda asked, spearing a tomato wedge and swirling it in dressing. "And that crap about 'sentinel events.' If we reported every mistake, we'd all be fired. By the way, you hear the rumor about her? She's been telling all the staff nurses that they'll have to join the union if we get one. Whether they want to or not."

"I think she's right. They have to pay dues for it anyway." I stirred sugar into my iced tea and took a sip. "She is trying to fix our accreditation problems. If we don't have a better nurse-to-patient ratio when the evaluators come back. . . ."

"You hear we had to divert another ambulance last night? That's the third night in a row we've been on diversion."

When an ambulance picks up a patient, they call the nearest hospital and if that hospital doesn't have the staff to care for any more patients, the patient is diverted to another hospital and so on. Some patients had been driven miles away from home before an available hospital could be found.

"Anyone hurt by the delay?" I asked her.

"Not that I heard. No wonder we don't have enough business, no open beds."

When there were not enough nurses to take care of any more patients than we already had, any available beds were not considered "open," and the hospital was, in effect, closed to new patients.

"I'm moving on," Wanda said, popping the last bit of roll in her mouth.

"You're leaving St. T's?"

She swallowed. "I've started grad school at Milburn, in anesthesia," she said, wiping her hands and tossing the napkin on top of her plate. "I'll be here for a couple more years, at least 'til I finish. I'm taking evening classes."

I frowned.

"What's wrong? You don't think I should go?"

"That's not it. You just reminded me of one of my nurses who just started there too. Bart Mickelson."

"Someone told me another nurse from here was going there. He's in the day program, isn't he? That's why I haven't met him yet. What's the matter, you don't like him?"

"Just something he did."

"What?"

I looked around to the cafeteria filling slowly, but no one was within earshot. "More what he didn't do."

"Screw up?"

"You might say that."

"Does he know what he's doing? You have to really have your skills down pat to do anesthesia. Fine motor skills, especially. He any good?"

"His skills are fine. It was just one case that we didn't agree on. That's all," I added.

"What'd he do?"

"I can't really talk about it, Wanda."

"I wouldn't report any of my staff unless they killed someone. We need every nurse we can get even if they're slow or need watching." She laughed. "Warm bodies with a license, that's all it takes."

"Don't you think that could be dangerous?"

"What would you want, Monika, a licensed nurse who knows something—there are always other qualified nurses and doctors around in ER—or no nurse at all? I try to assign the easy cases to the less-experienced staff."

"Are there any easy ones in ER?"

"Not many. And I don't always have a choice. We never know what's coming through the door."

"Like ICU. We just do the best we can with the nurses we have," I said with a sigh. "Maybe, with what Judyth said today, we'll have more soon."

"And we're going recruiting on Saturday."

"Oh, that's right, the bazaar," I said referring to the career fair for student nurses that some of us had been ordered to attend.

"That's a hoot, isn't it? Throw them some bait and reel them in." She pretended to cast a fishing line and roll it up. "And then wave signing bonuses around and, who knows, maybe a free trip to Bermuda thrown in to seal the deal."

"Signing bonuses?"

"You don't know about that? Yes, Miss Administration neglected to announce that, didn't she?" Wanda snorted. "Okay, here's the deal." Wanda leaned across the table and tapped her finger on my tray. "Every new hire gets two thousand dollars."

"Two thousand dollars! Just for signing on?"

"Not all at once. That's the catch. They get five hundred after three months, another five hundred after six months, and a thousand after one year. Add it up. Two thousand bucks."

"And the people who've been here the longest get nothing unless they recruit someone."

"Students have the upper hand right now. No doubt about it."

"They've had hospitals after them the minute they started school." I gathered my trash on the tray.

"They can't graduate soon enough for me," Wanda said as we made our way out of the cafeteria.

"SHE BACK," RUBY said as I walked up to the nurses' station.

"Huh? Who?"

"His wife." She pointed toward Huey's room. "While you was at lunch."

"What'd she want?"

"She went with Jessie and Lord down to the waiting room."

"And?"

"She say it's okay to let him die."

"What?"

"Ruby," Jessie said, joining us. "We just explained what her options are if he's unconscious."

"What code?" I asked.

Jessie answered. "We agreed on B: CPR, drugs, no intubation. Fluids, yes. Feeding tube, no." Jessie closed the chart she'd been carrying and shoved it into the rack.

It wasn't much, but at least she'd accepted there might be a point at which we should stop trying to keep him going.

Ruby leaned closer to me and whispered, "You gonna tell him there?" she asked, nodding toward Huey's room. "That his wife's giving him up to die?"

"Ruby, I'm sure she realized the situation, and this is only used if he can't speak for himself. And two doctors have to agree he won't regain consciousness."

"May be, Missy, may be."

JUDYTH WAS MAKING ICU rounds with a visiting physician when I caught up with her later. Once she had sent her visitor on her way, we went into my office, a tiny, cramped space located in the hallway immediately outside of intensive care. I suspected it had been a closet in earlier days. I cleared off the chair beside my desk and piled the papers, journals, and files on top of the unopened mail that spilled across the desk top.

Judyth arranged herself in the chair and pulled her skirt together over her knees. Her expression was noncommittal.

"I've got a problem," I began, "with the salaries for new hires. I've got one nurse—Jessie—who's been here her whole career, twenty-five or thirty years," I went on, ignoring her frown. "With the new salaries you're proposing, a brand new grad will make more than she does."

"We've got to get more nurses, Monika," she said, waving away my concerns. "The only way to do that is to try to top the competition and, believe me, that's not easy. They're upping the ante all the time."

I hesitated, then said, "You know she's black, don't you?"

"What does that have to do with it?" Her tone was sharp. "I hope you're not implying we'd treat her any differently. And, just for your information, no, I didn't know she was black."

"So what should she do, quit and reapply? At least then she'd get the signing bonus."

She chewed on her lower lip, biting off a corner of lipstick. "If she's been here her whole career, sounds like she's committed to us."

"And you're counting on that. Once again, nurses are supposed to sacrifice for the good of the institution." I slapped my hand down on my desk, sending a stack of mail sliding to the floor. I left it there.

"And their patients. Don't forget their patients," she said, a note of sarcasm tinged her words. "That's the business we're in, isn't it?"

"Is it? I thought the business we're in is business!"

"Okay, okay. Listen, Monika, we're in this together. I'm just trying to do the best I can with what I've got. That's what you're doing too, isn't it?"

I kept my face neutral.

"So let's just keep trying." She smiled as if we were colleagues. "You're a top-notch manager, Monika, if I haven't told you that lately, I'm sorry. I think you know that, don't you?"

I waited.

"As long as we can keep the union out, you can keep on doing your job."

"We can't keep working people like we are and keep the union out. These people are working overtime—mandatory, I might add—split shifts, doubling back after only eight hours, and floating to units where they don't know how to care for patients—again, no choice—and now this, you hire a fresh grad and give her more money." A whine had crept into my voice. "Where's the sense in that?" I asked, lowering my tone.

"Let me tell you about my experience with the union. Then maybe you'll understand how bad it can be." She leaned back in the chair and stretched her long legs in front of her.

I gathered up the dropped mail as Judyth began.

"I had a nurse once with good clinical skills. She worked herself up to head nurse in peds, the kids loved her, she was well-liked by everyone who worked with her—nurses, ward clerks, orderlies, even the docs loved her. She was especially good during the difficult times, you know, when you lose several in a row? She seemed to know just the right thing to say. Some of those kids were in and out a lot and the nurses got really attached to them, but this nurse kept everyone's spirits up. She was like the frosting between cake layers—you could eat the cake without the filling but it was so much better with it.

"Then her mother got sick and needed care, so the nurse needed more money to pay for that care during the day while she worked. Her salary was lower than the other head nurses because she had been there so long. Just before this happened the nurses had lobbied for a union and got it. I wanted to raise her salary to more than the other managers—she deserved it and she'd leave if she didn't get it. I put in the request, thinking everyone knew how good she was and how important she was to the hospital. All salary changes for nurses—even those in management—had to be approved by the union. They said no. Wasn't fair, they said, meaning equal. The only criteria for salary increases were seniority or advanced education or certification. Nothing extra for the nurse's special expertise or value to the institution, according to the hospital's contract with the union." Judyth's beeper sounded. She looked down at the message and stood up. "You know, Monika," she said, "fair and equal aren't always the same thing."

I sat there thinking about what she had said until Ruby called me out to the desk.

"Him there's been calling for you," Ruby said. She jerked her thumb toward Huey's room.

"Where's Jessie? She's his nurse."

"She says she's done all she can. He just wants more drugs, she says."

"When'd he last have something?"

"Don't ask me nursin' stuff. I got enough to do with all this paperwork." She knew what time Huey had his medication, I was certain. She kept strict boundaries, though, on what each person's work was, especially where her responsibilities began and ended. Since she had been at the hospital so long we acquiesced to her rules. She kept ICU running much better than other units, especially now that we had too few staff.

Sighing, I pulled his chart off the rack. Jessie had given him 25 milligrams of morphine IV push twenty minutes earlier.

"THERE YOU ARE, sweetheart," Huey said, straining to talk.

"Oh, so I'm another of your sweethearts, eh?"

He smiled weakly.

"Noni was in to see you while your wife was here."

"Uh oh."

"Uh oh is right. You better talk to your girlfriend. We don't want to have to separate those two fighting over you. God knows why."

"I'm still a stud, ain't I?" He jerked his sheet up, revealing his naked body.

"Cover yourself, Huey," I said, and flipped the sheet back over him.

This wasn't the first time he'd done this; he tried it out on every new nurse, especially the young students, sending one screaming out of the room.

"You've been giving everyone trouble, I hear," I said, checking his IV. Huey had a central venous device, so-called because a triple-lumen catheter was inserted into a central vein—in his case, the jugular vein. The bag attached delivered total parental nutrition, known as TPN, and contained dextrose with vitamin B added that turned the solution a distinctive bright yellow. If any of the solution spilled, it left a sticky residue. We called it a banana bag because of its color and sweetness.

"I need that PGA. One that works this time."

"You mean PCA. The pump." Patient-controlled analgesia allowed patients to administer doses of pain medication intermittently.

"I'm really hurtin,' Monika."

"Where?"

"Everywhere." He waved his stub of an arm across his trunk, wincing as he did. "It's a ten."

I didn't doubt he was in pain. What I doubted was if it was as bad as he was saying.

"The PCA didn't work for you, Huey."

"It wouldn't work. It were broke."

"You kept pushing it all the time. It's set to allow only a safe amount. You wanted more."

"I need it!"

"Listen, if we give you too much now, then if it gets worse we won't be able to give you enough to control your pain."

He moved restlessly in the bed. "I don't care about that. I need it now!"

"I'll send Serena in when she gets a chance. She can give you a back rub."

"That won't do no good. Talk to that doctor. The black guy. Tell him I'm hurtin.' Bad."

"I'll tell him," I said, straightening his sheets.

"How 'bout that thing they put in my back? That made it numb." He jabbed his thumb toward his abdomen. He said that wouldn't stop me breathing."

"The epidural. They put that catheter in during surgery so you could cough and do breathing exercises afterward, that's so you don't get pneumonia. And it only works on the nerves going to your abdomen. Your pain is everywhere."

"Maybe, but I still think it would help."

"Even if it would, Dr. Lord wouldn't do any more surgery on you. Not in your condition." Huey had slid down in the bed so I positioned myself over him, grabbed him under the arms and pulled him up. He seemed lighter than he'd been the day before. "Now," I said, resting back on my heels, "have you thought any more about what you want us to do—what we talked about yesterday."

"You better do everything to keep me alive. Everything! If I stop breathing. . . ." He looked around, his head jerking back and forth as if he was expecting someone. "You better bring me back. You don't let nothing happen to me, you hear?" He looked at me, his eyes clear and focused. "I told lots of people to make sure you don't let me die."

"Huey," I started, trying to think how to say this. "You've got too much life in you to be willing to just exist, hooked up to machines, not knowing anything. That's not you."

"Don't talk like that. And don't go asking Mavis what to do, neither. I don't want her deciding anything," he said with more emphasis than I expected. He grinned and his pointed, yellow teeth gave him a feral look. "She's gonna get a big surprise."

"Your girlfriend?"

"They're both gonna be surprised." He rubbed his thumb and first finger together on the only hand he had. "Money," he added, lying back on the pillow, a smile on his face.

I started for the door.

"Hey," he said.

I turned back.

"Father Rudolf been up here? He's bringing some cops into see me."

"The police are coming to see you? Why?"

"Don't you worry about it. Just don't give them no trouble about getting in to see me."

"We haven't been keeping people who aren't family members out, as you know," I said, my reference to Huey's girlfriend apparent.

I came out of Huey's room and Ruby jerked her head toward a man with his back to me standing at the counter. He was searching through the files in his briefcase open on the ledge.

"Can I help you?"

The man turned around. He was about my age or a little older, dressed in a finely-tailored navy suit, white on white shirt and light-blue tie with a subtle sheen on it. His dark hair, a sprinkle of gray along the temples, had been professionally styled. And not at a clip joint either. He'd been brushed and buffed to perfection.

"You're . . ." he ran a manicured finger down the file in front of him. "Monika Everhardt?"

I nodded. "What can I do for you?"

"Phil Silverman," he said, handing me a card. *Phillip B. Silverman, Attorney at Law*. His initials were embroidered on his shirt cuffs.

"Is there somewhere we can talk?" he asked, looking around.

"What's this about? We're busy here."

Ruby was staring, and Serena lingered at the counter pretending to read a chart.

He leaned toward me and lowered his voice. "Just a few questions about a patient. It will only take a moment." His soft gray eyes crinkled into a disarming smile. One front tooth, slightly crooked, marred its perfection. "I know you've got a lot more important things to do."

I led him into the conference room where I knew a meeting was scheduled to begin shortly. An empty cup and a wadded paper napkin sat among crumbs littering the table. I motioned Mr. Silverman into a chair as I scooped up the trash and grabbed a paper towel to wipe the table.

"What do you want to know?" I asked, joining him at the table.

"I'm here on behalf of the family of Antonio Guardino," he said.

I groaned inwardly. "What's the problem?"

"There isn't a problem. They know he was dying. It's just that Joe—that's the younger son—he's so upset that they asked me to check into it."

"Even so, I can't say anything, especially now with the HIPPA regs."

The Health Insurance Portability and Accountability Act was the federal privacy act that restricted access to patient information far more stringently than earlier regulations.

"You'll have to talk to administration," I said.

"I have power of attorney; I'm executor of his estate," he said, placing his briefcase on the table and fishing out a document apparently signed by Mr. Guardino.

I handed it back. "I still can't talk to you."

"I'm not here officially," he added, his smile revealing a dimple on one cheek. He closed the briefcase. "You know how upset his sons were."

I nodded, absently rubbing my head.

"I just need to be able to tell them that I followed up and that everything possible was done for their father. Can't you tell me that? Just to reassure them." His eyes lingered on mine, and I felt a warm flush spread up my neck.

Serena popped her head in the door. "Mr. Swenson's pulled his catheter out again," she said.

"You'd better get Tim to put it back in, and also call Dr. Lord. See if he wants to order some kind of restraint for him."

"And Ruby says," she went on, "that Mrs. B's chart's missing."

"Check her room. I saw it on the bedside table." I turned back to Mr. Silverman, trying to remember what it was he'd asked me.

"I just want to reassure the family that everything was done for Mr. Guardino. And I'm sure it was."

I studied his hands resting on the table, square-trimmed nails, lightly buffed, cuticles trimmed. "Everything's down in records now," I said at last. "We don't have anything up here."

"I'll get the official records—" he began as the door opened again.

"I need a cup of coffee," Ruby said pointedly.

I scooted my chair back. "You need to see administration and our legal counsel even if you're here unofficially."

Ruby had her back to us as she dumped sugar into her coffee.

"I don't know anything," I told Mr. Silverman. "I wasn't here."

"Thank you for your time, Ms. Everhardt," he said, standing. We shook hands and he held mine a fraction too long.

I pulled away.

He walked out, leaving a trail of expensive cologne in his wake.

Stirring her coffee, Ruby said, "Uh huh."

"What?" I picked up his card and shoved it in my lab coat pocket.

"Why you so flustered, him looking at you like that? You know, you're a good looking woman." She looked me up and down. "For a skinny, white girl."

Chapter 6

THURSDAY, 09 AUGUST, 1435 HOURS

I WALKED IN on an argument.

"He's got a wife. She's the one who should be able to see him," Jessie said firmly. "Not some girlfriend. It's not right."

"He's dying," Serena offered. "I think we should let him see anybody he wants. Don't you, Monika?" she asked as I settled in a chair at the head of the table.

We were meeting in our conference room, also called the break room, located behind the nurses' station. The room held a small refrigerator, microwave, employee lockers, and the ever-warm coffee pot.

All my regular day-shift staff were there while agency nurses—at least this shift we had some experienced ones—were watching our patients. A student nurse joined Tim, Jessie, Serena, and Laura, who had been off the day before. Bart and my two evening nurses were missing but Jessie would take responsibility for catching them up on our meeting when she saw them at change of shift.

A nurse for only a year, Laura was on probation with the licensing board. She'd abandoned a patient who had died, but she hadn't caused the woman's death. Nonetheless she had to report to the board every three months and I had to submit regular reports on her as well. Her clinical skills weren't up to speed yet either, and I was beginning to feel frustrated, wondering if she'd ever be the nurse I needed for the fast-paced work in intensive care.

"We can't keep anyone out if he wants to see them," I said, arranging my notes in front of me.

"We could if we wanted to," Jessie said, in a rare display of pique. "Family members only, that's the rule."

"You're right, Jessie, but that's not the policy anymore," I told her. "With our census down, we're supposed to let anyone in the patient wants to see. Just not for long. That's still true."

"Any more talk about intubating him?" Tim asked.

"Not at the moment. I convinced Jake to wait until we can let him talk about what he wants done. If he gets a tube down his throat, it'll just be that much harder for him to communicate. And he's having such a difficult time accepting his prognosis, I just don't want anything to interfere."

"Yeah, but if he can't breath, he won't live to tell us," Tim said.

"What about his pain control?" Jessie asked, her smooth brown forehead creased in a frown.

"We're going back to the pump," I told them. "Judyth got onto Jake after she was up here and Huey told her his pain was a ten. She said we can't have Huey telling Joint Commission that. So Lord agreed to put it back on and he's also getting a fentanyl patch."

"What's a patch?" a student nurse asked. She had been assigned to Huey that day.

"Fentanyl is a different narcotic, and it's on a patch that the patient absorbs through the skin," Jessie explained. "It gives those with intractable pain more consistent relief. It's non-invasive and better tolerated as well."

"A pump and a patch?" the student asked.

"Sometimes it takes several different medications to control pain in severe cases like Huey's," Jessie said.

"How do you know he's in that much pain?" she asked, chewing on the end of her ballpoint pen. "He was laughing and joking around when I went in there this morning,"

"That's the problem," Tim said. "He's an alcoholic and it takes more analgesic to relieve his pain, but then again he might just want to get high."

"Or he might really be in that much pain," Jessie added.

"Aren't you worried about him getting addicted?" the student asked.

"It doesn't matter now," Tim told her.

"He doesn't have long," Jessie explained to her.

"But he seems so alive I just thought. . . ." Her voice trailed off and she lowered her head, scribbling in her notebook.

Jessie patted her shoulder. "Some of them are like that right up to the end. Others are never conscious. It just depends on the person, what's wrong with them, and on their pain tolerance."

The student smiled a thank you to Jessie, and I shifted the conversation to the agenda. I told them to expect the Joint Commission surveyors soon and to just go about their business as usual.

"Now about the union," I began, glancing at the copies of the union flyer strewn on the table.

"Union supporters can lobby you in any public areas, including the cafeteria, the gift shop, the lobby, or outside. Or send something to your home, for that matter. What they cannot do," I said, ignoring Tim's angry scowl, "is talk about it on the floor or during working hours. If you're clocked in, you have to avoid discussions about the union until you clock out. Everyone understand?"

"Where do you stand, Monika?" asked Tim. He tipped back in his chair, hooking his feet on the rungs and lacing his fingers behind his head. Brown hair flopped over his forehead. "You for or against?"

"Tim, you know I can't take a stand on this."

He looked around for support. The swelling on his face had gone down but the skin beneath his eye was streaked with black and purple, giving him an obvious shiner and belying the seriousness of his manner.

Jessie kept her eyes on the file in front of her. Serena looked toward the door.

Laura, who had been off the day before, piped up. "I'm in favor of it."

"Really?" I asked.

She swallowed. "I know I'm not as fast as I could be yet, but I know we don't have enough help. And I can see how administration just blows that off, telling us to do more and more." She stopped, blush staining her naturally-pale face. She picked at a piece of lint caught on the hem of her scrub top and brushed it away.

Tim dropped his chair to the floor. "That's right, Laura, and they won't do anything about it until we can speak with authority. That's what the union will do for us."

Jessie spoke up. "Isn't there any other way? Can't we convince them we all want the same thing—good, safe, patient care?"

Tim snorted. "You know what I heard?" He went on without waiting for a reply. "That I can't vote because I'm a charge nurse. Management," he added with a sneer.

"Are you sure?" I asked him. "I thought it was only full-time managers who couldn't vote, not those who took charge occasionally or frequently, even."

"That's what I heard," Tim said, sounding not so sure.

"I think you're wrong," Jessie told him. "That was just a rumor."

"Or something they," he jerked his head toward the door, "tried to pull on us."

"You'll each have to decide this for yourselves," I told them, ending the meeting.

After they left, I picked up one of the flyers. "NURSES CARRY THE PATIENT LOAD" it said over a drawing of a nurse of indeterminate gender bent over double at the waist, a stack of occupied hospital beds piled on her back. "GET BACK YOUR POWER—VOTE UNION" was followed by the union website and phone number. I laid the flyer back on the table and went out.

I WAS HEADING back to my office to try and get in a few minutes to attack the work multiplying on my desk when Judyth, her penciled eyebrows drawn together in a furious frown, stomped off the elevator and headed toward me.

"In your office," she hissed through clenched teeth. "I told you to keep you mouth shut!" she screeched as I scrambled to close the door behind her. An elderly man peeked in as he passed by.

"Calm down, Judyth, I have no idea what you're talking about." I motioned toward the chair beside my desk, but she ignored me.

She tapped one patent leather toe on the tile floor. "That lawyer, the one the Guardinos have. You talked to him, didn't you? After I told you specifically, do not talk to anyone!"

"Yes, but it's nothing to worry about. For godsakes, settle down and listen to me."

She took a measured breath and motioned for me to get on with it.

"He told me he was only trying to appease the family by making a routine visit. Just so he could say he talked to someone at the hospital."

"And you believed him? What planet are you on? You know damn well not to talk to a lawyer without our attorney present."

"Of course I know that, and I didn't tell him anything. In fact, he didn't even ask me any questions. And besides, I said I wasn't here when Mr. Guardino died."

"So what made him want to see me, you tell me that."

"What did he ask you?"

"I haven't seen him yet. He's waiting downstairs right now."

"It's probably the same reason he came to see me. He's just trying to placate the family."

She took a breath. "Maybe. . . ."

"Are you going to talk to him?"

"It looks too suspicious if I refuse," she said, biting a corner of her tongue. "But, I'm going to have our attorney with me, that's for sure."

"It's going to be all right, Judyth," I said. She did have a tough job; everything that went wrong in patient care circled back to her eventually.

"Okay, Monika, I'll let you go this time."

Let me go?

"I won't write you up for it, but you make sure you never talk to a lawyer without legal and me with you. Understand?"

Write me up? For what? My sympathy for her fizzled.

AS I NEARED the round table in the corner of the bar, the conversation dropped off suddenly. All the nurses from ICU had been invited to hear Serena's boyfriend play in the band at Bubba's Bourbon Street, a New Orleans-style hangout. On the mural behind the table a laughing jester cavorted among Mardi Gras revelers. Art Deco posters adorned the adjoining wall, interspersed with feather-decked masks, their delicate ribbons fluttering in the breeze of ceiling fans that kept the smoke-ladened air moving. A favorite of local St. Louisans, Bubba's was crowded, as it was most evenings.

Only Serena, Tim, Laura, and Peggy, who used to work in ICU, had shown up so far. The table was full so I pulled up a chair from the next table, and they squeezed together to make room.

I gave everyone a nod as I sat down, adding a small smile for Tim. He kept his face blank. Others shuffled in their seats or looked around the room. The band was apparently on break.

I broke the silence. "Glad you could join us, Peggy," I said. Peggy had transferred from ICU to psychiatry after she had returned to St. T's following treatment for drug dependency. She had said there were fewer narcotics in psychiatry and, more importantly, less stress.

"I gotta go," Tim said, dropping a five on the table. He left with a quick glance at me.

"What's wrong with him?" Peggy asked. Statuesque with a rosy complexion and auburn-hued brown hair, Peggy wore a turquoise short-sleeved camp shirt with white capri pants.

"It's about the union," Serena said, glancing sheepishly at me. "We were talking about it before you came in."

"I figured as much," I told her.

"He had just told us to not be swayed by the insurance that administration offered us," Peggy said, referring to the announcement that had come with our last paycheck about how the hospital was now providing life insurance in the amount of our annual salary. "Tim said it was just a way to pretend they were trying to be fair. For myself, I'd rather have more money in my paycheck," Peggy said to the table. "Not for my sister after I die."

A blast of hot air hit us as the door opened and Bart walked in, his arm around a woman with short, dirty-blond hair cut pixie-style. She wore cutoffs, a snug yellow top that almost reached her waist, and sandals. Bart's navy T-shirt stretched tight across his muscular chest, and he wore khaki pants and loafers without socks. They pulled up more chairs and crowded around the table. Finally, Bart let go of his companion.

Laura said hello to them.

I introduced myself to the woman, whose name was Lisa.

"Lisa's a nurse in the ER and helped us out one day last week when you were off," Laura explained. "She's Bart's fiancé."

"Girlfriend," Bart corrected.

"Anyone else coming?" I asked.

"Jessie isn't," Serena said as a bored-looking waitress propped a small black tray on her hip and stood waiting, pencil poised over her order pad.

"Margarita," Lisa said quickly.

Bart frowned.

Lisa's chin went up. "I'm not working tonight. I can have anything I want."

"Sprite for me," Bart said. "I am going to work tonight," he said, giving Lisa a sideways glance.

Laura and I ordered beers, and Peggy and Serena asked for Cokes.

"What do you think about the union, Bart?" Laura asked.

Bart kept his eyes on Lisa.

Laura repeated her question.

"I don't. Think about it," he said finally, turning toward the group.

"He thinks unions are just for the masses, the 'worker bees' as he calls them," Lisa explained, giving him a too-bright smile.

"I just don't think it's very professional, that's all," Bart said with a note of defensiveness.

Laura spoke up. "What's not professional is the way the hospital cuts staff and expects us to make up for it."

"Yeah," Serena said, turning to me. "You're the boss. Why don't you do something about it?"

How could I make them understand that I didn't control the hospital budget, I couldn't hire people when my budget had been cut, and I had next to no influence on administration about anything?

"She's just middle management, Serena, she just manages on what she's given," Peggy said. "The best she can," Peggy added with a smile to me.

"That's why we need the union," Laura said, looking around at each of us. "Then we'll have some power. Collective power."

Bart snorted. "You've been listening to the propaganda. Only you can get yourself ahead." He tapped a forefinger firmly on the table. "You can't depend on anyone else to do it for you."

"Maybe for the rest of you," Laura said. She'd changed from her scrubs to a sleeveless white blouse and stone-colored pants, her clothes as nondescript as her hair and skin. "You've been in nursing for a while, but I'm just starting out. I need to pay off school loans. This job's got to work out for me!"

"Listen, I know about unions," I said, knowing I was probably going to say too much. "My dad was in the union all his life. At the brewery."

"They have to belong, don't they?" Serena asked. "If they want to work there."

"That's true. Everyone eligible has to pay dues."

"Did they ever go on strike?" Serena asked.

"Once," I told them. "I was pretty little, but I remember he said they needed the union to protect them from the big guys."

"That's why we need one, too," Laura said.

"What worries me," Serena said, "is what would happen to the patients if we ever went out on strike?"

"Nurses can't strike," Peggy told her. She turned to me. "That's what I was arguing with Tim about. Why should we be getting in all this trouble when we don't have the leverage of striking?"

"That's not exactly true," I told them, reluctantly. "Nurses can strike with notice. They have to give the hospital time to prepare."

"For what? To fire us?" Laura asked, splotches of red creeping up her pale neck.

"Transfer patients, cancel elective surgery, train supervisors, that sort of thing. They can't fire anyone." I had slipped into my administrative role in spite of myself. I was torn between wanting them to know I understood how difficult it was to care for patients when we were understaffed, how afraid we all were that something would go wrong, and knowing that I couldn't get involved.

A police officer came in, glanced our way, and straddled a stool at the bar.

"Lots of professionals are in unions," Laura said. "Police." She nodded toward the man at the bar. "Ball players, pilots."

"Musicians," Serena added, looking toward the empty stage. Tonight she wore low-rider jeans and a filmy black short-sleeved blouse open to reveal the scrunchy magenta tube top underneath. A row of gold and colored stud earrings marched up one ear, and a dangly earring of filigreed gold on the other ear swung wildly as she looked around. "Hey'd you see where police cars are gonna have ads on them?" she asked.

"Like taxis?" Lisa inquired.

Serena giggled. "Next thing you know we'll have ads on our scrubs."

Conversation drifted to Serena's boyfriend as the canned music stopped and we turned toward the stage.

"They're starting," Serena said, bouncing on her seat. She squeezed my hand and smiled up at the stage.

Five young men shuffled up onto the stage perched on a wide pedestal behind the bar. They fiddled a bit with guitars and cords and speakers, and soon started up. Talk was impossible. The drinks arrived along with a basket of peanuts in their shells.

Lisa stood to excuse herself and reached behind her to snag her bag hooked on the chair, revealing a small gold ring in her navel. Peggy joined her and they headed toward the restroom. Bart stared at Lisa's back until the restroom door swung shut. I leaned over and asked him if she was all right. He nodded and stirred his Sprite with the straw, glancing toward the restroom until Lisa and Peggy finally emerged.

Between songs, the talk turned back to the hospital. Accreditation was on everyone's mind.

"We'll do fine," I tried to assure them. "Joint Commission's just doing their job, and it really helps us."

"Helps?" Serena asked. "How can it help to be on warning?"

"It makes the hospital do what they're supposed to. Hire more people."

"And pay them more than many nurses who have been there for years," Peggy added.

"If that's what it takes," I said, defending administration.

At the next break, Serena introduced us to her boyfriend, Ray, the band's drummer. Ray sported multiple piercings—nose, eyebrow—and a braid of brown hair dangling down his back. A straggly goatee marred what might have been a good-looking face. I thought I detected a glint of metal in his mouth and wondered idly what it would be like to kiss someone with a tongue stud. Ray apparently let his music do his talking, his mumbled answer was lost in the noise of the bar. He acknowledged the group with the briefest of nods. The sickly-sweet odor of marijuana lingered after he left.

After another set, I told them I had to leave, and Peggy joined me when I stood up. Outside the smoky bar we stopped and took a breath of the still-hot evening air.

"What'd you think about Bart's girlfriend?"

"What about her?" I asked, pulling my keys out of my shorts pocket.

"She's on drugs," Peggy said simply.

"Drugs? Maybe she just had too much to drink. You heard her. She doesn't work tonight, and Bart's driving."

"I saw her in the ladies' room. Her pupils were dilated." Peggy's hair, which she had let grow long, swung across her shoulders as she shook her head.

"She had just come from a dark room," I said as we reached Peggy's car. "They should have been dilated. Yours probably were, too,"

"Nope, this was when we were washing our hands. She'd been in there long enough for her pupils to constrict. I looked in the mirror. Mine were tiny slits; hers were huge. She was acting funny, too."

"Maybe she's on some medication that dilates her pupils. I think she was just having fun."

"It's no fun," Peggy said, unlocking her car door. As she slid into the driver's seat, she looked at me and said, "Believe me."

I didn't say anything. I thought Peggy was seeing drug problems in others because of her own problem in the past, and now that she worked in psychiatry, maybe she was diagnosing mental illness all around her. Much like nursing students do when they develop symptoms of every disease they study.

"Addicted people will do anything to get their drug of choice. Anything," she added, slamming her door.

After she left I climbed into Black Beauty and fired her up. Let Bart handle her, I thought as the top slid back and I looked up into the night sky. Earthbound problems seemed minuscule at that moment. A pickup truck squealed around the corner, spewing fumes. I reluctantly slid out from the curb and headed home.

Chapter 7

Friday, 10 August, 0713 Hours

I HEARD THE PAGE announcing the code as I stepped off the elevator. I ran through the double doors to ICU and followed Laura, who was heading toward Huey's room with the crash cart, hoping Huey had just pulled a lead off his chest.

I was wrong.

Huey lay still, his prosthesis uselessly hooked on the IV tubing and his amputated arm wrenched loose from its straps. His eyes were open, staring at the ceiling. A thought shot through my mind—if Huey died now, he'd be spared. Then the adrenaline kicked in and I shifted into automatic.

Oxygen hissed into his nose through a cannula but his chest didn't move.

"Huey," I said, loudly. "Wake up!"

No response.

"Come on, Huey, wake up!" I shook him. I checked his carotid pulse. It was weak and fluttery.

Respiratory arrest.

I pulled on gloves, grabbed the reversal kit hanging on the PCA pump, pulled out the syringe of Narcan, and drew up two doses. I noticed that the foil covering was off the rubber end of the access port on his IV line that we use to inject additional medications, and that it was discolored from the other drugs Huey had been getting. I cleaned the port with an alcohol wipe that Laura tossed me and stabbed the needle in, pushing in the drug that should reverse the effects of excessive narcotics.

"Wake up, Huey, come on, come on, wake up!" I shook him again. His body felt flimsy and his good arm flopped on the bed until I let go.

A minute had passed.

I injected the second dose of Narcan and waited, watching the monitor. Uneven lines jerked across the screen, the alarm screaming.

"No respirations?" Laura asked.

I shook my head, then yanked Huey's head back, slid an oral airway through his mouth and down his throat, grabbed the Ambu bag off the wall, hooked it up to the oxygen flow valve, and slapped the bag over his nose and mouth. I cranked the oxygen flow meter up as high as it would go—to 15 liters—and began squeezing the bag, trying to push the hundred percent oxygen into his lungs.

His chest resisted.

I squeezed harder, pushing in as much oxygen as I could.

Tim came in, quickly surveying the scene. "V-tach," he said, glancing at the erratic rhythm on the monitor.

Huey's heart was in ventricular tachycardia.

Laura pulled Huey's hospital gown loose from his body and bunched it up under his chin. She took over bagging him as I slapped the florescent-orange jelly pads on his chest, one on his sternum, the other over his left nipple, and put the defibrillator paddles over them firmly on his bony chest.

"Go directly to 360 joules," I told Tim, "since he's in V-tach."

Tim nodded and set the defibrillator charge for the first jolt.

"Stand clear!" I yelled.

Pressing hard on the paddles, I pushed both discharge buttons simultaneously. I let up and looked at the monitor.

A single line bounded wildly up and down across the screen, its shrieking the only sound in the room.

"360 again," I ordered.

"360 joules," Tim responded.

"Stand clear!" I shocked Huey a second time.

No change.

A third jolt.

Nothing.

An anesthesiologist rushed in to intubate Huey. Laura moved to the head of the bed to assist, pulling an intubation tray off the code cart. She tore it open and tossed the equipment onto the bed while the anesthesiologist squeezed between the head of the bed and the wall. As the anesthesiologist called for equipment, Laura handed it to him.

The doctor struggled to get the tube down Huey's throat and into his barrel chest distended by pulmonary emphysema. "What's his O_2?" he asked, glancing toward Huey's hand where the pulse oximeter should have been clipped to a finger to record oxygen levels in the blood. The finger clip lay on the sheet.

"His clip's off," I told the doctor.

"BP? Pulse?"

Tim wrapped a blood pressure cuff around Huey's arm and inflated it. It deflated downward quickly. "80 over 30," Tim said, grabbing Huey's wrist. "No palpable pulse," he reported.

A squiggly thread rippled across the monitor's screen. Asystole.

"V-fib," I said out loud. Huey was in ventricular fibrillation now.

Four minutes had passed since the alarm had sounded. Huey's face was bright blue, his eyes still staring at the ceiling.

Dr. Lord came through the door, breathless.

I reported our progress. "He's in cardiac arrest. No pulse. Shocked 360 joules times three. No response."

He glanced at the monitor. The wiggly line continued.

"Epinephrine," he ordered. "One milligram, IV push."

Tim was already drawing it up. Swiping the access port on the IV tubing with an alcohol wipe, he plunged the needle into the stopper and injected the epinephrine.

The screaming alarm was the only sound.

"Shock," Lord ordered.

"Stand clear." I shocked him again.

Nothing.

Frowning, Lord said, "Epi again."

Tim gave it.

"Shock again, 360."

No response.

"Stat blood gas," Lord said.

Tim grabbed a blood gas kit off the code cart, turned Huey's hand over and expertly inserted the needle deep into the inside of Huey's wrist. Dark red blood backed up into the syringe.

"Is that venous blood?" Laura asked.

"Nope, I got the artery. His blood is so saturated with CO_2 it's turned it dark." Tim put the syringe in ice and handed it off to a student. "Get stat blood gases," he ordered as she scooted out the door.

"Push epi again?" Tim asked Lord.

"Yes."

We continued alternating shocks—360 joules—with epinephrine as Lord ordered it.

"Other drugs?" Tim asked finally.

"It won't help now," he said, rocking back on his heels.

"Don't quit yet," I said, my voice rising. "This is just what he worried about, that we wouldn't keep trying if he coded."

Lord shook his head.

"Please. Please keep trying," I begged even as I stared at Huey's still, blue face.

Cyanosis colored Huey's arms and legs bluish-purple, and streaks of purple and blue mottled his chest. Even with the jelly pads, the paddles had left burn marks where I had shocked him.

The respiratory therapist came in to report on Huey's blood gases that Tim had drawn. She handed me the lab printout strip.

"His O_2 is 37, CO_2, 65," I read.

Incompatible with life.

"How long's it been?" Lord asked, "since the alarm."

I looked at the clock. "Thirty-three minutes."

"Too late now," Lord said. "Stop drugs." He moved to the bedside. He checked Huey's neck for a pulse, listened to his chest and, finally, bent over with his ear next to Huey's mouth. He shook his head and glanced again at the monitor now humming a straight line across the screen, whining our failure.

"We're calling the code," he said.

"You're calling the code." I said, trying to keep my voice steady. I glanced at the clock behind me on the wall. "I have the time as 0749 hours," I added, for the record.

"Yes, patient pronounced, 0749," he said, and walked out of the room.

I stood a moment after the others had gone, feeling the emptiness. Even in death Huey looked somehow alive, as if his spirit was too strong to let go. He still stared at the ceiling, a surprised expression on his face. Sighing, I peeled off my gloves and threw them in the trash.

"YOU OKAY?" JESSIE asked me back at the desk.

I clutched Huey's chart to my chest and swallowed.

Ruby snorted.

"What?" I asked her.

"Now we got a room."

"Huh?"

"Well, we do," she said, lifting her chin. Loose flesh jiggled underneath. "They got a accident victim in the ER needs a room." She picked up the phone.

I opened Huey's chart and glanced at the record for the PCA pump. "He got a fresh morphine syringe on his pump right before he coded."

"Wasn't he due?" Tim asked

I checked. "Yep."

"So what's wrong?"

"I was wondering if it was too much. This is what he worried about, that we might not be able to resuscitate him."

"We did all we could, Monika. The damage had been done. His brain was fried."

"I know," I said with a sigh.

I checked the night shift report.

"Something else?" Tim asked.

"Could Bart had given him morphine, too, and not charted it?"

"What makes you think that?" Tim asked.

"Uh, he's not always as accurate as he could be," I explained, equivocating.

"I don't blame him if he missed something," Jessie said, coming through with a wash basin. "What with all the work we've got. . . ." Her voice trailed off as she headed into Huey's room to help Laura, who had started cleaning up Huey's body for the morgue.

"Nah, Bart was gone before," Ruby said. "With that Lisa."

"Lisa? Was she in here?" I asked.

Ruby sat down, creaking the springs in her chair. "Yep. She came in right behind me and she saw him in the med room, but I stopped her. No, sir, I weren't having her in there with all them drugs, not in my med room."

"Then what happened?"

"She just followed him out."

"So she never got into the med room? Or in a patient's room?"

"Nope. I didn't take my eyes off her until she left."

"Jessie," I said as she came out of Huey's room with a wash basin. "Did you and Bart do the narcotic counts this morning?"

"He got away before we could do them," she said over her shoulder.

The same nurses aide who'd thought a blanket was the treatment for a reaction to a transfusion came out of Huey's room carrying an IV bag, the PCA pump still attached, and the tubing dragging behind her on the floor.

"What are you doing with that?" I asked her.

She looked at the almost-full bag. "I thought maybe you could, like, reuse this."

Ruby rolled her eyes and looked at me pointedly.

"We never reuse anything that's been used on someone else. *Never.*" I squinted at her name badge. "Josie."

"I just thought, like, save some money. . . ." Her voice faded away as Ruby and I stared at her.

"Take it back into the room. Laura or Jessie will tell you what to do with everything."

"They hiring people with no sense now," Ruby said, shaking her head.

I sighed. Poor training and too little of that, was to blame. Not the nurses aide.

The phone rang and Ruby told me it was ER. Wanda filled me in on the patient, and I told her to hold up until we could have the room cleaned. She agreed but complained about having to keep other patients waiting in the hall.

"Yeah? Well, we got a dead one," I said louder than I intended. A man waiting for Serena to finish with his mother looked up. I lowered my voice. "Sorry, Wanda. We're all stressed out, I guess."

"Just hurry," she answered. "We got them piled up down here."

The morgue attendant had left the special gurney we use to stash bodies so it can be moved through the halls without anyone realizing it is anything but an empty stretcher. The obvious effort it takes to maneuver it, though, belies our subterfuge. After Jessie and Laura had cleaned up the body, taped the dangling tubes to the body, slipped a tag on Huey's toe and another around his neck, I had helped them lift the body onto the shelf that was stowed beneath the plain top, and we had pulled the gurney out into the open area to be picked back up by the attendant.

I was on the phone to housekeeping trying to convince the supervisor that we needed the room cleaned stat when the attendant came through the door.

"'Bout time," Ruby said.

"No hurry, is there?" he asked, popping the wad of gum in his mouth.

"For us, they is. Now you git moving."

He grabbed the cart and pushed it toward the entrance. He glanced back at Ruby and as he did the gurney hit the swinging doors with a bang.

I cringed.

He backed up and the doors swung open and hit the gurney again.

Mavis came striding through the door, passing right by the cart hiding her husband's body.

For a moment no one moved. Then Mavis, glancing at each of us, headed toward Huey's room. I grabbed her arm and asked her if she'd come with me to the visitors' waiting room down the hall.

"Why?" she asked, jerking her arm away.

The attendant shrugged, bobbing his pony tail, and pushed the gurney through the doors as we all turned to watch.

"What's going on here? Why's everybody just standing around? What's wrong?" Mavis asked.

Laura came out of Huey's room, shoving the curtain open as she did, revealing the empty bed.

The next sound was something between a wail and a sob as Mavis slumped against me, and Serena and I grabbed her before she hit the floor. We helped her sit down on the floor and I shoved her head between her knees, my arm firmly around her shoulders. She smelled like stale cigarettes and greasy hair, and her breath came in ragged bursts. Serena stared at me across Mavis' head as she hung on tightly to the woman's arm. Neither of us spoke. Finally, Mavis raised her head and struggled to stand. Holding her firmly by the arms, we led her off the unit and into my office. Serena brought her a cup of water and some tissues.

"Can I see him?" she asked after blowing her nose.

"He's already downstairs, but as soon as you have a funeral home, you can see him there."

Beads of sweat had broken out on her forehead. She dabbed at her face with a tissue and took a sip of water. "What was it? The cancer?"

"I imagine so. It was pretty bad, as we'd talked about."

"I want to know," she said. "I want you to find out for sure what killed him."

"You want an autopsy?"

"I want to know for sure. He told me to make sure."

I called Ruby and asked her to bring the forms to order the post. By the time Mavis had signed them, she seemed composed. I asked her if I could call someone for her, but she shook her head. I insisted that someone take her home, though, explaining that she was too distracted to drive. I assigned a student to take her to the waiting room and sit with her until her friend arrived. As soon as they left, I hurried in to see the patient who had just been wheeled up from ER.

I HAD JUST heard an update on the new patient when the doors swung open, and two men in suits came through followed by Father Rudolf, the hospital's chaplain.

Rudolf smiled hesitantly. "Uh, Monika." His hands behind his back, he shifted back and forth on the balls of his feet. He was a small man with a full head of wavy, brown hair lightly sprinkled with gray, a cheerful demeanor, and crinkly blue eyes.

"Uh, these men are here to see Huey," he said, his face breaking into a quick smile.

"You're too late," Ruby said, coming back to the desk.

"Was he moved?" Father asked.

"You might say," Ruby added.

I turned to the men. "I'm Monika Everhardt, head nurse here. Why do you want to see Mr. Castle?"

I recognized the older of the two men. I'd met him a few months ago when he'd investigated another death at St. Teresa's. It looked like he was wearing the same navy blazer and gray pants I'd seen him in before, but he'd replaced the frayed-collared shirt with a more stylish one in wide royal blue-and-white stripes with a solid-white collar. His wing-tip shoes could have used a shine, though.

Detective Harding nodded to me as he showed me his identification badge. "Father Rudolf arranged for us to see Mr. Castle," he said after introducing his partner, Tom McNeil.

"What's wrong?" Rudolf asked. He turned toward Huey's room as the housekeeper pulled open the curtain. The room had been stripped bare, the bed was glistening with still-wet antiseptic cleaner.

"I'm sorry, Father. And detectives. Mr. Castle died earlier this morning."

"Oh my," Father Rudolf said.

"It wasn't unexpected, Father," I said.

"It's not that, Monika." He looked around. "It's just that . . . he wanted to take care of something first." He moistened his lips. "And I promised I'd help him."

"Sorry, Father. Not our timing, I'm afraid."

Rudolf glanced upward. "His." A fleeting smile crossed his lips.

"Hers," I said, automatically.

Rudolf looked puzzled, then asked, "When'd he pass?"

I checked my watch. "About an hour ago. I can check the record for the exact time, if you want."

"No, no." Rudolf turned to Detective Harding. "I'm sorry, Martin. I guess we're too late."

"Twenty years too late," Harding said.

"Probably not much help anyway," McNeil said, looking toward the doors as if he wanted to get away.

"Humph," Ruby commented, heading into the now-clean room carrying supplies.

"But I thought he was doing better," Rudolf said. "He'd really perked up the last few days," he said to the officers, smiling. "He was glad you were coming."

"That's sometimes how it is right before they die. They seem to rally," I explained.

"What you gonna do wit this?" Ruby asked, waving Huey's hook as she came out of the room.

"Oh." Rudolf seemed to crumple.

"Steady, Father," I said, taking his arm. "That's Mr. Castle's prosthesis," I explained to the officers.

"You want it?" Ruby asked them, sticking it in the younger man's face.

He backed up.

"It belongs to his wife, Ruby. Put it in a bag out of the way."

She swung it over her shoulder like a rifle and marched out to the supply closet, the pincers flopping against her fleshy back.

"He was worried about this," Father Rudolf said, almost to himself.

"Oh," Harding said. "Worried about what?"

Rudolf shrugged. "I don't know exactly, but he was afraid of something."

Harding turned to me. "Anything unusual about his death?"

"What do you mean, unusual?"

"Unexpected. Strange. What did he look like?"

"Dead," Ruby said, returning. "He look dead."

"Not really. He had stomach cancer. He was terminal," I told them.

Laura came out of the med room, gave us a glance, and headed into a patient's room.

"Was *she* here?" Harding asked.

"Laura?" I said.

"Don't tell me this guy was her patient, too," Harding said to me.

"As a matter of fact, he was."

"She was the one I was telling you about," Harding said to McNeil. "The one who ran out and the patient died. It was a few months ago. Now," he said, turning back to me, "it seems as if you have another death."

I drew myself up to my full four feet eleven inches. "She did not do anything wrong. Then or now," I said, my voice getting louder.

Harding and McNeil exchanged glances.

"Did he have any visitors this morning?" Harding asked.

"I don't think so. Ruby?"

"I can't watch everthing."

"Where's the body now?" Harding asked.

"In the morgue," I told him.

"You going to do an autopsy?"

"The wife requested one."

The phone rang, breaking the tension. A patient's daughter wanted to talk to me, Ruby said.

"Do you need anything else?" I asked, holding my hand over the receiver.

Harding looked around as staff members scooted in and out of patients' rooms, stealing curious glances at us.

"I'll walk you out," Rudolf said to Harding, smiling an apology to me.

I CALLED OUR pathologist, Max, to ask him to save the specimen Tim had drawn for Huey's blood gases. I'd be down later to tell him why, I told him.

Judyth came through the door, carrying a stack of paychecks. She had started delivering paychecks on Fridays to everyone who didn't have direct deposit. She said it was to save the nurses time; Tim said it was to remind us who signed their paychecks.

She moved aside a vase of flowers in order to place the paychecks on the counter.

"I have something to talk to you about. Come to your office."

"This is just precautionary," she said when we were seated. "I'm worried about the amount of narcotics we're using, and I want to take your narcotic records to match against patients' charts."

Uh oh.

"I need to tell you something," I said, sighing. I might as well get this over with. "A few times we've missed doing the change-of-shift counts."

"What? With Joint Commission breathing down our neck?"

"You're not up here, Judyth," I said, my voice rising to match hers. "I need twice as many nurses as I've got. I can't afford to have two nurses standing in the med room just to count boxes of drugs while patients need care. Sometimes two nurses to a patient aren't even enough."

She held up her hand. "Okay, okay. We can't do anything about what's happened. I've just noticed that your unit's been using a lot of narcotics recently. More than usual."

"It's the new pain-control regs. We're constantly checking pain levels and giving so many more dosages now to try to control it."

"I imagine that's it," she said. "I just don't want to take any chances that there are any discrepancies so I'm taking the drug books to match up with patient records.

"What do we do in the meantime? Where do we record them?"

"I brought some blank sheets to use for now." She released several lined sheets of paper from her clipboard. "They're coded and numbered, so don't lose them."

AS I CAME back onto the unit, Ruby waggled a pudgy, ringed finger toward the flowers Judyth had pushed aside on the counter. "You gonna open your card?"

"Huh? What card?"

"The one on your flowers."

"Aren't these for a patient?" I pulled out the card tucked between the stems of roses artfully arranged in a tall, milk-glass vase. "Don't you have anything to do but tease me?"

"To Monika, you're as competent as you are attractive. With admiration, Phil Silverman."

I felt the tell-tale warmth of a blush as I smiled to myself. "Don't you say a word, Ruby," I said as she opened her mouth.

I had known since the age of eight that Rick was the only man for me. Dressed in a baseball uniform, he'd been in his front yard tossing a ball up in the air when my bike had careened into a tree and I'd been tossed off, bringing him running. Embarrassed more than hurt, I'd let him help me up. From then on I'd watched him, mostly from afar. He was two years ahead of me at St. Aloysius where we'd both been grade-school students.

We'd met up again at a dance at his high school, St. Mary's. He'd been a junior and already determined to join the Army when he graduated. We'd married when I started nursing school and shortly thereafter he shipped out to Vietnam. Even though it had been many years since he'd been killed, I'd never thought of anyone else in that way.

Ruby smothered a giggle and asked me, "So what do I do with this?" She held up a paper sack, lunch-bag size. "Bet you can't guess what it is."

"I don't have time for games," I snapped, turning toward the door with my roses.

"OK, Miss Smarty Pants. She left it." Ruby nodded toward Huey's room.

"His wife?"

"Nah, the girlfriend. She came back while you were out to lunch yesterday."

"Why didn't you give it to me then?"

"I can't keep track of everthing. I just took it. We're supposed to keep everybody happy, ain't we?" She spread her lips into a Cheshire-cat grin. "What you want me to do with it now?" she asked, waving the bag in my face.

Sighing, I put my vase down and looked inside the bag. A small baggie, zipped shut, held four hand-wrapped joints, their papers twisted at the ends. A few leaves of the tell-tale light green matter spilled into the bag beside a yellow Bic lighter.

"Just what we need—more trouble," Ruby said.

"I'll get rid of it." I folded the bag into itself and shoved it in my lab coat pocket.

"Right now we've got work to do."

MAX WAS SIGNING reports when I found him later, perched on a stool in the lab. He looked up and smiled. "Hey, Monika, got more work for me? Like I need it." He nodded toward the open door of the exam room. A gleaming steel table stood below overhead lights, a tray of dissecting instruments was next to a backless stool, and a recording microphone hung suspended from a stand next to the stool. Lockers held the bodies that waited in cold storage for their turn on the table, Huey's among them. I'd only had to witness one autopsy while I was in nursing school. It was one too many.

"Are you short-staffed too?" I asked Max.

"I'm down to two techs, both inexperienced."

"I know what you mean. We're so low on nurses it's not safe."

"At least our patients can wait around until we get to them," he said, sighing. A rotund man with a fringe of white hair that formed a sort of halo on his otherwise bald head, Max had been St. Teresa's pathologist for as long as I could remember. "So, what can I do for you?"

"I came down to tell you why I wanted you to save that patient's blood, Castle's."

"One of the techs put it in the refrigerator. We usually save a couple of tubes for a few days anyway in case they're needed."

"Would you check it for alcohol? The last time he was in a buddy of his snuck him some booze and, along with all the narcotics he was getting, his respirations were depressed enough to scare him."

"You're worried that might have contributed to his death?" He peered at me through the thick lenses of his glasses.

"Let's just make sure it didn't."

"I'll run a blood alcohol and let you know."

"Another thing. Have you done the post on Guardino? He died Wednesday."

"I'll check," he said, stepping off the stool. "If it's typed up, it should be in my office." He gathered up the stack of reports, and I walked with him out of the lab into the administrative area. He handed the papers to a man who was listening through earphones and typing on a keyboard.

Max motioned me into his office and scooped several books off a chair for me. He sat down and rummaged through a stack of files on his desk. "Yep, here it is." He pulled out a manila folder and flipped it open. "Primary cause of death," he read. "Acute cardiovascular accident. Secondary causes: intervening pneumonia right lower lobe and cardiac arrhythmias." He closed the folder. "Stroke, complicated by pneumonia and heart problems, in layman's terms. Why'd you want to know? Isn't this consistent with his diagnosis?"

"It is," I said, chewing on my lower lip.

"And? What's the problem?"

I reached behind me and closed the door. "The nurse on duty when he coded didn't intubate him. Or shock him. He thought the man was a B code when he was a full code."

Max shook his head. "It wouldn't have made any difference, Monika. I doubt he could have been resuscitated no matter what anyone did, and even if they did get his heart pumping again, it was only a matter of time before it gave out." Max opened the folder again and adjusted his glasses. "This guy was seventy-nine years old, he had multiple health problems. Just let it go."

Max's phone rang. I waved a goodbye as he picked up the receiver.

Chapter 8

SATURDAY, 11 AUGUST, 0925 HOURS

"AUNT MONNY! Aunt Monny!" screamed the twins, slamming through the gate. Catastrophe, my white angora, streaked toward the opening.

"Stop her!" I yelled as my cousin Hannah scooped her up, snuggling her nose in Cat's warm fur who, in turn, nestled down in Hannah's arms as if she hadn't just been trying to run away a few seconds before.

I was in the back yard trying to tame the weeds that threatened to overrun the spindly annuals I'd planted along the fence row. The bedding plants had been displayed so enticingly at Shades of Summer, our local garden shop, that I'd bought too many and ended up giving some plants to Hannah. She had told me to fertilize them when I planted, and then re-apply fertilizer every few weeks, but I kept forgetting to buy the fertilizer. When she finally brought some over, the only plants I'd fertilized were the weeds.

Hannah sat down beside me on the warm grass, continuing to stroke Cat, who lay back with her belly exposed, purring softly. The girls, both talking at once, elbowed each other to be first to show me her treasure. Tina proudly displayed the latest Goosebumps book while Gena shoved Yu-Gi-Oh cards in my face.

"Those are for babies," Tina said, pointing to her sister's cards. She tossed her blond pigtails for emphasis.

As usual, the girls were dressed nearly alike in matching halter tops, one pink, the other a pale green, and blue-jean shorts. Tina had folded the legs of her shorts up higher, and Hannah absently rolled them down as we talked.

"No they're not," Gena argued, chewing on the end of one braid. "Are they Aunt Monny?"

Strictly speaking, I wasn't their aunt. Their mom is my cousin and we are both only children of twin brothers. So while we were growing up Hannah and I had pretended we were sisters. Her ten-year-old twins and their three older brothers were the nearest thing I had to children of my own.

"I thought everybody wanted Pokemon cards," I said, looking at Gena's cards as Tina shoved her book onto my lap.

"Oh, Aunt Monny, those are old," Gena said with a sniff. "Nobody wants those now."

Cat pounced on one of Gena's cards on the grass, and she snatched it up. Squealing, the girls ran after Cat and chased her inside.

Hannah examined my gardening. "You need mulch," she said, not for the first time. Hannah was appropriately attired for gardening, a loose T covering long denim shorts, her unruly auburn curls caught up under a bandana.

"I wanted to do it myself."

"Uh uh."

"I did," I told her. "I want to feel the earth in my fingers, to feel like I'm really a gardener. I don't want to smother the weeds with some phony mulch." I sat back on my heels.

"That's how nature does it," Hannah said. She picked up a trowel and began to loosen the soil between the flowers. "Old plants die or trees lose their leaves and you have instant mulch that builds up, layer over layer, year after year, the bottom layer disintegrates, providing nutrients, and the top layer prevents weak seeds from getting in, or other sprouts from poking through." She tamped down the soil around a geranium and wiped her face with the back of her hand. Ginger-colored freckles stood out on her face, and I could smell the sunscreen she wore religiously all summer.

"Okay. So it needs more work," I said, calculating the distance to the end of the fence row. My backyard had looked so small when I had bought the simple brick bungalow on a quiet street a little more than a year earlier. Now the yard seemed to have grown in size along with the weeds.

I sat down cross-legged on the ground and rubbed dirt and grass off my knees. Sweat had plastered my T-shirt to my body and my gray gym shorts were soil-spotted.

Next door white sheets were stretched tight on the clothesline, motionless in the August heat. On the other side, play equipment in bright, primary colors stood empty, waiting for the two toddlers who lived there to return from vacation. The temperature was predicted to reach 100° by afternoon; it felt close to that now.

Saturday morning cartoons on TV blared through the door the girls had left ajar.

"I'll tell you what," Hannah said. "As soon as it cools off a little I'll bring the boys over and we'll help you get this weeded." She shoved sunglasses up on top of her bandana and squinted at me. "So what's wrong? Something's bothering you, I can tell."

I sighed. "It's work. As usual."

"Come on, Monika, you've dealt with a lot of work problems over the years. It can't be that bad."

"Oh, no? I'll tell you what," I said, digging up a clump of grass and tossing it aside. "Administration's so caught up in accreditation, derailing the union, and a few missing meds that the important problems are being ignored."

"Like what?"

"My boss has her priorities mixed up. She's worrying about meds we've been too busy to chart instead of helping improve the staff's morale. It's in the toilet now." I stabbed a recalcitrant dandelion through its middle. "Just so we look good. That's all she's worried about." I pulled the severed weed out but the roots stayed in the ground.

"Have you lost any more nurses lately?" Hannah sat back on her heels and pulled off the gloves she'd been smart enough to bring along. She tucked a strand of hair back into her bandana.

"No, thank goodness. But it's probably just a matter of time."

"So then you have enough for now."

"No, Hannah, we still have open positions that haven't been filled. That's the problem. We've been understaffed for months."

"Then I'm glad you agree with me."

"Agree about what?" I studied another dandelion's fat, white root.

"That gardening is a stress reducer."

"Sure, I'm not stressed anymore." I flung the weed toward the pile I'd been accumulating before Hannah had arrived. "I'll tell you one thing," I said, pushing my trowel under a clump of crabgrass.

"Yes?"

"You don't want to be a patient at St. Teresa's now. Or any other hospital for that matter." The crabgrass came loose with a jerk, spraying dirt into my face. "I say a prayer every day," I began, spitting dirt out of my mouth, "that nothing happens."

Hannah tamped down the earth around a cluster of marigolds that had come loose when she'd picked out sprouts of grass around them.

"I'm worried someone did something or didn't do something they should have." I unfolded my knees and stretched out on my back on the grass with a sigh and examined my dirt-encrusted nails.

"Didn't you get more nurses this summer? When they graduated?"

"Not enough to fill all the open positions in St. Louis. And every hospital in town competes for them. It seems like the hospital administrators steal staff from one another, trying to top their competitors' offers with higher bonuses. Or they entice nurses with goodies, like housecleaning for a year." I raised up on my elbows, stretched my legs out in front of me and wiggled my bare toes.

"Wow. Sign me up! For a year of housecleaning, I'll go to nursing school." With five children and a husband, Hannah often said she never got the whole house clean at one time.

"Another hospital is offering a full-body massage for every forty hours worked. That would do it for me," I said, sitting up and rolling my shoulders.

The back door banged open as the twins ran out, chasing Cat into Hannah's arms.

"I think I'm done gardening today," I said. "Too hot."

"Are we still on for tomorrow?" Hannah asked, dropping Cat and scooping up the pile of weeds.

"The Deutsch Fest?" I asked, referring to Hannah's question about Sunday's plans.

"Even in this heat?" Hannah asked.

"Of course we're going. We couldn't miss it," I said. The annual German street festival in South St. Louis was a tradition for our family and many others. "I can smell those brauts already."

The girls chased Cat around the yard until she slid under a peony bush and refused to come out.

"Why do you think they moved it?" Hannah asked, standing. "At least by Labor Day we had a chance for cooler weather."

"Politics."

"Politics? What does a street fair have to do with politics?"

"The election's next week. This gives the politicians time to meet-and-greet in the flesh," I said.

In unison the girls reminded their mother that she'd promised to take them to Ed Crewe's for a concrete at St. Louis' famous frozen custard stand, a landmark in South St. Louis. And they were ready to go, now.

"Help your aunt carry everything to the garage first," she said to them with a nod toward the tools scattered in the grass. Hannah went out my back gate to deposit the weeds we'd dug into a dumpster in the alley.

After we'd stowed the last of my garden tools in the garage I wiped my face with a rag I'd left on the shelf.

The girls giggled.

"What?" I asked them.

"You look funny," Gena said.

Even Hannah was trying not to giggle. "Well," she said, "that rag left black smears all over your face."

"The better to scare you, my dears!" I jumped toward the girls. They squealed in delight. I growled and chased them out to the street and into Hannah's SUV.

"You can't catch us now!" Tina shouted through the closed window. She stuck out her tongue, put her thumbs in her ears, and wiggled her fingers at me.

Hannah opened the driver's side door and Tina leaned out the opening.

"Ha ha ha ha," she taunted in the time-honored sing-song children's chant. I waved them a smiling goodbye, grateful for the help and the distraction. Hannah was right. Gardening *is* good for stress.

THE PARTY WAS in full swing by the time I arrived at the career fair in a downtown hotel. A jazz combo played on a dais at the far end of the ballroom, which was crowded with display booths. I squeezed my way through the aisles jammed with students. Interspersed among the hospital booths were equipment companies, book publishers, and representatives from graduate schools. Hospital recruiters hawked their giveaways—candy, penlights, key chains—and grabbed any takers with their spiel. Most glanced over me, my age and determined look discouraging them. Young, energetic ones were the prize they all sought.

I'd grabbed a quick shower after Hannah left and donned white pants, a red-and-white striped top, and white clogs that I usually wore with scrubs to work—the ones without any bodily fluids left on them.

St. Teresa's had a small exhibit space along one wall. Dressed in khakis and a moss-green polo shirt, Tim stood beside a table spread with brightly-colored brochures that touted the benefits of working in a small, urban hospital. Pictures of nurses caring for patients—mostly photogenic infants, of which St. T's had precious few—were tacked on the felt board propped atop the table.

Tim watched me approach, his one black eye giving him a lopsided owl-like appearance.

"Any traffic?" I asked him.

"Some," he admitted, handing a smiling young woman a brochure.

"Any live ones, really interested?"

He turned to me. "What does administrations want us to do? Tell these kids how wonderful it is to work at St. T's? Lie?"

"Tim, I'm sympathetic to you. And everyone. But we have a job to do here."

"Some job," he said. "We don't even have recruiters like the other hospitals. Or a real booth—just a table and a few feet. On top of that we're expected to do this on our own time." Tim had a family—a pregnant wife and two young girls—and he treasured his days off. "Anyway, you're here now. I'm going to take a break." He left without telling me what I was supposed to do.

A group of students approached, and I gave them my best smile.

"What do you have to give us?" asked a young man dressed in a navy golf shirt, tan slacks, and expensive-looking loafers.

I looked around on the table. "I have some brochures here about St. Teresa's." I smiled again.

"Humph. That all?"

A couple of the girls with him giggled and then the group moved on. I kept busy after that as a steady stream of students grabbed brochures as fast as I could hand them out.

At a break in the crowd, I spotted Bart and Wanda standing behind a counter in a booth down the aisle. Milburn University had twice the exhibit space St. T's had. A tall display board stood at the back and held photos of smiling graduates proudly displaying diplomas. Waist-high, narrow counters surrounded the booth on three sides and were covered with colorful brochures.

Wanda saw me, spoke briefly to the older man, and then made her way to my side.

"Are you the advertisement for graduate school?" I asked her, smiling.

"Ain't I the one who'll grab them?" She laughed. A little on the chunky side, Wanda had wavy brown hair, turning gray, and a no-nonsense attitude.

"Him, there. He sure seems to know where he's going." She waved toward Bart, who had a couple of young women intently listening to what he was telling them.

Bart bounded back and forth from in front of the booth and around to the back table, collecting information for interested students, talking all the time.

"He's pretty energetic," Wanda commented.

"And he worked last night. Bart Mickelson. He works nights in ICU," I explained.

A group of students approached, read the name on our sign and moved on.

We looked over to watch Bart's girlfriend, Lisa, interrupt his conversation with the women, and push herself up close to Bart. He frowned at her and turned back to the women, but they had taken the hint and moved off. We couldn't hear what Bart said next, but Lisa turned away, and then she jerked her arm away from him when he tried to grab it. She moved on to a pharmaceutical company's booth where she picked up a syringe and examined it. Another woman stopped at Bart's booth and he launched into an animated discussion with her, gesturing widely.

I handed a student a brochure, but she wasn't interested in talking. She dropped it in her plastic bag and moved off, swinging her arm.

"I wonder where he gets all that energy. Me, I can hardly stay awake sometimes in my evening classes." She picked up one of my brochures. "Yeah, this captures it. Smiling nurses working side by side with equally-cheerful doctors. That's us. Every day." She tossed the pamphlet back onto the table.

"What made you decide to do it? Go to graduate school," I added, offering a reluctant young man a brochure.

Wanda leaned back and folded her arms across her plaid blouse. "Aren't you sick and tired of it, Monika? Fewer and fewer staff, sicker and sicker patients. And all administration says is, 'Work smarter.' Damn, I've always worked smart." Wanda had once told me she was the oldest of six; now she was divorced with a teenage son. "This way I'll be able to work decent hours, make a good salary, and have a life, too."

"But won't all your patients be asleep?"

"Hey, that's how I want them." She grinned. "I'd choose sleeping patients any ol' day over all those crabbing people in the ER, mad because they have to wait. The other ones who are really sick, they're just waiting to sue us." She shoved off from the table. "I'd better get back."

"Who's that?" I asked her, nodding toward the man talking to Tim, who was over at the Milburn booth.

"Dean Swanson. We're supposed to bring him in when we get a live one."

"I hope that doesn't mean he's leaving St. T's. He works for me."

"Aren't you the lucky one?"

"Huh?"

"He's sooo good looking."

"And so married."

"Aren't they all? But that other guy isn't married, is he? He is definitely a hunk."

"Oh, you mean Bart. I never noticed."

"Wow, Monika, you dead or something? Those blond curls, burly arms, big smile, blue eyes—"

"Okay, okay, that's enough. He's just not one of my favorite people, that's all. Tim, on the other hand, is very conscientious."

She squinted toward the booth. "Isn't he the one pushing the union?"

"Yeah," I said.

"He'd better watch out. I just heard they fired a nurse at St. Michael's. She was one of the union leaders."

"They can't do that. At least not for supporting a union."

"No? You're way too naïve, Monika. Of course they can. They just say it was for 'attitude.' It gets them off the hook, legally."

"You're really burned out, aren't you, Wanda?"

"You know, even if someone resigns they can change the record to say they were fired. Who's to know?"

"Why don't you just quit? Do something else?"

She looked surprised. "I can't, Monika." She stopped and pulled herself up. "I'm a nurse," she said, looking me in the eye. "It's who I am."

Tim returned when Wanda went back to Milburn's booth, and for a few minutes we had a rush on brochures. A couple of students asked questions but none wanted to give us their names and addresses. The room was clearing out. A voice on the loudspeaker invited everyone to the program beginning in the next room. I told Tim I was going to see what they had to say and he nodded his agreement.

Out in the hallway three models, wearing the latest in uniform fashion, pirouetted on a small stage. With their perfect makeup and equally-perfect figures, they sashayed back and forth, displaying snappy scrubs in sun-splashed prints under crisp white jackets and lab coats. None had any blood on them.

"Monika!" Lisa said, grabbing my arm. "Can I talk to you?" she asked, her round baby face marred by dark smudges under her eyes. "Please."

Shaking off her arm, I said, "Come on. I'm going in here." I started toward the crowd heading into the auditorium.

"No, no, someplace we can talk." Her eyes darted back and forth. "It'll just take a minute."

I looked at my watch. The program was due to begin in five minutes but, judging by the size of the crowd still lined up to get in, they'd be late starting.

"We could get a Coke or something," I said, nodding toward a refreshment stand doing a brisk business in hot dogs, ice cream, and soft drinks.

After we bought our drinks we found an empty table among the few scattered along the wall. We settled ourselves, carefully balancing our cups on the black grill-work top of the wobbly ice cream table.

"I wanted to ask you about Bart," she began, stirring her drink with a straw, its paper cap still on. She stared at the dark liquid swirling in the ice. Finally, she looked up, her green eyes serious. "He's a good nurse, you know," she began as if I'd argue with her. "He really is." She stirred some more.

Her knit top looked a size too small for her, or maybe it had shrunk in the wash. But that had been a while ago; perspiration stained the underarms and the front showed the remains of more than one food group.

"I was still living at home in Louisville and working my first nursing job on nights in the ER," Lisa said, looking off in the distance. "Bart came in with his father." She turned to me and shook her head. "Nothing we could do. Alcohol and pills. Looks like he did it on purpose. Bart said he'd just been fired from another job."

Inwardly I sighed. I never have been able to understand suicide. Life is just too damn precious, no matter what.

"Bart was upset, his mom too, of course. He told me he was a nursing student but he said the instructors had it in for him, him being a man."

I knew what she meant. Tim and other men in nursing had told me how difficult some women made it for them. The ones who stuck with it were all the more noteworthy, I'd always thought.

"You've been together since then?"

"Most of the time. I got hurt lifting a patient. He came up here for school, and I came a month later when I finished physical therapy. It still hurts, though," she said, pressing a fist into her back and straightening up. A smile spread across her little-girl face. "We got this cute little house in Dogtown I've been trying to fix up when I feel up to it."

I finished my drink and looked around for a trash can.

"Wait," Lisa said, her hand on my arm. "He's a good nurse, you know that, he just made a mistake. We've all made mistakes." She ducked her head and looked up with a small smile. "Even you."

There was one time. I tried not to think about it. I was just out of school, working nights on a medical floor with no help, as usual, and I'd thought the man—one of the twenty-two I'd had that night—was asleep.

At least he was quiet. It wasn't until my supervisor called me the next day, waking me from some badly-needed sleep, to tell me the man had died during my shift, his body cold when the day nurse checked him shortly after I'd left. He'd been dead several hours.

"And he's got to keep this job," Lisa said, jerking me back to the present. "Until he finishes school."

"Lisa, I can't talk to you about this. It's a personnel matter."

"But I'm his fiancé, we need the money!" She scrubbed at her head, leaving a spike of her pixie-cut hair standing on end.

I shook my head. "I can't talk about another employee no matter what."

"Tell me one thing."

A security officer motioned a few final stragglers toward the auditorium door.

"I've got to go."

"Tell me you're not going to report him to the board." She looked up at me, her eyes pleading. "Monika, please, please. I don't know what we'd do if. . . ." Her voice drifted off as she looked down into her cup at the few remaining ice cubes.

The security guard, hampered by a straggle of giggling students, tried to shut the doors to the auditorium.

"I'm going to the talk." I stood, slurping the last dregs of my drink.

"Just tell me he can keep his job. Just that."

I shoved my empty cup under the lid of a trash can overflowing with ketchup-smeared sandwich wrappers and paper cups dripping ice cream. "Don't worry about it," I said, wiping my hands on a napkin and tossing it in the can. "He'll be okay."

I smiled an apology to the guard and squeezed through the closing doors with one last glance at Lisa. She sat looking down into her cup.

I took a seat in the back and looked around at the students settling in. As I'd often thought recently, they looked young. Scattered talk muffled the introductions of the dignitaries—some St. Louis hospital administrators and the dean of one of the local nursing schools. Then a young woman took the stage. She wasn't beautiful—not like the models parading outside—but when she started speaking, the room quieted down. She leaned into the microphone and spoke directly to me.

"I first became aware of what nurses do," she began, "after my little sister Sally was hurt in a boating accident at Lake of the Ozarks." The woman went on. "I was only sixteen. My mother and I stayed at the hospital with her and my dad went back and forth between St. Louis and the hospital."

The woman looked down for a moment and seemed to collect herself.

"I remember one night I was asleep on the sofa right outside her room. I woke up when I heard the nurse talking to Sally. I thought Sally had awakened from her coma, but she hadn't. The nurse, though, was talking to her as if she were awake. She was telling her that her family was nearby and that we all loved her and wanted her to get well. Her voice was upbeat but gentle and caring. And calm, I remember thinking, as I lay back down. Just before I dropped off to sleep, though, I realized Sally's nurse was talking to her as if she loved her!

"That," she said, "is the essence of nursing care."

I could hear our collective breath let out as she continued.

"I couldn't imagine any career other than nursing after that. So I got serious about school, enrolled in college and studied hard to make it through the science courses that schools use to weed out students who won't make it in clinical courses (there were a few chuckles at that) and celebrated the day that I was accepted into the nursing major.

"I wasn't an honor student, I won't try to tell you I was, but I graduated in the top half of my class. Then as most of us do, I started working on a medical-surgical floor to hone my skills and pick up speed."

She still worked in nursing, she said, although most of her time now was spent traveling around the country and speaking to groups of nurses and students.

"I know it's true, what I learned back when I was sixteen and watching my sister being cared for by nurses who didn't even know they were becoming my role models, that nursing is the most satisfying career anyone can have, caring for people when they need us, when they're most vulnerable."

The auditorium was silent.

"Yes," she said, "there are problems in nursing, in health care. As there are in any worthwhile endeavor. But the main problem is that there are too few nurses now and not enough people entering nursing to care for the millions of baby-boomers on the cusp of developing serious health problems and needing nursing care."

She had some suggestions for the audience. "Every one of you can be an ambassador for nursing. Tell other people what you do, what nursing's really like, what it takes to be a nurse. It's up to you to tell people how rewarding nursing can be."

She stopped for a sip of water and began again.

"The world has changed since 9/11. People are asking: What am I doing with my life? Is it worthwhile? Does it make a difference?" She looked around the room. "That's one thing you know for sure: You know that your lives and the work you do has meaning."

She looked up from her notes and smiled. "You're wondering what happened to my sister." She motioned to someone off stage. "Meet Sally—a brand-new RN!"

A smiling, younger version of the speaker came onto the stage, using a wheelchair. The speaker thanked us for coming and joined her sister, giving her a hug. She waved goodbye as she and her sister started off stage.

The room exploded with applause, and people were on their feet clapping. The speaker stopped and smiled, seeming a little embarrassed by the fuss, then she bowed to the audience and mouthed a thank you.

When the lights came on, two girls next to me wiped their eyes and I heard several people blowing their noses. I needed a tissue, too.

Walking out with the crowd, I remembered why I'd become a nurse.

"MONIKA," AUNT OCTAVIA greeted me, a broad smile creasing her plump pink cheeks. She pulled me into her small apartment and pressed me to her soft bosom in a hug. She smelled like talcum powder. "Come in, come in, and cool off. That hallway's hotter than outdoors, I'll swear." She fanned herself with her apron.

"I didn't know if you were back yet but I thought I'd stop by and see," I said, dropping my keys and wallet on a table by the sofa.

"I just got back last night," she said, nodding toward a basket of laundry by the wall. Several white nurses' uniforms—all dresses, no pant uniforms for Aunt Octavia—were piled on top of the sheets and towels crammed in the basket.

A timer went off.

"Make yourself at home," she said with a backward glance at me.

I sat down at the round table by the window in the dining area that was an L-shaped extension of her living room. Aunt Octavia had lived in the same apartment since I was a little girl, and she still had the same furniture, too. Most of the wood pieces—various tables and cabinets—had been handed down through the family, worn smooth from many polishings. One cabinet had been originally built by a distant uncle in the mid-nineteenth century shortly after our family had first come over from Germany. Being at Aunt Octavia's always felt like home.

"It smells like pumpkin pie in here," I said as she came back in from the kitchen.

"You must have smelled these," she said with a smile. She moved aside some handwork that was neatly piled on the table and placed a plate of sugar-topped ginger cookies in front of me.

She left again and returned with two glasses of milk and a stack of napkins, then she settled herself opposite me. I took a warm cookie and dunked it in my milk.

Aunt Octavia wiped her face with the dish towel hanging on her shoulder and pushed a few damp curls up into her gray hair. As we sat there eating the cookies she studied the materials spread out on the table covered by stacks of small fabric cutouts of identical shapes—some solid-colored, others in plaids, polka dots, and tiny floral prints. An open sewing box stood nearby next to a bowl of raw navy beans.

"It's already August," she said, nodding toward the piles on the table. "I usually try to start in July."

Every year Aunt Octavia, whom we fondly call "Auntie O," made a small gift for every child in the family. An only child with no children of her own, she doted on the grandchildren of her late husband's four sisters and five brothers. Her nieces and nephews totaled twenty-seven now.

"They're going to be frogs." She held up a finished one, bright in kelly green. "A bean bag," she added as the frog's head flopped over her hand, black button eyes staring straight ahead.

"Where'd you get the idea for that?" I asked her, taking another cookie.

"From the rummage sale at church one year. I bought one and took it apart, then made a pattern of it." She shrugged as if anyone could have done it.

But Aunt Octavia isn't just anyone. She's my favorite aunt, great-aunt by marriage, to be specific. She had become a private duty nurse after she'd left St. Teresa's about the time I graduated and went to work there. She now worked for families wealthy enough to afford a live-in registered nurse to care for their dying family member.

She had inspired me to choose nursing as a career after I'd watched her care for my grandmother who had died of breast cancer when I was thirteen. Grandmother's dying was long and drawn-out, and I realize now that her death had been made easier by the attentive, meticulous nursing care Auntie O had provided. She was the one family member I could talk to about things that happened at the hospital without having to sugarcoat the bad stuff.

She placed the right sides of two pieces of pink-flowered fabric together, strapped a pin cushion onto her wrist, and began to pin the edges together.

"So how's things at St. T's," she asked, stabbing the fabric with a pin.

The timer dinged again.

"You wait right here." She patted my hand. "This is the last batch. I'll be right back and we can talk."

After she had refilled the cookie plate and topped off our glasses of milk, I told her about the two deaths the past week, the accreditors due to arrive, and the battles over the union.

She chewed slowly, digesting my words. "It seems to me," she said finally, "that the union is one way to get some power."

"I can understand it even if I can't support it. And God knows, we need some clout. Administration doesn't listen to anything we say. A union—if the organizers are not just doing their own empire building—can help patients." I stopped. "People think it's all about money but it isn't."

"Of course it isn't. No one goes into nursing to get rich." She jabbed a pin through the corduroy fabric and stuck herself. She sucked on her finger. "You know what I think?" She went on without waiting for my answer. "I think forming a union is about getting respect. Plain and simple. Respect from doctors. . . ." She looked out the window, remembering, perhaps, the times when a doctor had berated her for doing the right thing after he had made a mistake. "And from administration," she added, turning back to me.

"We know what we need in order to do our job," I said, "but the bottom-line folks—how they can afford to keep hiring more and more of those guys, I don't know—keep pushing until now the nurses are pushing back."

"So you think a union's the answer?" she asked me.

"I don't know. One thing I do know, though, it pulls everyone apart, even before it happens. Management—that includes me—is told to stay out of it, but how can we? We work with these people on a daily basis, you know how it is."

She nodded and picked up a green-and-red plaid cut-out.

"In ICU anyway, we're crammed in there together with all the equipment and everything to do and we have to be fast because just as quickly the patient can go bad. We're like a basketball team, playing off the other. We can't, or at least, I can't, just ignore it when my nurses—some of them—are lobbying for a union. Administration says I'm not even allowed to have a civilized discussion about the pros and cons." I dragged my finger across the table, tracing a thread in the tablecloth.

"Do you think the nurses will vote for it?"

"If they do, I'll be on the other side of the table from the people I know best. And some contract will spell out for me what I can and cannot do, instead of letting me use my own common sense. You can't manage by the book. Every nurse, every situation is different."

She didn't say anything until she'd finished pinning the frog and placed him on the stack to be stitched.

"No one really knows what nurses do," she said as much to herself as to me. She'd said it many times, as had most nurses I knew. We're the invisible majority in health care, this afternoon's speaker had said, and she was right.

"You watch ER?" Aunt Octavia asked.

"Nah, I've never've seen it."

"I haven't either, except one time at a patient's house. He wanted to see it." She shook her head. "I told him, 'you see that many doctors in the ER looking down at you, you're dead!'"

I laughed as Auntie O passed me the cookie plate.

Chapter 9

Sunday, 12 August 1050 Hours

I FOUND HANNAH, Roger, and the girls at our pre-arranged meeting spot waiting for the parade just as snare drums signaled the start. We exchanged quick hugs and turned toward the street to watch.

Deutsch Fest was a South St. Louis tradition, a street fair begun by German immigrants early in the twentieth century to celebrate their heritage. Now, nearly one hundred years later, St. Louisans of all nationalities joined in the festivities at the annual event.

Leading the parade was a troop of boy scouts, Hannah and Roger's older twins among them, marching to a drum's beat. Then came a contingent of police officers in uniform, complete with gun belts, holsters, and batons. Motorcycle cops rode alongside them.

Following next were the politicians, out in force with their aides and campaign managers because there was an upcoming mayoral election. The current mayor, who wasn't running for reelection, made his way along the line of spectators. He gave me a quick handshake and a tight smile and moved on. Two of the three candidates for mayor came next, working opposite sides of the street. The woman candidate gave out candy to squealing children, and the man tossed bubble gum into the crowd. Our district's Congressional representative and his wife walked in front of a contingent of his supporters, all waving placards with his name prominently displayed.

Other local dignitaries followed, riding in cars and pickup trucks sponsored by Southside auto dealers. A giant replica of an Ed Crewes' ice cream concrete sat atop an open convertible with the genial Mr. Crewes waving to the crowd.

A drum major walked backward in front of a high school band and blew his whistle to signal the downbeat. The crowd rallied from the heat to scattered cheers as the band broke into "When the Saints Go Marching In." The sun blazed down on the band members, dressed in heavy wool uniforms, sporting their maroon-and-yellow school colors. But they soldiered on, the trumpet players' faces beet-red as they passed. A trombone player stopped to wipe his face with the back of his sleeve then hurried back into formation. A tuba player near the end of the group let her instrument droop on her shoulder as she passed in front of me. Suddenly the tuba dropped to the ground with a crash and the girl toppled over on top of it, her cap rolling away into the crowd. I reached her before anyone else did.

"Give her room," I yelled as curious onlookers crushed around us. Her skin was hot and dry, her breathing shallow. Several cops pushed through the crowd and ordered onlookers to back up. A paramedic ran up, his case banging against his legs. He crouched down beside the unconscious girl.

"Heatstroke," I said.

The girl twitched with what looked an impending seizure but quieted as the paramedic slid a needle expertly into a vein, starting fluids from a bag his partner held aloft. The paramedics' ambulance, positioned on a nearby side street for just such an emergency, squealed around the corner, scattering the more determined onlookers. Soon the girl and her tuba were loaded onto the ambulance and on their way.

I moved to the sidewalk, snagging a scrap of shade to watch the remainder of the parade, and rejoined Hannah and her family when the clowns finished tossing balloons to the children.

A few stragglers, children and some teenagers, followed in the street, pretending to be marching. A police officer shooed them over to the sidewalk and the street was reopened to traffic.

Hannah handed around small water bottles and smeared sunscreen on the girls' bare shoulders. Their sleeveless tops were damp with perspiration. Tina had her balloon inflated but Gena was still struggling with hers, her face red with the effort. Roger blew it up for her and handed it back as BJ joined us for a round of hugs. She'd been a part of our family since we'd met in kindergarten.

On duty, BJ was dressed in full uniform, light-blue shirt for summer, black pants, and black oxfords shined to a gloss. Her hair was pulled back in a French braid and her cap sat forward, shading eyes covered by reflective sunglasses.

The girls wanted to see her gun. She showed them how it wouldn't come out of the holster. Gena bought the story, but Tina put both hands on her hips and stuck her chin out. "That's not so. It's a trick. You have to get it out. What if you see some bad guys?"

BJ leaned down to the girls. "I say a secret word," she told them. "It's magic."

Their eyes opened wide.

"Speaking of magic," Roger said. "How about some rides?"

"Yes, yes, yes," the twins squealed, jumping up and down and tugging their parents toward the fair's midway.

"What's new?" BJ asked, keeping her eye on the crowd as we walked along the side street now filled with festival activities rather than its usual traffic.

German dancers, the women in brightly-colored dirndl skirts and the men in lederhosen, demonstrated an intricate folk dance to the delight of fair-goers who had gathered around them. A canopy-shaded band, consisting of an accordion, two trumpets, a trombone, a tuba, and a snare drum, accompanied the lively dancers. We passed a temporary post with signs directing fair-goers to games, rides, food, and the first-aid station. "Stuttgart 4733 miles," one hand-lettered arrow read.

"Your detective was at the hospital," I told BJ as we joined a line to buy tickets for food, drinks and carnival rides.

"Mine?"

"Harding. The guy I met last spring."

"Oh, yeah. When that woman was killed," BJ said, referring to a death in ICU just before Easter. "So what'd he want? Was it about that guy that your nurse, uh, didn't. . . ?" BJ asked.

"He didn't kill him, BJ," I said in a whisper, "He just didn't do all he should have to revive him."

"Same thing," she said. "He's still dead."

A woman ahead of us turned around.

We didn't talk again until we reached the ticket seller. I pulled a ten out of my shorts pocket and ordered ten tickets. We moved on to the next stand. BJ had said she was officially on break, but she kept scanning the crowd.

"This was someone else. The detectives were there to see him." I gave the volunteer four tickets and we took our root beers and hand-rolled soft pretzels to a picnic table under the scant shade of a scraggly tree. We arranged ourselves, sitting on the table top and resting our feet on the bench. BJ laid her cap beside her and scooped sweat off her face with her fingers, flinging it to the side. She wiped her hand on her pants.

"Apparently he wanted to tell them something," I said after taking a long drink of root beer. I pulled my T-shirt out of my waistband and wished I could take it off like some teenage boys who were walking by had done.

"Do you know what it was about?" BJ asked. She broke off a piece of pretzel and dipped it in mustard.

"The patient died before Harding arrived. Just a few minutes before, as a matter of fact."

"So you don't know what he was going to tell the detectives?"

"No. Except Father Rudolf said something about twenty years ago."

"Was the patient someone I know?"

"I doubt it."

"I might. If he had something to tell Harding, he's probably been in trouble." When I didn't answer, she said, "Come on, Monika, just between us."

"Confidentiality doesn't end with death," I said, somewhat sanctimoniously.

"The guy's dead, he won't complain."

I told her Huey's name. "Ring a bell?"

"Not off hand. Maybe he wanted to confess. Clear his conscience before meeting his maker."

"He'd already talked to Father Rudolf, you know, our chaplain. That's who set up this meeting."

"Father say what it was?"

"Nope.

"Might clear up a case."

"I guess it died with him."

BJ checked her watch and told me she needed to return to duty. I tossed our empty cups and napkins in a trash container and walked with her toward the police booth at the end of the midway. She told me her next job was to sit in the booth beside a target. For a donation to the fund for families of police officers and fire fighters killed in action, fair-goers could throw a softball at a target. If they hit it, BJ's seat would release and she'd drop into a tub of water. Hot as it was today, she was hoping she'd get dunked at least once.

We passed a tent-covered booth selling chances on a spinning apparatus that looked suspiciously like a roulette wheel.

"You know, they have a program." BJ stopped, her hand on my arm. "To help people with a problem." I tried to pull away but she held onto my arm with an iron grip. "They said family and friends should confront people. That it would help just to let someone know it's available."

I shook her off. "I don't have a problem. I just don't gamble anymore. Period."

She looked at me for a minute, then shrugged. "Okay. Glad to hear it."

"I'm fine, BJ, really I am." Truth was, I did feel a familiar tug, as if I were being drawn in against my will. Someone had told me that this was how an alcoholic feels about alcohol. How could I explain it to BJ? I didn't understand it myself.

After BJ left to be dunked, I caught up with Hannah and Roger, who were watching the girls—their faces flushed with the heat—on the Caterpillar, a snake-like ride that wiggled its way around a track. Roger sported a button that read, "WHEN YOU'RE GERMAN, IT'S HARD TO BE HUMBLE" clipped to his polo shirt. Stumbling off, the girls waved small German flags at us and pushed each other aside to show me their colorful face paintings.

Joining the crowd, we headed toward the booths with antiques and hand-made items for sale, passing a German-dressed organ grinder hand-cranking a polka while a mechanical monkey danced on top. We spied Auntie O tending a booth from her church, selling hand-made quilts. Business was brisk so we gave her a wave and moved on. Hannah found a Christmas wreath she liked, and Roger studied some wooden furniture while the girls and I checked out doll clothes for their American Girl dolls. I made a mental note of what each girl liked.

Soon bored with our ambling perusal of trinkets and crafts, the girls begged their father for more rides. Hannah's freckle-splashed fair skin was already flush with the heat so Roger told them they could each choose one more ride before they headed home.

Her pigtails bouncing up and down, Gena clapped her hands. "I'm in suspenders!"

Her mother and I laughed.

Gena ducked her head, and I hugged her to me. "Sorry, sweetie. We're not laughing at you. It's suspense, not suspenders," I explained as her father smiled at us.

The girls begged me to ride the scrambler with them and I let them lead me along, pretending to be afraid. Our heads were still whirling and twirling when we stumbled off. I left as the twins headed for the Ferris wheel, their parents in tow.

I caught up with BJ at the police booth as she was putting her shoes and socks back on. She stood up and pulled her wet uniform shirt away from her body and patted her blond hair, tucking loose strands back into her braid. She donned her cap and smiled at me from under its shade.

"You should try it, Monika. Go get dunked. Feels great." She nodded to two uniformed cops who passed us. They were still dry.

"I'm ready," I said, fanning myself with a flyer advertising the police benefit dunking station as we waited for our frozen custard at Ed Crewe's busy stand. A preschooler ran into me, and his mother smiled an apology as she grabbed him.

"Hey, here's a new flavor. 'Rich chocolate sauce and tart cherries whipped together into the world's best vanilla frozen custard,'" I read from the hand-lettered sign above the stand. "Perfect for these days, I'm sorry to say."

"Oh, yeah?" BJ studied two men who noticed her stare and walked away.

"Cardinal Sin Concrete," I read.

"Yikes! That hits too close," she said, referring to the recent spate of indicted priest molesters, including a few BJ and I had known when we were in school.

"Too much of a good thing," BJ said. "I'll stick with a chocolate-chip concrete."

We had our treats in hand and were walking back toward the street when I asked her why she was working the fair that day.

"It was either this or funeral duty tomorrow."

"Ballgame tomorrow night," I said. We had tickets to a Cardinal's game—they were playing the Cubs—and the game was sold out. Our seats were in the bleachers, but BJ's husband, Don, was working security. If any seats opened up after the game started he'd move us into them.

"You don't need to remind me, Monika!" she admonished. "Even if I had signed up to work the funeral, it's in the afternoon. I wouldn't let a little thing like my job interfere with a ballgame!"

I'm a Cardinal fan, but BJ's a fanatic. She knows all the stats, tapes the games she can't see (not many) and won't let anyone tell her the score so that she can watch the game play out herself.

"Whose funeral?" I asked, scooping cherries, chocolate, and ice cream into my mouth.

"No one we know."

"Why do they need police if it's not somebody important? Are they expecting trouble?" I stirred my ice cream, dragging cherry juice and chocolate into swirls.

She leaned toward me. "Connected."

"Connected? Connected to what?"

"Shhh. To the mob. In fact, they say he was the boss. Antonio Guardino."

I stumbled, my ice cream toppled out of the cup and splattered on the hot concrete.

"You okay?" BJ asked.

I looked helplessly as the cherry juice and chocolate sauce spread like blood-tainted milk on the hot concrete. The paper cup stood upside down like a drunk's hat sinking into the mess.

"BJ, that was our patient. The one Bart didn't resuscitate."

"Ohhh."

"Ohhh is right. His son's the one who hit Tim and me." I rubbed my head where the lump had been. "Why are the police there? You expect trouble?"

"Nah. Show of force mostly. They're all getting old, the wise guys. Dying off," she said, signaling a rookie cop to get someone to clean up my mess on the sidewalk. She offered me a bite of her concrete and when I shook my head, she went on. "Even mobsters die of natural causes. I wouldn't worry. Sounds like the guy died of old age, not a blast to the chest."

"I wonder if Bart knows who Guardino was." I chuckled. "And he was worried I'd report him to the state board. The licensing board," I explained to BJ.

She snorted. "That'll be the least of his problems if the Guardino family finds out what he did."

"What he didn't do," I amended.

Chapter 10

MONDAY, 13 AUGUST 0722 HOURS

THE SIGN WAS handmade, with heavy black marker on white paper. "DO YOU KNOW WHO YOUR UNION'S IN BED WITH?" it said. An arrow pointed to a copy of a newspaper article. Several people were gathered around the placard pasted on a concrete pole on the top floor of the parking garage. I'd seen similar signs on other floors as I'd wound around looking for a parking space.

The article had been copied many times and wasn't as readable as it had once been. But the message was clear. It told the story of the conviction of several St. Louis mobsters for fixing union votes, committing fraud with union funds, carrying out strong-arm tactics over right-to-work laws, and intimidating union candidates and employers. The story sounded familiar but I couldn't remember the details. It had happened several years ago, as I recalled.

The temperature was already hovering around a humid ninety-five degrees so I decided to use the underground tunnel from the garage to the hospital, joining other employees. Few visitors knew they could descend to a lower level in the garage and walk under the street that ran in front of the hospital.

I had a lot on my mind. The battle over the union promised to heat up this week before voting took place on Saturday. I said a silent prayer that I and everyone else would keep our tempers until it was over.

Would anything come of Guardino's death? We hadn't heard any more from his son nor their lawyer, thank goodness. The funeral was today. That usually helped the family accept the reality. Maybe that would be the end of it for us.

Huey's death puzzled me, coming so quickly. Had someone sneaked him some booze? Or marijuana? In spite of our best efforts to keep it from him? I tried not to think the worst: that he'd had too much morphine. At least he was at peace and no longer in pain.

I grabbed the door to the hospital and yanked it open. Time to go to work.

"You in trouble," Ruby said when I came into the break room an hour later.

I poured myself a cup of coffee, added powdered cream and a two sugars and sat down next to her.

"Don' you wanna' know why?" she asked, reaching into a bag of bagels. She wore a shocking-pink top stretched wide over her ample frame. She dumped two bagels out of the bag, tore them apart and popped the tops back in the bag.

"Ruby! Why'd you do that? Do you expect someone else to eat the tops?"

"Sure. Everbody like those better. Anyways, I can't eat those seeds. They get caught in my plate." She dropped her upper false teeth down for me to see.

"Yuck, Ruby. Put those back in. I'll eat the tops."

"See, I told you," she said, smirking.

After pouring the extra poppy seeds onto a napkin, I wadded up the empty bagel bag and tossed it toward the trash can. A slam dunk.

"What happened? You missed breakfast?" Ruby asked.

"Cat upchucked in my bed," I told her as I spread the last of the cream cheese on the two bagel tops and sprinkled the seeds on top. I bit into the bagel, scattering more seeds on my napkin. Those went on the cream cheese, too. "She ate a plant during the night and made me a gift of it in the morning. I lost my appetite after that."

"Lordy, that's more than I wanted to know."

That was probably the only time I'd heard her say she didn't want to know something.

"Don't you wanna know what's got Miss Judyth's underpants in a knot?"

"I'm sure you're going to tell me." I wet my finger and blotted up the last of the tiny black seeds.

"She scared," Ruby said as I came back onto the unit.

"Oh?"

"Your lawyer scared her."

"Mine? What about?" I certainly wasn't going to tell Ruby anything more for her to add to her store of gossip.

"You'll find out." She flipped her head in the air, her top knot bouncing as she waddled out the door.

So she didn't know.

A FEW MINUTES later Jessie and I were turning an obese comatose patient so Serena could wash her backside when I heard Judyth asking for me at the desk. Her voice was curt and sharp.

"There you are." She motioned for me to follow her out of the patient's room and into my office.

"There are some discrepancies," she said when we were seated. "In our drug records."

I moved aside the vase of roses I'd received from Mr. Guardino's attorney. "And?"

"Some are missing. We checked all the records against patients' charts."

"Don't you think it might be a mistake? Everyone's so busy, we don't always have time to check them out. And with the new regs about pain control—"

"Morphine is missing and I think, I think it's nurses stealing it," she said with reluctance in her voice.

"That's hard to believe. In fact, it'd be hard to do, wouldn't it? Anything missing would have been reported."

Morphine, premixed in ten, fifteen and twenty milligram dosages, came in glass tubes with a rubber-covered needle attached called a Tubex. The tube fits into a metal applicator, and a plunger pushes the drug through the needle and into the patient. It's quick, safe, and reduces the chance for theft.

"We think maybe they took a whole box of five. That way no one would notice any discrepancy in the numbers."

"What about the pharmacy? Couldn't it have happened there? Pharmacists steal drugs, too."

She flushed. "You think we didn't think of that? We've checked their records, and every box was signed off by two pharmacists, different ones at different times, so they'd all have to be in collusion to do it. On the other hand," she leaned forward, tapping newly-lacquered nails on the desk top, "half the time change-of-shift counts haven't been done, or the signatures are so scribbled we're not sure who signed the record."

I flopped back in my chair. "Where? ICU?"

"And the ER and OR. We're going to start urine screens on all the nurses right away."

"On the nurses who work on those units?"

"We're testing every nurse at St. T's."

"Why?"

"Because we don't know who took them or who they might have given them to," she said, her voice carrying a note of exasperation. "Someone's stealing our drugs. And we're going to find out who. Starting today, every nurse who wants to keep her job is going to give us a specimen. Observed," she added, standing.

"Observed? Someone's going to watch them pee?"

"That's the only way to be sure they haven't tampered with it."

"How could they tamper with their urine?"

"Wake up, Monika," she said with a flap of her hand. "There's all kinds of ways. Dilute it with water from the toilet bowl. Add soap. Or other substances. Substitute someone else's urine." She turned and her suit jacket fell open. A tiny coffee stain marred the perfection of her silk shirt where it bloused out over her waistband. "Someone will be up from the lab shortly. And," she added, "This information should only be shared on a strictly need-to-know basis, Monika."

"Don't you think the people who are going to have someone watch them pee need to know?"

"Don't be silly. That defeats the whole purpose. We've got to surprise them."

"What about the docs? They have to pee, too?"

"Why?" she asked, her hand on the doorknob. "They don't sign out drugs."

BEFORE THE LAB tech arrived I took staff members aside and told them about the impending tests. I tried to make it sound routine, which some of the younger nurses believed, but the more experienced nurses knew otherwise. Jessie, as usual, took it in stride, and also reassured me that the narcotics had been counted that morning. All were correct. Tim, on the other hand, tightened his mouth when I told him about the urine test, mumbling about "invasion of privacy" as he walked away. This action by administration would just add to the union supporters' grievances, especially since only the nurses were being tested.

Two lab techs—a man and a woman—came together. The man looked embarrassed but the woman just looked weary. I went first. The woman followed me into the restroom, tacked up an out-of-service sign on the door, and handed me a cup already labeled with my name, "Everhardt, M." I propped the door open with my knee, pulled down my pants, and peed. She glanced my way briefly. I sent Jessie in next. When one nurse came back, another went in. The woman had her tray of specimen cups full in less than ten minutes.

Tim had refused, Ruby told me.

I WAS STOWING the meds from our pharmacy order when Serena came into the med room with an empty IV bag. She tossed it into the trash and leaned against the counter until I finished checking off the last of the order. I closed the cabinet and asked her what she wanted.

"Why are they doing all these drug tests? What's going on?" She worried the cuticle on her thumb with a fingernail.

"Some narcotics are missing, and for some reason Judyth thinks nurses are taking them," I explained. "We're just so busy. Everybody's grabbing what they need, and I'm sure people are just forgetting to check them out."

A few months ago Serena had given a patient a medication when she shouldn't have. She'd received a warning from administration, and she'd been extra careful with meds since then.

"What's wrong? If you're worried about the drug tests, don't be. You don't have to be tested. You don't have access to narcotics."

"It's Judyth. She called me in and grilled me this morning." She rubbed her hands on her scrub-suit top and shoved her hands in her pockets.

"Grilled you? What about?"

"Everything!" she said, her eyes filling. "Had I made any more mistakes? Did I ever get into the narcotics' cabinet? She said she'd received complaints about me. Did you do that, Monika? Complain to her but not to me?"

"Of course not, Serena. That's not my management style. I tell people right away when something's wrong, you know that." When she didn't answer I added, "Don't you?"

"I do, Monika. It's just that with another patient of mine dying. . . ." She played with gold stud in her ear, tugging on her earlobe.

"I didn't know you'd been taking care of him that morning."

"I didn't do anything to him! I didn't! I just went in to see how he was. He asked me for some black coffee. I didn't touch him!"

"Calm down, Serena, I didn't say you did."

"So, why did he die like that? Just stop breathing. I didn't think that's how it'd happen to him."

"He was terminal, Serena. They can die in a number of ways. This was Huey's."

"I can't have another patient of mine die and not know why!"

"Serena, a lot of your patients are going to die and you won't always know why. It happens. It's important to care, but you can't get too involved. You have to keep a professional distance." I put my arm around her thin shoulders. "I know it's hard."

She shook me off. "That's not it. I thought Huey was kinda spooky with that arm and all. I just don't want to be accused of doing anything wrong. I didn't do anything, Monika, I didn't. You have to believe me." She bit her lip.

"Pull yourself together, Serena," I said, my annoyance showing. "The post should explain things. In the meantime, you've got work to do."

She turned away with a jerk of her head.

I CAUGHT MAX sorting through the piles on his desk. Stacks of papers, bulging file folders, books stuck full of post-it notes, and an assortment of medical journals all competed for space on his oversized desk. The chest piece of a stethoscope peeked out of the pile, dangling precariously over the edge.

"I'm glad you stopped by," he said, reaching his arm in between some folders and pulling out a slide. "Ah ha," he said, carefully aligning the pile before it toppled over. "I knew it was in here someplace. Hazelman wanted it for grand rounds tomorrow," he explained, smiling at me. He waved me toward the chair in front of his desk but it, too, was overflowing so I stayed where I was, closed the door behind me, and leaned against it.

Max took off his thick-lensed glasses and wiped them on his lab coat. He looked up, his eyes unfocused. "What can you tell me about the patient, Castle?" he asked.

A knot of worry began in my stomach.

"You've done the post?" I asked him. At his nod, I took a breath and went on. "Cancer of the stomach. Alcoholic, we think. He had a respiratory arrest and died. Why? What did you find?"

He slipped his glasses back on, hooking wire temple pieces behind his ears. "Respiratory arrest. That's a pretty unusual way for a cancer patient to die. His arteries were good, no CVA, like your other patient, or MI. In fact, his heart looked good."

"Are you saying his death wasn't related to the cancer at all?"

"Well, the cancer still doesn't explain the respiratory arrest. Any indication that he was going bad?"

"I haven't seen any change recently, nothing that would be a sign that he was about to die. Laura had him that morning and she thought he looked about the same."

"You saw him when he coded?"

I nodded.

"And he wasn't breathing? Not moving at all?"

"His eyes were open," I said. "But his heart was still beating, according to the monitor."

Max stood and came around to the front of his desk. He leaned back and crossed his arms, resting them on his paunch, lab coat spread open. "I got a call from the medical examiner about him."

"Oh?"

"He's going to rule the death 'suspicious'."

"Suspicious? Why? Just because we didn't expect him to die this way doesn't mean there's anything suspicious." When he looked as if he was about to disagree I asked, "Is there?"

"There's nothing in my report that indicates his death was anything other than natural, but I'm not the law. I've already talked to Lord. He's puzzled by it, too, but no more concerned than I was. But once the ME gets ahold of something like this it's out of our hands, Monika. Nothing you or I or anyone else here can do. The ME's ruling has the force of law behind it. In fact, he is the law. And if I remember correctly you had some questions yourself. You asked me late Friday to check Castle's blood for alcohol. You were wondering about something other than the cancer, weren't you?"

"Well, that complicates things," I said, ignoring his question. I told him about Huey wanting to talk to the detectives before he coded. "They acted like they thought that Laura might have had something to do with his death."

"Let's wait and see what they do. The police are as overworked as we are. Maybe this is one they'll let go."

"Well," I said. "I don't care if they do investigate. I'm sure a nurse didn't do it. So they're welcome to do all the investigating they want to do."

"Respiratory arrests are awful, aren't they?" He scratched his bald head and smoothed the surrounding white fringe of hair. "Death by asphyxiation."

"What about his alcohol screen?" I asked.

"Negative. The ME is running a tox screen as well."

"His narcotics' levels will be pretty high. He had stomach cancer and pain control was a constant challenge."

"I'm sure they'll let us know the results."

"That's all we need," I said as much to myself as to Max. "On top of the drug tests."

"When I heard about those this morning, I knew you'd be upset."

"Damn right, I am," I said, my voice rising. "My nurses are already overworked and then administration has someone come in to watch them pee into a cup. It's humiliating."

He winced. "I can imagine it'd be terrible. But, Monika, we have to find out who's taking the drugs before they harm a patient."

"I suppose so," I said, with no conviction in my voice.

"I know so. There's no other way, short of catching someone in the act, to identify who's doing it."

"When will you have the results?" I asked.

"They should be back in a day or two," he said, sitting back down in his chair.

"You don't do them here?"

"We can't handle that volume. But it shouldn't take long, they contracted an outside agency for stat urines." He glanced at a stack of reports awaiting his signature.

"Doesn't that cost more?"

"Of course, but we can't have people working here who might be on drugs. Anyway, these are just screening tests. If any come back positive, they run a confirmatory test. And, yes, that also costs more," he added, anticipating my question.

"What's the probability of a mistake in the testing process? Could anything go wrong with how they're done?"

"Nothing's one-hundred percent, you know that. But we take a number of precautions to make sure the results are accurate."

"What about when it's going to the lab? How does it get there?"

"Monika, listen, we're both busy here." He tapped a plump finger on the papers behind him. "I wouldn't worry about them."

"Please, Max, just explain it. Please."

He stared at me, his eyes magnified by the thick lenses. "All right," he said. "We maintain strict chain of custody on all drug tests. In this case, only two techs collected the specimens and handled them. Then they hand-delivered them to the lab. Don't worry. Nothing will go wrong. Satisfied?"

"Could it be labeled incorrectly? Or mixed up in the lab?"

"They do it every day. Why are you so worried? For goodness sakes, Monika, they know what they're doing as well as you do."

"Okay, okay." I held up my hand as if it were a stop sign. "If they say there are drugs in a nurse's urine, I'll believe it."

"If anything, it's more apt to be a false negative."

"So the person could be on drugs and not get caught?"

He nodded. "Or the test could accurately be negative, but the nurse could be stealing drugs for someone else. Or to sell."

"No nurse would do that. And why does everyone think it has to be a nurse? If someone is stealing narcotics they're a criminal, and a criminal could find ways to steal meds even if they aren't the one who signs out drugs." Max didn't say anything so I went on. "What about a false positive? Does that ever happen?"

"It's possible, but they usually set the cutoff high enough so that it doesn't."

"What would cause a false positive?"

"Lots of things. Medications—narcotics, certainly—but over-the-counter things, too. Antihistamines, cough syrup, some pain medications, those for sleep. Food even."

"Food?"

"A few things, but don't worry, Monika. That's why they set the cutoff high. To rule out those things."

"Let's hope."

BY THE TIME I saw what was happening, I'd already stepped off the elevator at the lobby floor and joined the surge of people moving into the melee.

Tim and other nurses—most I recognized—had formed a sort of gauntlet through the lobby, shouting at employees as they left. Behind the chanting nurses stood several unsmiling men, bulky with muscles, their hands crossed in front of them.

"Hell no, we won't pee!" they screamed in unison. "NURSES WON'T DO IT TILL DOCTORS DO IT," read a placard waved aloft by a short nurse.

Two elderly women came through the entrance doors but turned away, frightened, and hurried back out. One young couple trying to leave looked confused, were caught in the crush and yelled at. They escaped, running across the street to the parking garage.

The chanting continued as another elevator opened, discharging more tired employees. The press of the crowd pushed forward. Some employees assessed the scene in time to realize what was happening and slid into the line of protesters. Quite a few of them slipped on through to the back of the crowd and out of the building. I walked straight ahead, trying to tune out the shouts as I kept my face purposely blank, and kept moving. I passed Tim, his face screwed up in anger, one eye still puffy and streaked with yellow, as several uniformed security officers hurried in the door. I turned into the garage as two police cars squealed to the curb. I looked back and caught a glimpse of Judyth standing beside a post down the hall, her arms crossed over her chest and her mouth curled in satisfaction.

Chapter 11

Monday, 13 August, 1822 Hours

"You hear any more from Harding?" BJ asked me as we waited in line to go through the turnstile into Busch Stadium.

"Not from him or his partner."

After work I'd changed from my green hospital scrubs into cream-colored shorts and a Cardinal-red T-shirt. Standing in the sun, I could feel both already damp with perspiration.

"I didn't know there were two of them."

"I don't remember the second one's name," I said over my shoulder. A large man, pot-bellied and chewing on a used cigar, bumped me from behind. I scooted out of the way and waited for BJ to catch up with me.

"McNeil, Tom McNeil's Harding's new partner," she said. "Dark hair, our age, about six foot, good looking?"

"That's him."

"Be careful around him," BJ said.

"Why? He looked okay. Seemed a little lost on the unit, but, that's pretty normal. Intensive care's pretty intense." I laughed. "No pun intended."

"He's a hot shot, out to make a rep for himself."

We started up the ramp, winding around to the upper levels.

"It's too late, now. Whatever Huey wanted to tell them went to the grave with him."

"Don knew who Huey was. Said he'd been picked up for some minor stuff over the years."

I giggled. "He listed pick-pocket as his profession on the admitting form."

She tilted her head, puzzled.

"He only had one arm, BJ, and a metal hook. He'd have had a hard time picking anyone's pocket."

"Apparently he was a runner for numbers' guys back when they had those. Liked to hang around the action," she said as we wiggled through a line waiting before a concession stand.

"Action?"

She gave me a look I couldn't read. "Gambling."

"Uh oh. Was he in debt, do you think?"

"Don't know. Maybe. He was a regular at the Ambassador, I heard. He's one of those guys the department keeps an eye on. They're never going to do the really bad stuff, they just hang around on the fringes."

We stopped to catch our breath at the top level.

"Umm," I said, sniffing. "There's nothing like a ballpark hotdog."

"And a beer," BJ added. We stopped and BJ checked our tickets again. "Straight ahead . . . to the nose-bleed seats."

The game was sold out and the stands were a sea of red. Cardinal shirts, ball caps, and banners were interspersed with a few blue shirts of the Cubs' fans. BJ sported her Cardinal T-shirt, slightly faded now. It was the one she'd worn the day McGuire had hit his record-breaking homer. We settled in our seats, the shade almost reaching us and promising some relief from the unrelenting heat. BJ took off her cap, shaking her blond hair loose, and fanned herself with the cap.

I hesitated. "BJ."

"Yeah?" She was watching the players warm up. The Cardinals' mascot, Fredbird, was running around on the field, goofing it up for the fans.

"You know a guy they call Dog? He's probably called that because of the way he looks like a basset hound. He used to run numbers."

Fredbird bounced up the steps into the stands and shook his feathered booty at a woman sitting at the end of a row, eliciting laughs from the crowd.

"Do you know him, BJ, Dog?"

She pulled her eyes away from the field and squinted at me.

"I'm not gambling, BJ. And besides, nobody runs numbers any more. Not now that it's legal—the lottery."

"Yeah, I know him. Well, I know who he is. A CI."

"CI? What's that, short for CIA?"

"No, silly. Confidential informant. Don knows him. He's given them some good intel, Don says."

"What's he do? Just hang around with the bad guys?"

"He works for the casinos. Sits at the table, gambles—they front him the money—and he watches for cheaters—players or dealers."

We stood so a family of four, lugging Cardinal pennants and balancing drinks and hot dogs, could get by us to their seats.

"Sounds like a perfect job for him," I said as we sat back down. "Anyway, Dog was in to see Huey a day or so before he died."

"What's that got to do with his death? He wasn't there when Huey died, was he?"

"I don't think so. I didn't see him."

"So what's your point?"

"Nothing, really," I said. "I'm still wondering what Huey wanted to tell Harding."

"Didn't you say he talked to your chaplain? Maybe he knows." BJ turned her attention to the field where the team was warming up.

"I doubt he'd tell me if he does. If it was Huey's confession, that survives death."

The noise died down and we stood for the national anthem. The sun had dipped below the stadium and a puff of air momentarily straightened the flag to attention.

"Maybe it wasn't a confession," BJ said, when we were seated. "Strictly speaking. Maybe Huey just told Father something. You can tell a priest something and, as long as it's not a formal confession, it's not sacrosanct."

"Boy, BJ, you paid more attention in religion class than I did."

"Yeah, well, I didn't have any choice. Not with Uncle Joseph—Father Joseph to you—teaching the class."

"Ah, yes, the good old days. 'Brandon Julia'. . ." I deepened my voice. ". . . give us the answer!" I poked her in the arm. "And then he'd snap his ruler down on your desk!"

"I am not amused," she said, but laughed to show otherwise, and we turned our attention to the game.

"DID I TELL you about the missing narcotics?" I asked a little while later when the umpires were discussing a disputed call. I had gone out in the meantime and brought us back hotdogs—two apiece—and a beer for each of us.

"I don't think so," she answered, her eyes on the field.

The game resumed amid cheers.

"Some are missing." I bit into my mustard-and-relish covered hotdog.

Another Cardinal player walked to first base. The pitcher sped a ball to third but the runner jogged back to second.

"They think some nurses are taking them," I said.

"What do you think?" she asked me as another strike was called and the inning ended. She unwrapped her first hotdog, studied the mustard and ketchup inside, and took a bite.

"It's a mistake, or a series of mistakes. Maybe a dose gets wasted—the patient changed his mind and didn't want it, or the doctor changed the order after the nurse checked it out—and then the nurse gets busy and forgets to chart it."

BJ wiped her fingers on a napkin. "That sounds dangerous," she said, taking a sip of beer.

"It is. And illegal." I tucked my trash under my seat and drained my beer. "It never used to happen, or if it did, then we knew some nurse was taking it. But these days we're just so damn rushed that we have to focus on the patient and not worry too much about record keeping."

"I guess it would be pretty easy for nurses to take drugs. Couldn't they just grab two doses and keep one for themselves?"

"It's not that simple. There are lots of checks and balances. Narcotics are kept in a locked cabinet, and only one nurse on each shift has the keys. We have to count every vial, ampule, and tablet in the cabinet at the beginning and end of each shift. Both nurses sign, the one leaving and the one coming on. Well, usually."

The first Cubs' batter struck out.

I went on. "Except when we're busy and when are we not these days? We hand off the keys like we're in a relay race. That's what it feels like every day these days—a relay race."

The next batter hit a double, running to second base. I pictured nurses jogging around the unit passing off the keys to the next runner.

"So now they're testing the nurses for drugs. I had to pee in cup this morning." I clenched my teeth.

"What's the big deal? You don't have to worry about them finding drugs in your piss."

"I'm not worried. It's just the indignity of it. And they're not testing the docs."

"Why not? Don't doctors give drugs, too?"

"Doctors can only write the script, the pharmacist fills it, and the nurse gives it. And the pharmacy would have a record of it."

"I thought some doctor in Ohio did that. Overdosed his patients. How'd he do it if they can't get drugs?"

A ball shot in between first and second base, sliding by the player who grabbed at it. The next batter hit a foul ball, eliciting a sigh from the crowd. He tapped the plate and readied his stance. The pitcher adjusted his cap, squinted at the catcher and leaned back, then released the ball at ninety miles an hour, according to the scoreboard. The bat hit the ball with a crack and sent it spinning into the outfield and over the fence. Cheering Cubs fans jumped to their feet as two runners jogged home.

When the noise died down, I went on with my story. "That doctor in Ohio did it very creatively. He wrote scripts for fictitious patients and picked up the drugs at the hospital pharmacy."

A ball zinged into the outfield and the fans jumped to their feet as the Cardinal outfielder caught it easily. The Cardinals came up to bat again.

"I'm just keeping my fingers crossed they don't make a mistake with the nurses' tests. That's all we need, to lose more nurses."

"Don't worry about the tests. We use them all the time with perps."

The first batter struck out.

I explained what Max had told me about chain of custody, contamination, and how they set the cutoff.

"See what I mean? They know what they're doing. Believe me, if someone tests positive for a drug, it means they really took it."

"It sure set off the nurses who want a union." I told BJ about the demonstration in the lobby earlier.

"So that's what that was about," BJ said, applauding the player who slid into first base, just beating the ball.

"You heard about it?"

"Just that there was some kind of ruckus at St. Teresa's."

"It was the nurses and they were mad."

"That doesn't sound too bad."

"Oh, no? You didn't see it. They were screaming at visitors and staff alike."

"What happened?"

"I don't know. I left. I don't know what happened to them."

"They got hustled outside, Don told me."

"Any arrested?"

"Cops don't want to arrest people for union stuff if they can help it."

"Oh yeah, you have a union, don't you?"

"We can't. We can't bargain and we can't strike."

"Really? I thought you did."

"I wish. Then we'd have some recourse when the board—the police board—comes down on us. For trying to do our job," she added.

"So why do you like union members?" I asked, forestalling her litany about injustice for cops, something I'd heard before.

"It's a brotherhood thing. Working stiffs like us."

"Sounds like you don't have much power."

"So what's new? We do have an association. Two, actually. One for uniforms: Police Officers Association, and another for sergeants and above: Fraternal Order of Police."

"I heard something about those, something about them supporting different candidates for mayor."

BJ laughed. "Yeah, that's how it always is, isn't it? Somebody gets a little ahead and suddenly their politics change. But all cops, whatever their rank, are ruled by the police board. Did you know that the board's appointed by the governor?"

"Why does that matter?"

"The *state* governor appoints the *city* police board. What kind of sense does that make? The members of the police board don't even have to live in St. Louis, yet they can make it a requirement that we have to live there."

There was an ongoing battle between officers on the force who wanted to move out of the city and into the suburbs mostly because of the sad state of our public schools, and the police board that wouldn't let them, thinking cops would work harder to protect their own neighborhoods if they lived there.

"What about the bad cops, though, BJ. I've seen some of those videos on TV."

"Yeah, well, they don't tell the whole story. You ever try to arrest somebody who doesn't want to be handcuffed?" she asked, downing the last of her beer. "You know how dangerous that is?"

"Okay, okay. But the union fight at the hospital is detracting from what we should be doing—taking care of patients. I think administration and some nurses have lost sight of that."

"Nobody's getting violent, though, are they?"

"No, but there were some rough-looking guys hanging around. You know, all muscle, no brain types."

"Who were they? Cop wannabes?"

"They looked liked gangsters."

BJ laughed.

"You think that's funny? Remember the man who died last week? You told me who he was yesterday," I said, keeping my voice low.

She turned serious. "What'd they do?"

"They just stood around, looking mean."

"Maybe they're from the union supporting the nurses. Or maybe the hospital hired them to intimidate the nurses."

"Hmm. You could be right about that. I wouldn't put it past them to try to frighten us. They looked like they could hurt someone, that's for sure."

"Stay away from them, Monika. Guys like that play rough, regardless of whose side they're on."

I told her about Judyth watching in the background.

"You think she knew who they were?" BJ asked.

"I don't know. She did come from Chicago, though, and they have a lot of gangsters there, don't they? Maybe the Guardinos sent them to scare Bart, the nurse who was caring for Mr. Guardino when he died."

"Nah, those guys wouldn't fool around with anything so subtle." She chuckled, standing for the seventh inning stretch. "They want you dead, you're dead."

Chapter 12

Tuesday, 14 August, 0732 Hours

I hurried to cross the street from the parking garage as thunder boomed around me and dark clouds threatened another downpour. Why hadn't I had remembered to use the tunnel? I had voted in the primary election and it had made me late. The woman in front of me had argued with the officials who had told her she wasn't registered in the precinct. She kept waving her registration card and yelling that they were just trying to keep black people from voting. Finally, two police officers—both white—arrived to escort her out of the building. Luckily, the rain had held off while I had waited outside but had let loose when I came back out and made a dash to Black Beauty. Just as quickly, the sun came back out, steam rising from the rain-slick streets. By the time I reached the hospital, my scrubs were wrinkled, my hair had frizzed, and I wasn't in my best mood.

Lisa scooted through the outer doors just ahead of me and stopped to look around. She was dressed in cutoffs and an oversized navy T-shirt. Her unfocused gaze slid over me until I called her name. She gave me a weak smile; her pupils were dilated.

"Are you all right?" I asked, taking her arm.

"Fine, fine, I'm just fine." She giggled.

"Lisa, I think you should go home. You can't work in your condition."

She pulled away. "I'm not working today. Just picking up a paycheck." She moved through the automatic doors as they slid open.

"Let me find someone to drive you home after you get your paycheck," I said, hurrying to keep up with her. "You shouldn't be driving."

"I'm not. Bart's waiting." She flailed an arm toward the street.

A beat-up sedan sat parked at the curb.

Judyth stood in front of the public information booth in the lobby, her arms folded across her chest, a frown on her face. "Come with me," she said, motioning to Lisa.

Lisa seemed to shrink beside me.

"Now," Judyth added, leaving no doubt that she meant it.

"I didn't do anything," Lisa whined, throwing a quick glance back at me as Judyth led her toward the administrative offices.

UPSTAIRS, RUBY WAS bursting to tell me the latest news. I held her off until I had checked the day's roster of patients, asked if anyone had called in sick (they hadn't), and answered a visitor's questions about her husband (condition unchanged) before I'd let her tell me.

She made me wait, grinning when I asked her what was going on.

"Never mind," I said. "It must not be important."

"Very important, Miss Monika." She crooked her finger for me to come closer.

I scooted my chair over to her and waited.

"They found drugs," she said, satisfaction coloring her black face. "In three nurses. Including that Lisa goes with Bart."

"I'm not surprised. I saw her coming in. She looked high."

"She's been fired, too," she added, trying to get the upper hand again.

"Judyth was waiting for her and she didn't look pleased."

"And . . ." she hesitated just long enough to annoy me. "Bart ain't gonna be happy 'bout it. Her paycheck's been helping pay for his school. Now what you think he gonna do?"

"You know anyone else who's been fired?" I asked.

The phone rang.

"Wouldn't *you* like to know." she said, picking up the receiver.

I HAD JUST finished talking with the social work department about a nursing home placement for Mrs. Faust when the doors swung open and Dick Gerling, our new chief of security, came through accompanied by McNeil, the younger partner of Detective Harding. Speaking loudly, Dick demanded to see Laura, who pushed open the curtain to a patient's room when she heard her name.

"Yes?" she asked.

"That's her," McNeil said.

"Over here," Dick ordered, jerking his head for her to join them.

Several staff stood around the nurses' station pretending to be busy, but Ruby made no pretense of eavesdropping.

"You have to come with me," the detective said. "We have some questions for you."

Laura clutched an empty IV bag as if it were her first-born.

"What's going on here?" I asked them.

"This is not your affair, Monika," Dick answered. "It's a police matter."

"Let's go in here." I took Laura's arm firmly, steering her toward the conference room. The detective looked at Dick, who shrugged and followed us in. I shut the door and leaned back against it. "Now what do you want with Laura?"

"I told you—" Dick started to say.

"We have some questions about the death of Huey Castle," McNeil interrupted, "and since she was his nurse, we'd like to talk to her. This is just routine."

"What do you want to know?" I asked him.

"This is the second time this has happened, isn't it?" McNeil asked. "That one of her patient's died under suspicious circumstances."

"That wasn't her fault. She didn't do anything wrong then and I'm sure she hasn't now."

"That's not how I heard it," Dick interjected. "I have knowledge that she's on probation."

I turned to him, feeling my face getting hot. "She did not cause anyone's death," I said, enunciating each word. "You weren't even here then."

Dick puffed himself up. "How about other patients of hers? Any of them die?"

"Of course!" I said, getting louder. "In case you haven't noticed, this is a hospital. And this is ICU where they send the sickest patients. Lots of people die here."

"Unexpectedly?" McNeil asked.

"Sometimes. And sometimes they live unexpectedly, too. Medicine is not an exact science," I said.

"Do you know what time she arrived that morning?" McNeil asked me, nodding toward Laura.

"She clocked in at 6:32," Dick said officiously.

McNeil looked at Laura. "What did you do to him before he died?"

"Uh, I only went in there for a minute."

"He died at . . ." McNeil flipped open a notebook. ". . . 7:56. What'd you do all that time?"

I jumped in. "Don't you know about the privacy laws? She can't say anything and neither can I. You'll have to talk to administration and our legal office."

Dick jumped in. "It's already been cleared. They said we don't have anything to do with a criminal case."

"I think you'd better come with me," McNeil said. "We can talk better downtown."

"She can't go now. We need her," I explained, biting my lip to keep from losing my temper.

"No," Laura said firmly, startling us. She had barely moved from a spot next to the wall. Her white-blond hair, pulled back in a clip, framed her face, which had regained a faint color. She stood tall, her arms at her side now, the IV bag still clutched in one hand, its tubing dangling toward the floor. "I'm not going anywhere," she said, pushing off from the wall. "I have work to do. I have patients. I'm not leaving," she added.

"It's not a request," Dick said. "This guy is a St. Louis City cop."

"If you won't come willingly, I don't have a choice," McNeil said with a quick glance at Dick. He reached behind him and pulled out a pair of handcuffs. "Laura Schlesinger, you're under arrest for the murder of Huey Castle. Put your hands behind your back." She dropped the IV bag and her newly-found backbone collapsed as the detective started to read her rights.

Chapter 13

Tuesday, 14 August, 0947 Hours

"Get back to work," I ordered everyone within hearing distance after Laura and the officers had gone, taking out my anger on them. Two students scurried away and the rest of the staff went back to work, but Ruby just shook her head. "I'll be in my office," I told her.

I tried to reach Judyth, telling her secretary I had an urgent matter. The secretary insisted Judyth was unavailable. I hung up and sat thinking. What had made the cops think Huey's death was anything but natural? He was terminally ill with stomach cancer. Max had said he wouldn't have expected Huey to die in a respiratory arrest, an "unusual way to die" is what he'd said. I'd never seen a cancer patient die in respiratory failure either, but that didn't mean it couldn't happen. And why did Detective McNeil think Laura had anything to do with it?

Tim popped his head around the corner of the door. "You find out what they're going to do about Laura?" The swelling on his face had gone down although the bruise remained mostly purple but was turning yellow. He looked almost normal.

I told him I couldn't reach Judyth and motioned for him to sit. "What do they consider important?" I waved my hand across the desk, knocking a stack of envelopes onto the floor.

"What are these?" Tim asked, picking up the envelopes. He looked at them and wrinkled his brow. "These are all written to people who don't work here anymore," he said.

"I meant to take those back to Judyth but I keep forgetting. It must have been a mistake."

"See what I mean, Monika? See how inept administration is? They keep crying they can't afford more nurses. No wonder they're over budget when they make salary mistakes like this."

"I'm more concerned about Laura at the moment," I said, stacking the envelopes back on my desk.

"What made them think she did anything to Huey?"

I explained about the medical examiner's ruling that labeled Huey's death as suspicious.

"What does that mean? Suspicious? Sounds like they don't have much to go on. My brother's a defense attorney. I could call him," Tim offered, ruffling a hand through his dark hair. He smelled like antiseptic soap.

"I don't know if Laura could afford it."

"Don't worry about that," Tim said, punching in the number. "He likes nurses," he added with a grin.

Tim spoke to his brother for a few moments. "He says he'd be glad to help her," he told me after he hung up the phone.

"That's terrific."

I watched Tim head out the door, glad that he had put aside our differences about the union to help Laura.

Tim's brother called back a few minutes later, asking me where the police had taken Laura. I reached BJ on her cell phone and she told me Laura would be downtown at headquarters on Clark Street for booking.

"Can he get her out right away?" I asked her.

"I doubt it," BJ said.

"But she didn't do anything. They just jumped to conclusions."

"Even so, if he didn't have a warrant he has to apply for one and wait to see if he gets it."

"What does that mean?"

"They can hold her for up to twenty hours."

"Even though they don't have any evidence."

"Yep. He has to cover the arrest with a warrant even if it's refused. Any chance she did it?"

"No, BJ, I'm sure she didn't. I'm sure it's a mistake."

At least I hoped so.

I called Tim's brother back and told him where he could find Laura, adding how much I appreciated his help. He said he was glad to help a nurse in trouble.

"Would you get Father Rudolf on the phone for me?" I asked Ruby when I returned to the unit. "Tell him I want to see him."

"You got sins to confess, girl?"

"Just get him." I was in no mood for a hassle from Ruby.

She hung up the phone and told me he was on a retreat until Thursday. "Just don' die till then so's you have time to confess your many sins."

I ignored her. "I'm going to see Judyth now, Ruby, please keep quiet about Laura."

"Yes, ma'am," she said, saluting military-style.

ON THE WAY to Judyth's office I passed Max, who was deep in conversation with another doctor. He glanced up as I passed, but when our eyes met he creased his brow, and then his face slipped into doctor mode. He returned to his conversation without even a brief nod to me.

What was that all about?

JUDYTH'S DOOR WAS closed. Norma, her secretary, smiled and asked me if I wanted anything to drink while I waited. For years Norma had been secretary to our former chief nurse, now retired. Norma knew secrets in hospital administration but, unlike Ruby, kept her own counsel. She was loyal to the position, she'd once told me, regardless of who was in the job.

Putting aside my worries about Laura and Huey's death for a moment, I looked around the waiting area, which was tucked into a corner of the administrative suite. Norma was known for her talent for growing African violets, and the window sill held a plethora of the pink, white, and purple blooms, adding an atmosphere of calm in the midst of the chaos that reined outside in the hospital. And probably inside the office, too, if my experience with Judyth was typical of her interactions with others.

After a few minutes the phone rang and Norma sent me in. Judyth motioned me into a chair in front of her desk as she continued to study papers in front of her.

"Yes?" she said finally, looking everywhere but at me.

First Max and now Judyth. What was going on?

I pulled the three envelopes I'd stuffed in my lab coat pocket and tossed them on her desk. "You left these with me last Friday," I said. "None of these nurses work here anymore. In fact, they haven't worked here for a while." I crossed my arms and released what I thought sounded like an exasperated sigh.

She stared at the envelopes as if they were tainted with anthrax. Then she pushed them into the corner of her desk with the click of a fingernail. "I'll see that payroll gets them. And I'll talk to whoever's responsible," she added. "Is that all you wanted?"

"It's about Laura Schlesinger," I began.

She flipped her hand in the air dismissively. "I know all about it."

"Can you help her?"

"Monika," she said. "Laura is in police custody. Just what is it you think I can do for her? And, anyway, she's on suspension as of now."

"What? She didn't do anything that we know about. She's innocent until proven guilty, isn't she? Can't you call the police and vouch for her? We need her back in ICU!"

"We can't take any chances, Monika. She'll get paid, but she's on administrative leave. She won't come back to work until we know what happened. And don't forget that she's already on probation with the nursing board."

"But not with us."

Judyth dismissed this statement with a wave of her hand.

"Did Laura test positive for drugs?" I asked her. "Is that why you won't do anything?"

"We're in the process of running confirmatory tests on any test that came back positive before we do anything. Unless, of course, the screening test was exceptionally high. That's all I can tell you now." She checked her watch pointedly.

"With Laura gone, I'll be short another nurse. I'm already understaffed. What am I supposed to do now? What if the accreditation team shows up today?"

"I'll get an agency nurse for you."

"Who doesn't know squat about intensive care. Or St. T's."

"Monika," she said. "I'm doing the best I can here. I can't create nurses out of thin air, you know." Her eyes narrowed. "Tim. Schedule him for more overtime."

"Why?"

"Isn't he your best nurse?"

"One of them. Jessie actually has more experience. What's this about, Judyth? Because Tim's supporting the union, you want me to give him more overtime?"

"Of course not. You need the help, don't you? Although," she said, leaning forward, "his license is on the line if he abandons patients. Remember?"

"That's a pretty big stretch, don't you think?" I asked. "We're understaffed and an already exhausted nurse might refuse to work a double shift. If the board started after nurses for that, they'd be investigating all of us. He got hurt, remember? Working for us."

"Anyway," she said, straightening her suit jacket, "we've got a new class of nurses in orientation. Ten or twelve, I think. You should have a replacement next week. You'll be fine."

"Oh, sure. We're just dandy. A nurse marched off the unit in handcuffs this morning." I leaned forward to make my point. "Through the hospital."

"I told you not to let her come back after that last incident."

"But they had no reason to arrest her. She'd never have hurt him, even unintentionally."

"How do you know, Monika?"

I didn't answer.

"As you pointed out, Joint Commission's due back any time. Fortunately," she said as if to herself, "the record will show that we are adhering to our staffing plan." She drew herself up and looked at me. "Anyway, we don't defend an employee in a criminal case. We don't even have a criminal defense lawyer. She'll have to get her own."

I let that pass.

"And don't talk to any reporters. You or anyone on your staff. I'll hold you responsible if they do. I don't want any bad publicity." She stood. Our conversation was over.

AS I WALKED away from her office I thought about what had happened. Judyth was right, of course. The hospital couldn't defend a criminal case nor could they afford bad publicity. And, to be perfectly fair, Judyth had made some improvements since coming to St. T's. More, in fact, than any of us had expected. Equipment had been repaired and what couldn't be fixed she'd found the money to replace.

Heading toward the gift shop I noted that she'd improved it as well, adding medical products, equipment and supplies, everything necessary for patients released too soon and needing care at home. Even large medical equipment, such as wheelchairs, walkers and hospital beds, could be ordered for purchase or rental. Already the hospital had their pharmacy business because most people found it convenient to have them filled before they went home. Actually, her ideas sounded good to me. Patients' families could go to discount stores where they might find a cheaper price, but people who are taking home sick relatives usually value the convenience.

She had made the hospital auxiliary angry, though. She'd barreled into the gift shop, which had been the purview of the auxiliary for more years than I'd been at St. T's, and taken it over. The auxiliary members—most of them older doctors' wives—had been miffed, and they had threatened to boycott our annual fund-raising event. The banquet and silent auction, our big money-making event was supported by Southside businesses, organizations, and grateful patients. The benefit this year was going toward nursing scholarships, thanks to Judyth. Tim had said it was just a way to get on the nurses' good side, but I wasn't so sure. We needed more nurses and scholarship funds would help, benefiting the staff as much as administration.

She courted employees, too, by luring them into the gift shop with a ten-percent discount on every item, including candy, soft drinks, greeting cards, and gifts, and adding special promotions near holidays. Employees were now allowed to buy on credit, and the payments were deducted from their paychecks, a benefit that those without credit cards valued.

"Did you hear that charge nurses can't vote?" asked a female voice from beyond the candy aisle in the gift shop. "Any nurse who assumes responsibility for a unit or a floor when the nurse manager's not there is ineligible. That means all of us but brand-new grads," she added.

I was trying to decide whether to have a Hershey bar with or without almonds.

"Not so," her companion said, her voice raised. "Another hospital tried that and the board—the labor relations board—ruled against them. They said charge nurses don't hire and fire, so they're not considered management. It's just one more way they're trying to intimidate us. Don't listen to that."

The speaker was Lucille Pendergast, the head nurse in orthopedics, who towered above the counter. Lucille's six-foot height matched Judyth's, but there the comparison ended. While Judyth looked as if she'd been pulled up tall by her head, with her body stretched thin, Lucille's head and neck were oversized, matching the rest of her. She wasn't fat, she was just a big woman. I had often wondered what patients thought when they woke up after surgery to see her looming over them. But she had the back and arm strength necessary for the heavy lifting required in orthopedics.

Lucille reached a large hand up and grabbed a bag of cheese puffs from a rack near the cash register. I knew they needed me upstairs but I waited at the back of the gift shop, reluctant to go up to the cash register and get into a debate with Lucille, whose size, I had to admit, intimidated me. Two older women standing by the display of nightgowns watched as Lucille and her companion paid and turned toward the entrance.

"If we don't fight," Lucille said, raising her fist into the air, "we get what we deserve: nothing." She spread her hand wide, flinging off invisible injustices.

I grabbed both candy bars and hurried toward the counter. Outside I realized what had seemed confusing: Lucille was management just like me; she couldn't vote for or against the union.

A new patient had been wheeled up from surgery by the time I got back to the unit, and I went in to check on him.

"What are you doing here?" I asked Bart, my tone none too welcoming.

"Just giving her report on this patient after surgery," he said, nodding to Jessie, who was checking the patient's vitals. "I'm doing clinicals in anesthesia today and tomorrow, and this was my patient."

The young woman groaned. Jessie swiped a port on her IV with alcohol and injected a Tubex of morphine.

Bart scooped up some syringes left on the bed and deposited them in his lab coat pocket. "I'll take these back to surgery," he offered.

"What are they?" I asked.

"Meds we used in the recovery room," Bart said.

"You'd better be careful," I warned. "They're keeping a close check on the counts, now especially."

"These aren't narcotics. They're just meds we use in OR, but I have to return them so they can be logged out anyway." He turned to go.

"Bart, can I talk to you a minute?"

A flick of annoyance crossed his face. "Sure," he said, "but I've got to get back soon."

I nodded toward an empty room and when we were inside I asked him, "That morning Huey Castle died—"

"I wasn't here," he said quickly. "I don't know anything about it." He jiggled the syringes in his lab coat pocket.

"I know that. Did you see anyone around the halls or by the elevator? Anyone who shouldn't have been here?"

"I honestly can't say. I was in such a hurry to get to class, I don't remember. Now can I go?"

I waved him off.

"ALL SHE'S WORRIED about is our reputation," I told Jessie later, relating what Judyth had said.

"That affects us all," Jessie said, reasonably.

"What affects us?" Serena asked. She had had an early class and had just arrived.

Jessie explained what had happened to Laura.

"Oh, no. This is just like before when they thought she—"

"Shhh," I interrupted.

Serena leaned over the counter and lowered her voice. "I know Laura didn't do anything wrong. She cares too much about her patients. She just wouldn't," Serena added with a catch in her voice. "Can't you do something, Monika? Find out what happened to Huey? Do they think he died of something other than the cancer? Can't you find out? Can't you get Laura back?"

"I'm not sure there's anything else I can do, Serena. Tim's brother said he'd have her out of jail tomorrow morning, at the latest. And we don't even know that Huey's death was anything but what we expected."

She chewed her lip, fingers drumming on the counter, nails bitten to the quick.

"They're running a tox screen for narcotics," I said, not mentioning that it was the medical examiner's office who was doing it.

"I know Laura didn't do anything wrong," said Serena again.

"So how do we cover Laura's hours?" Tim said, returning after taking medication to Mr. Kleinfeldt. "More overtime for the rest of us? Mandatory, I suppose."

"I have some good news, though. They've got a bunch of nurses in orientation and . . ." I stopped when I saw Tim's face screw up in anger.

"Great," he said, sarcastically.

"It is! We need more nurses. With accreditors coming and Laura gone—for now, at least—this will help the whole hospital."

"Don't you know why they're doing this, Monika?" He went on without waiting for a response. "It's to stack the union vote!"

"We won't even be in business if we don't pass accreditation, Tim. We've got to have enough nurses to be safe."

"Oh, yeah, we'll be safe. But for how long? They're getting a two-fer, you know. Having new nurses will help us pass accreditation *and* they'll vote down the union. Two fer one." He squinted. "You think new nurses, just hired by Judyth, will vote against administration?" Serena had left so he turned to a student nurse standing by the counter, "Would you?" he asked her.

She backed up and didn't answer.

He went on. "They won't know how bad it is here. Then we won't get representation—that's what a union can do—and nothing will change." He turned on his heel and marched back into Mr. Kleinfeldt's room.

The student scooted away.

I'd have to broach the overtime issue with Tim soon, but not now. Not when I couldn't predict what he'd do or say with patients, visitors, and staff all listening.

BJ WAS LATE. Not for the first time, I worried. I knew that cops, like nurses, often spent more time documenting what they did than doing it.

But police work was more dangerous than working in a hospital, even though we had had our share of violent patients and their visitors. I also knew BJ would no more think of being anything but a cop than I would think of leaving nursing.

"Where've you been?" I asked her, my irritation concealing my fear.

She straddled the stool, smoothed loose strands of her blond hair back and smiled. "I'm happy to see you, too," she said, tapping the bar for a beer.

We were meeting at our favorite hangout, Hauptmann's, the corner tavern in our old neighborhood. Hauptmann's remained a working man's (and woman's) bar, but the clientele was more diverse than it had been when we grew up there. Back then the patrons were mostly of German heritage and worked at the brewery nearby, faithful to the Busch brands of beer.

"That your dinner?" BJ asked, nodding at the bag of chips I was rapidly devouring.

"Uh huh," I mumbled, my mouth full.

"Come right from work?" BJ asked with a grin.

It had been too late to go home and change so I was still dressed in my green scrubs, which, thankfully, were only slightly soiled, with what I didn't want to think about.

I wiped my hands on my pants and grabbed a drink of beer. "I didn't want to be late," I said to make my point.

We were there to watch the election results. The polls had just closed and the announcers, with no results yet to discuss, were rehashing the election. Democrats had controlled the mayor's office since 1949 so the primary election would decide the winner. The city was strictly divided along racial and economic lines. The north side was mostly black and poor, the south side was white and, while few Southsiders could be considered wealthy, they were more likely to be financially-comfortable. The central corridor, which consisted of the regenerated areas, was racially-mixed and more socially liberal. The candidates reflected these differences. A black man from the northside was opposing a white man from the south.

Both factions had been successful at city hall in the past, although the first African-American mayor had not been elected until 1993. In this election, however, a white woman, who represented the central corridor, was garnering as much support as the other two. According to the most recent poll the three were in a dead heat, but only one of them would be the Democratic candidate and, thus, the next mayor of St. Louis.

I asked BJ if she knew anything more about Laura's arrest.

"Isn't she the one ditched that patient a few months ago? Left her to bleed to death?"

"Well," I said. "Laura couldn't have saved her no matter what."

"I thought she lost her license over that. Nursing license."

"She's on probation. She can still work, and she's done fine. Until now. I'm sure Judyth will report her arrest to the board of nursing, and what they'll do I don't know."

I waited until the bartender left and went on. "Maybe not, though. Judyth's so worried about publicity and our accreditation. Maybe she'll wait and see what happens. She wouldn't let me report Bart, the guy who let Guardino die."

"Wasn't that different? Guardino was about to die."

"So was Huey. Just not so soon. Or so we thought."

A man approached the bar, noticed BJ's uniform, and took a seat at the end away from us.

"Why'd they arrest Laura, anyway?" I asked her. "Have you heard anything?"

"Don told me that ever since McNeil made detective he's been trying to rack up scalps. I told you he was a hot shot. But he's in a shit-load of trouble now." She smiled and took a long swallow of beer. "We call it 'jumping the gun.'"

"Sounds like a cliché."

"Well, cops ain't the most imaginative."

"In the meantime, Laura's sitting down there in jail."

"What time did you say they arrested her?"

"In the morning. I think it was about ten. Why?"

"They can only hold her twenty hours without charging her with something."

I checked my watch. "It's been almost twelve hours now. You mean they'll keep her overnight?"

"Probably."

"Poor Laura." I rolled my beer bottle around on the bar, leaving a pattern of wet circles.

"Unless they find something," BJ added.

"Like what?"

"Well, they'll try to get the results of her urine test from the hospital, and maybe try to get her to give some blood, too. See if she's on anything."

"I doubt the hospital would release her results without a court order. Judyth's too worried about our reputation. And with the accreditors coming back. . . ."

"Her lawyer wouldn't let her give blood anyway without a warrant. She have one? A lawyer?"

I told her about Tim's brother agreeing to represent her.

"Good," she said. "Too many perps say too much before they get a lawyer and then it's too late. Of course, most of the time we're glad about that." She smiled.

"Look, we don't even know that Huey didn't die naturally," I told her. "It's only the ME's office that decided to label it a suspicious death. We were expecting him to die. And Laura had only arrived a half hour or so before he coded."

"You said she was his nurse. Had she done anything yet? Given him anything?" BJ leaned back and looked me in the eye.

"She'd given him morphine. But he was due for it."

"Could that have killed him?"

"The flow is controlled. It's on a pump and the patient pushes a button to release the drug."

"What happens if he keeps pushing it? Wouldn't he get too much?"

"There's a mechanism that prevents it from releasing more that a set amount in a specified time, although it can be set for a continuous flow. Huey's wasn't like that because he also had a fentanyl patch." I dumped out the crumbs from the bottom of my bag of chips, popped them into my mouth, and took a drink of beer. An off-road vehicle navigated a sand dune on the silent TV. "Laura hung a bag, too, but I don't know why."

"What do you mean?"

"He had a central line—the IV was inserted into his jugular vein—"

"Yikes! Didn't that hurt?"

"I suppose, but he needed TPN—total parental nutrition—because he was so debilitated and he couldn't eat much because of the stomach cancer. Anyway, those bags are changed once every twenty-four hours, usually on nights, so the night nurse, Bart, should have changed it."

"But you say this Laura did it instead?"

"That's what she charted."

"Why would she do that?"

I shrugged. "It happens. The night nurse is usually pretty busy. He's there with only a temporary-agency nurse or two. This guy is somewhat careless anyway. He's more interested in grad school. He probably ran out at the end of his shift, Laura saw the bag laying there, and hung it."

"So could something have been in the IV bag?" BJ asked.

"No, the bags come up premixed and labeled with the patient's name. And they're calibrated too. They drip at a specified rate, depending on the patient and the solution."

I hadn't thought too much about the bag before telling BJ about it. I'd meant to ask Bart why he hadn't hung it, but I'd forgotten about it the last few times I'd seen him.

The bartender checked to see if we were ready for another beer but we waved him off.

"What makes Harding or McNeil think Huey's death was murder?" I asked BJ. "What evidence do they have? Or motive? What reason do they think Laura might have for killing him? So far all we know is that Huey had a respiratory arrest and we don't know exactly why, not for sure. Why is everyone making such a big deal about it?"

She shook her head. "Once the ME rules it suspicious, the cops don't have any choice. They've got to follow up."

"And arrest someone, anyone, just so they get an arrest?"

She kept her eyes on the silent television screen, not answering my question. Then she turned to me. "There's something else. They had a tip, Don told me. From that guy Dog, the one you know. Something about how Huey was afraid of someone at the hospital. It does seem weird that Huey was just getting ready to talk to the cops and then suddenly he's dead."

"What if Laura gave him what was ordered and it was too much? His liver was shot, so the drugs might accumulate," I said, thinking. "That wouldn't be her fault."

"Maybe the doctor who ordered the drugs would be blamed," she said. "Shouldn't he have known about his patient's condition and not ordered too much?"

"It's hard to judge exactly. And Huey kept clamoring for more. I'm not saying that's what happened. I'm just conjecturing."

Someone turned the sound up on the TV hanging from the wall in the corner. The first precinct results were coming in. The Southside candidate was leading in his own neighborhood. The announcers went on to rehash the campaign issues: the sad state of the city's public schools, another proposed increase in cigarette taxes, and regulation of the gambling industry. The sound went back down.

"What about those tests they did on the nurses? Did they find anything?" BJ asked.

"One nurse was high; I saw her. She was fired. I heard that a couple more tested positive, and they're running more tests on those samples. That's all I know now."

"Could this Laura have been on drugs when she took care of the guy? And wouldn't the tests show that if she was?"

I thought for a minute before I said, "Huey died Friday. They tested everyone on Monday. I'll have to find out, but I think most narcotics have a pretty short half-life."

"Half-life?"

"That's how long they stay in the body. That's why we give them to patients every three or four hours. I doubt it would've shown up after three days."

"So she could have been high, done something wrong that killed him, and still show up clean for drugs a few days later." BJ signaled the bartender, pointing at our empty bottles.

"What could happen to her?" I asked.

"I don't know. If they think she accidentally overdosed him on something, then it could be manslaughter—involuntary—or it could be a homicide, even first degree if they thought it was premeditated. Not accidental or spur of the moment, that is. First-degree murder carries the death penalty, you know," she added.

"Oh, god, BJ. Don't talk that way. I can't even think about something that horrible."

"Don't worry, Missouri's never executed a woman." She patted my hand. "I'm sorry I mentioned it."

I pointed to the TV screen. "If this breaks on the news right now and the accreditors arrive. . . ."

The television sound came back up, and an announcer said the vote for mayor was too close to call.

"Don't worry, the reporters are too busy with this election, especially after the brouhaha over announcers calling Florida for Gore back in 2000. They're way too busy to go hunting through the arrest records for something to write about."

After the bartender had deposited two more beers in front of us, BJ asked, "You ever talk to that priest? The one who brought Harding in?"

"I tried, but he's on retreat until Thursday. I'll catch him then."

"Maybe he'll know something that will help."

"Unless it was a confession."

"Then it went to the grave with him."

I HIKED MYSELF up on a barstool at the second tavern I'd been in that night and ordered a Busch Lite. The bartender was a large woman with too-blond hair who smiled at me as she popped the top and sat the bottle down on a stained coaster.

I smiled back and took a swallow.

"Is Mavis here?" I asked, looking around. A man with long, gray hair pulled back with a rubber band was counting bottles at the end of the bar. I was the only customer at the bar although some men were playing the 25-holer in the back. The machine was illegal unless they had a gambling license, which was unlikely.

"You a friend of hers?" the woman, whose name tag said "Bella," asked. She leaned against the cabinet behind her and lit a cigarette. The man counting bottles glanced my way.

Driving home from Hauptmann's I'd thought about Huey and who might have wanted him dead. I knew Laura wasn't on that list but I didn't know anyone who was. "I knew Huey better," I answered.

Bella nodded. "Sad," she said with a sigh. "Nice guy."

I took another swallow of beer.

"We all liked him." She nodded toward her co-worker, who seemed to be counting the same group of bottles over.

"Everyone did," I agreed.

She picked up a towel beside her and began to wipe the already-shiny bar. "Hell, that little guy could get more with his smile and one arm than most men twice his height and both arms."

"Here's to Huey," I said, raising my bottle.

She waved her cigarette in my direction. "One hell of a guy."

A fiftyish guy ambled up from the back and pulled himself up on a barstool at the end. Bella told him we were toasting Huey. He picked up the half-empty bottle in front of him and joined us. "To Huey," he said, "who never met a chance he didn't take."

"You knew him?" I asked.

"I knew this much." He took another swig of beer. "If you had anything Huey wanted, watch out. He'd find some way or 'nother to get it away from you. Never saw nothing like it." He shook his head in amazement. "And you'd end up thinking you had wanted to give it to him."

"Aw, shut up, Harry," Bella said, crushing her cigarette in an ashtray on the counter behind her. "You liked him, you know that."

"That's 'cause I never had nothing. He couldn't charm me out of what I didn't have." He tapped his empty bottle on the bar and Bella pulled another bottle out of the cooler. "That gal he got down at the boat," the man went on. "Wouldn't do for nothing 'til she'd go out with him. Told her he was separated."

"Was he?" I asked.

"Humph! Mavis would've separated him, that's for sure."

I took another drink and looked around. The man counting bottles had left. The two men in back were motioning for Bella to bring them more beers.

"When's she coming back?"

Bella looked like she didn't know who I meant.

"Mavis, Huey's wife."

"She's not." She nodded toward the men in back and slung the towel over her shoulder.

"Oh?"

"She quit," she said, pulling two Budweisers out of the cooler. "Said she didn't need to work any more."

Chapter 14

Wednesday, 15 August, 0932 Hours

I knew who they were the minute they came through the door. They were dressed alike in dark suits and white shirts, buttoned up tight. I was coming out of Mr. Dougherty's room carrying the dirty sheets that he had soiled when I tripped over a wheelchair someone had parked in front of the curtain. The place looked a mess, but it was too late to do anything about it.

The doors banged open again. "Coming through," the pony-tailed attendant ordered as he pushed a gurney strung with IV poles and loaded with an elderly man covered in blankets. The man moaned as the gurney rattled through the door. The three surveyors scooted out of the way. Tim grabbed the gurney and pulled it into an empty room.

"Dr. Hendricks," said the older visitor. "Lead surveyor, Joint Commission. And this is Ms. Holcomb, CEO of Hadley Hospital in Pennsylvania." He nodded to the woman. "And Mr. Lawrence, RN."

I shook hands with each in turn as I introduced myself.

Then all hell broke loose.

Tim yelled that our newest patient had arrested. Jessie grabbed a crash cart, banging it into a bedside commode left in the way. Just then an alarm screamed and Mr. Swenson emerged stark naked, his monitor leads trailing behind him. He was yelling that someone had stolen his clothes.

And the fire alarm went off.

Our three visitors left with a backward wave, saying they'd be back later.

Ruby found out the fire bell was a false alarm, and I got Swenson back into his gown and into bed. I told Serena to restart his IV and that I'd call Jake to see if he would order some kind of restraint for him, either chemical or physical. Tim would have to put in a new catheter; Mr. Swenson had pulled that out too.

Tim and Jessie were still in with the code, joined now by an anesthesiologist. A lab tech had been in to draw a stat blood. I stepped into the room as the anesthesiologist said, "We're calling the code."

"Calling the code," Tim intoned. "Time: 1012."

"SHE'S OUT," Tim said as I came through the door after a practice-review committee meeting. "Laura."

"I ain't heard that," Ruby said.

"Believe it," Tim said. "They didn't have enough to charge her."

"Thank goodness," I said.

"She's ready to come back to work, my brother said. Get this behind her."

"She's on administrative leave, according to Judyth. But maybe since she's not charged with a crime, Judyth will let her come back," I said, feeling a little bit guilty because I was more worried about having enough staff than I was about Laura.

"You gonna eat both of those?" Ruby asked, pointing to the Hershey bars I'd tossed on the desk the day before. "I can't eat the nuts," she said, picking them up. "But I like this one." She gave me a grin. "You don't need both, might make you fat." She laughed, her chins bobbing.

"Take it," I said, sorting through the phone messages Ruby had handed me. Mrs. Bauer's daughter had called again. She and her sister had been arguing about where their mother would go once she recovered enough from her stroke to leave the hospital. Apparently neither daughter wanted her mother nor did they want her to go to a nursing home. Another call was from the sister of a patient who had died a couple of weeks ago who wanted to know if she could come by with a gift for the nurses. Human resources had called as well to remind me to bring my renewed nursing license in to be copied for the file.

"You heard about what happened?"

"Huh?"

"You better pay attention." Ruby tore the wrapper off the top of the candy and took a bite.

I tried to remember if my new license had arrived in the mail yet.

"You see those guys hanging around the lobby?" she asked, her mouth full of chocolate. She took another bite.

"Those hulks? What about them?" I asked her.

She crooked a finger and leaned toward me. "They the mob," she said and bit another chunk out of the candy bar.

"What makes you think that?"

"That Judyth," she lowered her voice to a stage whisper, "she brung them here from Chi-ca-go," Ruby added, smacking her lips. "And that's not all."

Were they involved with the Guardinos?

"I've half a mind not to tell you the rest," Ruby said, folding the wrapper down on the candy bar.

"Spit it out, Ruby, I don't have all day."

"Some's money's gone missing."

"Where? Whose? What are you talking about?"

"Nurses, that's whose."

"If they kept it locked up, like we're supposed to—"

"It were locked up, but that don't make no difference to the man."

"The man?"

"The boss."

"Judyth?"

"Yeah, she the man around here."

"OKAY, SPILL IT," I ordered, cornering Max after a brief meeting administration had called to introduce the Joint Commission survey team I'd already met. Judyth and the other administrators had advised us to cooperate with them. No one mentioned Laura's arrest from the day before.

Max glanced around as if he were looking for a way out, but I stood in front of him, hands on my hips, the door shut behind me. "What gives? You've been acting like you hardly know me. What's up?"

He took a long breath. "It's your drug test. It came back positive. For opiates."

"What? How could it? I've never used drugs in my life!"

"They're running the confirmatory tests to be certain. Monika, I didn't want to say anything until we knew for sure."

"Maybe mine got mixed up with somebody else's and—"

"We maintained strict chain of custody, I told you that."

"Well, there's been a mistake. What could make it turn out positive, Max? You said something about how over-the-counter stuff might cause a false positive."

"Cold medicines, cough syrup, Tylenol PM, for example. You use any of those in the day or two before?" His eyes, magnified through thick lenses, were bright with hope.

"Nothing. I hardly ever even take an aspirin."

"I believe you, Monika. We've known each other too long for me to think you'd do anything like that." He gave me a hint of a smile.

"Does Judyth know? About my test?"

"She's the one who told me not to say anything yet. Especially with Joint Commission here."

"That explains why she acted so funny."

"Funny?"

"Not funny, ha ha. Funny, strange. I went to talk to her after Laura was arrested. She just acted . . . oh, I don't know, uncomfortable. I guess that was it."

"Let's just wait till we know more."

"When will that be?"

"We should have the results by Friday. In the meantime, don't worry about it. You know you didn't use anything. I'm sure it'll turn out fine."

I started to turn away, then stopped. "Max, what about Huey's tox screen? You hear about that yet?"

"They're running it today. Come by after work and I should have it."

RUBY HAD TAPED a message slip on my office door saying that Lisa had called. I was checking my email when the phone rang. It was Lisa.

"I need your help," she began.

"Yes," I said, try to remember where I'd hidden the package that Huey's girlfriend had left him.

"Will you help me?"

"What do you want, Lisa? I'm very busy." I rummaged through my desk. It had to be here somewhere.

"I know you are, and I'm sorry to bother you, but. . . ." Her words drifted off.

I thought I'd put it in the back of one of my drawers.

"I want my job back," she added, her voice firmer.

"I have a question for you," I said, switching gears.

"Anything," she said at once.

"Last Friday you were in ICU with Bart. Did you see anyone around who shouldn't have been there? Someone not a staff member?"

"Why? Is something wrong?"

"Probably not."

"A patient died right after you two left."

She was quiet.

"You thought of something?"

"No, no," she said.

"If you saw something, tell me, Lisa."

"Everything was normal," she said, "or as normal as it is in ICU. Now what about a job? Can you please help me?"

"Why don't you call Wanda? She was your head nurse. See what she can do."

I turned back to my search. Minutes from old committee meetings, a schedule of staff-development programs from last year, scraps of paper with phone numbers of long-gone patients' family members, and one very stale half-eaten package of cheese crackers jammed the drawer.

"I heard you lost a nurse. I can work in ICU. Ask everyone. I did great when I was there."

The bottom drawer wouldn't open. Something was caught inside. I shoved the drawer back and forth until it pulled loose.

"Please, Monika, I really need to work," Lisa went on.

Got it. The paper bag was torn where it had caught on the desk so I tossed it in the trash can. "I don't know what I can do," I told Lisa. I opened the baggie, releasing a pungent odor. I squeezed out the extra air and then zipped up the baggie, and tucked it into my lab coat pocket.

Lisa went on. "You can talk to Judyth. Everyone needs help and I'll work anywhere. I can do ICU, step-down, med-surg, anywhere, any hours, all nights even. Please," she said, her voice pleading.

"Why don't you ask Bart to help you? He's in school with Wanda."

"I can't tell him. He thinks I'm still working there."

"He doesn't know? Certainly someone's told him. And I'm sure he'd help you if you'd be honest with him."

"I can't tell him. He says I'm just like his dad." Her voice choked.

"I know he cares about you, Lisa."

She sniffed. "You don't know him, Monika. All he cares about is his career. That's it. That's the Holy Grail for Mister Bart Mickelson!" she said, her voice stronger. "One thing he's always said though."

"What's that?"

"He's not going to end up like his dad."

Silence.

"Drunk. And dead," she added just before I heard the dial tone.

"MONIKA," MAX SAID, stopping me in the hall later. "Tell me if you've had any of those poppy seed muffins they make in the cafeteria?"

"Not for a long time. Why?"

"It's the poppy seeds. You could get a positive with those."

"I had a poppy-seed bagel. Two, actually. Well, two tops. Ruby ate only the bottoms because of her dental plate, the seeds from the top half get caught, and then she has to take her plate out."

Max grabbed my arm. "That's it, Monika. That's why it showed up positive. If they'd used the cutoff I recommended, yours would have been below that, but they wouldn't listen. I'm sure your confirmatory test will bear this out." His face lit up in a smile and he put an arm around my shoulders companionably as we made our way along the hall. "Just remember that the next time you're going to have a urine test, don't eat poppy seeds beforehand."

"I'll be sure to remember that, Max, if I get advance warning, that is."

We waved goodbye as he turned toward the lab and then I headed back upstairs, bounding up the steps two at a time.

I WAS LATE to the meeting for nurse managers to meet with Mr. Lawrence, the RN surveyor from Joint Commission, but when I got there it turned out he hadn't yet arrived. As I looked for an empty chair I heard two nurses exchanging complaints.

"I'll tell him straight out," one manager said. "It's still not safe. There aren't enough nurses. People are being shifted to other units and working jobs they're not really qualified for. Or they're doubling back and working with not enough sleep."

"I'm afraid that's going to hurt our chances to get our accreditation status off warning, don't you?" her companion asked.

"That's exactly my point."

The room was full. I took a chair in the front row as Mr. Lawrence joined us. He opened a folder on the podium in front of him. He began by congratulating us on the improvements we'd made and asked if we wanted to add anything to the written report the hospital had submitted.

There were a few murmured comments, but no one volunteered anything out loud. I looked around for Lucille but she wasn't there. Maybe she'd resigned her management job to return to a staff nurse position so she could be involved in the union.

"I have here a list of nurses who have not provided the human resources office with copies of their current nursing licenses," he said, pulling out a single sheet of paper. "There are some nurse managers on this list as well."

A slight murmur rippled through the room.

"I'm sure it's nothing to worry about. Some of the licenses are out of date, people who've neglected to renew them, I suspect. In one or two instances, the license in the file is from another state. If a nurse doesn't have a Missouri license, that nurse is violating the law in addition to not meeting the standard for accreditation."

"Can we bring in a copy?" a nurse in the back asked.

"Originals, only," he told her. "That's the state requirement. And ours."

"DID LISA CALL you?" I asked Wanda as we took our lunch trays to a table by the window.

"No, why?" Wanda asked. She put her taco salad and chocolate milk on the table and set both our trays on the chair next to her. "Was she high?"

"She didn't sound like it. She wants her job back."

"After what she did to us," Wanda began. She leaned across the table and went on. "She stole our drugs, Monika. Stuff that should have gone to patients."

"Do you know for sure she stole anything? Have you been short?" I opened my carton of milk, stuck in a straw, and took a long drink.

"I'm not sure," Wanda admitted. "We haven't always had time to count as carefully as we should." Wanda broke off a corner of taco shell and nibbled at it. "You hear about the results on the nurses' drug tests?"

I busied myself with my salad and shook my head. Had she heard about mine?

"One nurse on call in OR nights—she'd just started—and Lisa, of course. You think her boyfriend—that cute guy who works for you—might have taken some for her?"

"From what I've seen Bart's more interested in his career than risking a drug arrest for his girlfriend."

"Well, I couldn't help Lisa if I wanted to," Wanda said, dipping into the meat sauce on her salad. "If we hired her back and someone got hurt because she was high on something. . . ."

"You could be fired."

"And sued. What is it they call it? Respondeat superior, that's it."

"Supervisors are responsible for the actions of their subordinates," I said, stressing every third word.

"Yep. I can't take that chance."

"Lisa will just go somewhere else. There are plenty of jobs these days."

"Well, I certainly won't give her a recommendation."

"What will you say if someone calls?"

"I'd answer the only question we're allowed to answer: would you rehire? I can't say I would." She broke of a piece of taco shell and scooped up some spicy ground beef, then popped it neatly into her mouth.

I cut off a bite of pork tenderloin, dipped it in mustard, and tasted it.

"Say, what's the story about the nurse on your unit they arrested?" Wanda asked. "The scuttlebutt is that she's another one stealing drugs. Wasn't she the one who got in trouble for abandoning the patient who died? She ended up in psych, didn't she? As a patient. Miss Loony-tunes."

"That's all over," I said, swallowing. "It was just a reaction to the trauma. She's fine, and she's a good nurse."

"Well, something's going on. I mean, they arrested her. I do have to say though, that I wondered why they didn't just fire her, like they did Lisa."

"Laura's in a protected class."

"Huh?"

"Peggy set me straight on that. Mental illness is one of the conditions under the Americans with Disabilities Act. They can't fire her."

"I never heard that. You mean that if someone's been diagnosed with a mental illness we have to keep them, regardless of what they might do?"

"No. It's just that we have to make accommodations."

"So what kind of accommodations do you make for crazy people?"

"Wanda! You're a nurse! You know that mental illness does not always translate into 'crazy,' which is not an accurate way of describing anybody, anyway."

"Well," said Wanda, "I heard they think she did something to the guy in ICU who died last Friday." She lowered her voice and looked around. "Do you think she murdered him?"

"Of course not," I said. "And, besides, the police released her this morning. I can't imagine what motive they think she'd have."

"Maybe they just think she made a mistake."

"They don't arrest people for making a mistake."

"Well," said Wanda, "maybe that nurse in Florida who did those mercy killings that's been all over the news has made them jumpy."

Peggy approached our table, tray in hand and a large book under her arm. Wanda stood, offering her chair to Peggy, saying she had to get back to work. Peggy slid the book onto the table and rubbed her arm where the book's edge had left a dent on her arm.

"Are you going to grad school?" I asked her.

"I'm thinking about it. I thought I'd try one class and see how it goes. Abnormal psychology," she added, tapping the book. She spread her napkin in her lap and took a sip of water. "You get those e-mails I sent?"

"No, I haven't had time to check my mail. What are they about?"

"Nurses United. The committee that's working to organize us. I guess he just sent them to staff nurses. That makes sense, we're the ones can vote."

"Who?"

"Tim."

"Tim sent them? From home?"

"I don't know. Why?"

"I just don't want him getting into trouble using the hospital's system for union organizing."

"That already happened." Peggy cut her pineapple rounds into tiny wedges and scooped one up with a topping of cottage cheese and took a bite. She dabbed at the corners of her mouth and went on. "Didn't you hear about Judyth," Peggy nodded toward administration's offices, "going off on him? It was after a meeting for staff nurses about the union, and it took the hospital's legal counsel to set her straight. It seems as if this issue already went to the NLRB, according to another e-mail we got this week. If your employer allows you to send personal e-mails on work time, they can't forbid you to send any sort of organizing information in the same way."

"When does any nurse have time to send personal e-mails?"

"That doesn't matter. If they've been allowed to do it even once, administration can't prevent them now."

"I didn't know."

"In another e-mail this week—you really should check your messages, Monika—they said that from now on, personal e-mails are not allowed. Sort of the barn door thing, I think." Peggy finished her pineapple, cottage cheese, and lettuce salad and took a sip of water. "Tell me what happened to Laura. I've been worried sick about her ever since I heard she'd been arrested. They can't possibly think that Laura killed someone."

"Well, you're the second person in half an hour who's heard that rumor. I guess it's all over the hospital. The truth is that the guy who arrested her is a new detective who wants to make a name, my friend who's a cop, says. And they released her this morning."

"In the meantime, she's still under suspicion, isn't she?"

"As far as I know."

"This is terrible, Monika. You don't need this to worry about on top of everything else."

"I know, Peggy, that's why I'm trying to find out how the patient died. We're all suspect until we know exactly what caused Huey's death. I'm waiting to hear from Max if he received too much morphine. That's the only thing I can think of that might possibly implicate Laura. Or any of us, for that matter."

"It's really unfair that that episode with the woman who bled to death is coming back to haunt her. She didn't do anything wrong then, and you've told me many times since then that Laura is doing a good job. She wouldn't have given a patient extra morphine. No nurse would. And since she's still on probation you know she'd be extra careful."

"Unless he'd already had a shot of morphine."

She set her glass down with a bang. A little water sloshed out onto the table. "You know who they suspect took the missing drugs, don't you?" She leaned back, her eyes squinted. "Moi," she said, jabbing her chest with her thumb.

"But you've been . . . uh, recovered for a long time."

"Recover*ing*, Monika, never recover*ed*. And yes, it's been four years, but they. . . ." She nodded toward the administrative wing opposite the cafeteria. ". . . never forget. It's on my record permanently."

"But your test was okay, wasn't it?"

"Yes, of course." She noticed the spilled water and began to mop it up with a paper napkin. "But that didn't stop them. I had to give two more specimens, the last time they put blue dye in the toilet water so I couldn't dilute the sample, I guess, and Judyth herself watched me." She shuddered. "It's so humiliating, Monika. Will it ever end? Will they ever stop seeing me as an addict?" she asked as if to herself. She turned back to me. "I heard about Lisa. Didn't I tell you? You get a sixth sense about that when you've been through it."

"You hear about any others?" I asked, wondering if word had leaked out about my test.

"Nope. They're . . ." Another nod toward administration. ". . . being pretty close-mouthed about it. I only heard that Lisa was fired. I assumed they found opiates in her urine."

"That would make her an addict, I guess."

"No, it wouldn't, Monika. It would mean that she had ingested the substance they're testing for. The test simply indicates the presence of a drug; it says nothing about abuse or dependency. For all we would know, she could have used it one time." She thought a moment. "Of course, in her case she exhibited addictive behaviors, too. That's when addiction can be diagnosed."

"Maybe she'll stop now. Since she lost her job."

Peggy shook her head. "That's not how it works. Her main concern is finding more drugs. Addicts always find a way to get something. They might substitute and feed their addiction with whatever they can get their hands on, but if she doesn't have something, she'll go into withdrawal." She swallowed hard. "And that's not something I'd let my worst enemy go through." She rolled the bottom of her glass around on the tray and watched the water as it swirled close to the edge and threatened to spill out again.

"She called me," I said. "She wanted me to help her get her job back. That's what Wanda and I were talking about."

"What'd Wanda say?"

"That she couldn't help. She said she'd be liable if anything happened, and Judyth wouldn't let her anyway, I'm sure."

"Maybe Lisa's ready for the diversion program."

"What's that?

"It's a program the state board and the nursing association put together. If a nurse enters the program and follows their recommendations and stays clean and sober for two years, she isn't subject to disciplinary action against her license."

"It worked for you."

"No, they didn't have the program then, although I could have used it. I was on probation for two years. I'm off it now, but that record will always be there. Always. If a nurse completes the diversion program, the record is wiped clean. That way the nurse is treated and the public is protected, too."

"Is that safe? Couldn't the nurse be using again?"

"Sure, but so could you."

I started. It was the poppy seeds that had caused the elevated opiate-levels in my urine, but, I was being treated by those who were privy to the results as if I were guilty. Is this how Peggy felt on a daily basis?

"The difference is," Peggy went on, "that the nurse in the program is being monitored, just like I was. There are unannounced urine analyses. There are regular reports from your supervisor. But if they do okay, there's nothing on their record."

I wanted to change the subject. I had heard more than I wanted to about drugs. Especially with the bag of dope in my pocket.

"You could talk to her," Peggy said.

"Huh? Who?"

"Lisa. Tell her about the program. She called you and asked for help. You could suggest she call about it. Or you could call them and find out the best way to handle her."

I put my hands up. "I don't want to handle her in any way. It's not my business and, I'm sorry, Peggy, I just can't stir up any sympathy for her. She seems so . . . so manipulative."

Peggy laughed. “Of course she is.”

“Well, why don’t you talk to her if you’re so hot to help her?” I said.

Loud laughter came from a corner of the cafeteria.

“What’s with him?” Peggy asked, nodding toward Bart who was entertaining a table of student nurses.

“He’s here doing clinicals for grad school,” I told her.

“The other night at the bar he looked depressed, now he’s bopping around like he’s juiced.”

“Too much coffee. From the espresso stand,” I added, referring to another of Judyth’s money-making ventures.

She squinted at him as if she were studying a rare specimen. “He looks bipolar to me.”

“Bipolar. Isn’t that what we used to call manic depression?”

She nodded.

“I remember a patient I had in school. She was way over the top, not like Bart there.”

“There are degrees. Cyclothmic, it’s called. Shorter ups and downs, not as severe.”

“That sounds like most of us. And not too serious.”

“For these folks, it’s more than that. And worse could happen. Paranoia, delusion, suicide even.”

We watched Bart going from table to table, greeting people and smiling as if he were a politician campaigning for votes.

“Or maybe borderline personality disorder,” she mused, tapping her book with an index finger.

“What’s that?”

“Explosive, driven, impulsive.”

“He’s pretty intense, I’ll give you that. But a lot of students are. Working and going to school, both full time. That would tax anyone’s mental health. I think you’re just seeing a psych diagnosis in everyone. You’ve been reading too much of that book,” I said, pointing to the textbook next to her plate.

Peggy flicked her hair behind her ear with a finger. “Those are bonafide diagnoses. In DSM IV.” The manual of psychiatric disorders.

“Yeah, a bunch of psychiatrists sit around thinking up an official diagnosis for every possible behavior so the insurance companies will pay. I heard a new one the other day: relational disorders. People who can’t get along with each other.” I wadded my napkin and stuck it under my plate. “I call that family.”

Peggy laughed.

Someone bumped me hard on the back and I jumped up as an elderly woman slipped behind me. Her knarled hands clutched the air as she fell onto the floor, spreading bits of lettuce and watery tomatoes everywhere. Her tray had flipped upside down and was now mashed into a glob of spaghetti. A broken glass lay beyond it. I shoved my chair out of the way and knelt to see how she was. She didn't move for a moment, her face frozen into a startled expression, then she started to whimper. Her companion, an elderly man held up by a walker, looked around as if he didn't know where he was as a woman about my age bustled up and helped him to a chair.

I helped the woman on the floor up into a sitting position and checked her for any obvious signs of injury. When she said she was ready, I helped her stand. Splatters of spaghetti sauce and salad dressing dripped off her green polyester pants. Peggy brought me a stack of napkins and a cafeteria worker used a damp towel to help wipe the worst of the mess off the woman. I slid a chair under her and asked her how she felt.

"Shaky, but I think I'm okay." She smiled tentatively.

"We need to get you to the emergency room and have you checked."

"I don't want to cause any trouble."

"It's no trouble; it's what we do," I said, watching Peggy negotiate a wheelchair through the crowded lunchroom. The cafeteria worker picked up pieces of broken glass as a man from housekeeping arrived with a mop and bucket. I left to deliver the woman to the emergency room.

RETURNING TO THE unit, I found Ruby and two staff huddled in a whispered conversation. "What are you telling them now?" I asked Ruby. "Don't have enough work, any of you?" I said. The nurses scurried away, but Ruby held her ground. She jerked her head toward the conference room. "Just see for yourself," she said, turning back to the desk.

I opened the door to the conference room to find Judyth and one of our young security guards rummaging through my locker.

"What do you think you're doing?" I said. I realized I'd really raised my voice when I saw the guard's startled face. "That's my locker," I stuttered.

Judyth had her hand inside my gym bag, which she had placed on top of the conference table along with an old spiral notebook I'd used for notes at a long-ago continuing ed program, a navy hooded sweatshirt, and a half-empty water bottle.

I'd almost forgotten about my locker since I seldom used it anymore. I kept my purse locked up in my office.

"Hospital property," she said.

"No, it's not." I reached for my bag, but Judyth moved it so that I couldn't touch it. "It's mine."

Judyth nodded toward the guard. "Tell her."

"No employee can assume an expectation of privacy in a place of business," he intoned, pulling out a smashed donut from I don't know how long ago. "If it's on our property, we have a right to know what it is." The guard dropped the donut in the trash can and dusted off his hands. "Everything here can be searched, and evidence can be confiscated."

I fingered the package lodged in my lab coat pocket and felt sweat break out on my face. "So what are you?" I asked. "The police?" I asked, my voice came out in a croak.

"Security personnel are empowered by the city," Judyth answered. "They're the law in here."

"What are you looking for?" I asked, trying to keep my voice steady.

"Evidence of criminal activity," Judyth said, flipping through the pages of my notebook.

"In there?" I pointed to the notebook.

She tossed it on the table. "Drugs, Monika. Someone's stealing drugs." She checked her watch. "We'd better go, three more floors to do." They left me there, my jaws clenched in anger.

With one swipe of my arm, I shoved notebook, gym bag and sweatshirt into the trash, trying to hold back tears of frustration before I had to face the distraught family waiting for me in their mother's room.

"YOU WANTED TO know about the tox screen on Castle," Max said. "I heard from the medical examiner."

"Please tell me he didn't get too much morphine."

"He had more than I'd expect," he said and stared at me through thick lenses. "It was at the upper limits of the usual therapeutic levels." He held up his hand as I started to interrupt. "But there's an explanation. Remember I told you he had a fatty liver? An impaired liver isn't able to process the morphine very well, so there'd be a buildup in his blood."

"That doesn't make sense. He kept asking us for more. No matter how much we gave him, he said he was in pain."

"I suspect he was right." He steepled his fingers under his chin. "The liver processes opiates, just like it does with anything toxic."

"I know all that, " I insisted.

"Okay, so when the liver doesn't work so well—such as in his case—drugs accumulate there but they're not circulating enough to help his pain. Eventually, of course, it'd sedate him. If there were enough buildup, it'd depress his respirations, just like any other patient."

I shook my head. "That's not it. We tried Narcan during the code and it didn't do anything. If he'd overdosed on a narcotic, the Narcan would have reversed the effects and we could have started him breathing again." I slumped back in my seat. "So what happens now?"

"Normally, the ME would run more tests."

"Normally?"

"But he says he can't. The city's budget is in crisis, tax revenues are way down, they're overspent on the year already and it's only August."

"Where does that leave us? And Laura?"

"I really don't know, Monika."

"How about another drug? With his liver, couldn't something else build up in his blood and cause a respiratory arrest?"

"I suppose."

"Max, work with me here. I'm trying to come up with some theories about how he died."

"I ran some routine tests. His potassium was elevated somewhat."

"That would stop his heart, wouldn't it?"

"He would have been in asystole if he'd had too much potassium. Do you remember what the monitor showed?"

"Not until the very end. V-tach, then he went into ventricular fibrillation."

"It would have stopped his heart right away. It wasn't enough to kill him, anyway.

"So what else?"

"Another metabolite, CPK, was elevated slightly."

"What does that mean?"

"He had some muscle damage. Did you notice him trembling when it happened?"

"He didn't move at all, Max. He looked like he was paralyzed."

"Monika, this probably is just one of those deaths that happen, and we're never exactly sure of the cause. Post-mortem tests don't always tell you exactly. You know that. We try to piece it together from the diagnosis, treatment, physical findings from the autopsy, and whatever lab tests are run. Just like when they're alive. We rule out some things and what's left is the diagnosis. It's not a perfect system, but it's the best we have. That's why they call medicine an art, not a science."

"Max, the medical examiner called this death suspicious. One of my nurses is under suspicion for murder. We've got to know for sure. I know she didn't do it. What if this happens again? Is there *anything* else it could be?"

"The only thing I can think of is succinylcholine, anectine is the trade name. It's a neuroblocker—a paralytic agent—often used in surgery. Do you know of any way he could have gotten it? You don't routinely use it on the unit, do you?"

"No, we don't but can't you test for it anyway? We've got to find out what happened to him! Laura and St. Teresa's are both on the line. All of us are."

"Monika, that test is expensive. Why do you think the ME won't do any more testing? And I don't even know if any lab in St. Louis does it. I think there's only one place in the country that will test for it and that's in Philadelphia, if I remember correctly. And even if we ran the test, it'd be unlikely to show up. Succinylcholine breaks down rapidly after death. I have no basis to run the test. Unless there's a good reason to suspect it or the police requested it, in which case the ME would handle it.

"Max—"

"I can't do it. My budget's stretched as far as it will go. And I just got the word that they're taking the costs for the drug tests on the nurses out of my budget. Several hundred nurses work at St T's full or part time. Where I'm going to find the money, I don't know. Not and keep the lab running.

"I have to use what little money I have for tests on live people, patients who might get well. Not on every cadaver that comes through here. Nothing we can do for them now." He closed the file and laid it on top of others piled on his desk. "I'm sorry I can't help you. You know I would if I possibly could. I'm convinced that his liver status explained the elevated morphine level. I don't know what would cause the respiratory arrest. That's the best I can do."

Chapter 15

WEDNESDAY, 15 AUGUST, 1735 HOURS

I SQUEEZED INTO Black Beauty and released the catch for the top. It had been a long day and, even though the temperature was still in the high 90s, I needed the wind tonight to clear my mind. I laid my paper-towel wrapped roses—the ones from the Guardino family attorney—on the floor and, wedging myself back out of the car, I snagged my lab coat on the latch and ripped the pocket. The plastic bag fell onto the garage floor, and when I stepped back to release my lab coat from the door latch, I inadvertently kicked the bag under the car.

It had been one of those days.

I crouched down and looked under the car. The baggie was sitting next to the right front tire, out of my reach. Why hadn't I tossed it in with the medical waste? I walked around to the other side of the car, squatted down and tried to reach it. No luck. My arms were just too short.

"What are you doing there?" a male voice demanded.

I squeezed myself back up and turned toward the security guard, not one I recognized. "Just looking for something I dropped." I said, feeling a familiar rush of guilt, even though I'd done nothing wrong. A legacy from my grade-school days at St. Aloysius.

"Can I help?" he asked, sounding less cop-like.

"I can get it." I levered myself back down and stretched out toward the packet. I couldn't reach it. But I couldn't leave it, either; he'd be sure to find it when I drove away. I scratched my fingers on the greasy cement and caught the bag's edge, inching it towards me. I rolled a little to one side and tucked the baggie into the waistband of my scrubs, and pulled my top down over it as I stood up, hoping the bulge wouldn't show.

The guard hadn't moved.

"Got it," I said. "Thank you!"

Keeping my arms crossed close to my waist, I inched around Black Beauty and slid into the driver's seat. As I started to back out, the unlatched top bounced on its frame. I stopped and fastened it back down.

Turning at the exit ramp, I looked in the rear view mirror. The guard still stood there, hands on his waist. If he'd been a nun, he would have seen through my subterfuge.

Chapter 16

Wednesday, 15 August, 1940 Hours

I stood near the entrance, trying to get my bearings. I'd avoided the St. Louis casinos from the day they'd opened. I figured I didn't need to test my resolve to not gamble. Now I knew I'd been right.

I felt right at home on the Ambassador, the casino built onto the old boat that paddled up and down the Mississippi in the Big Band era. Now it was docked and today's amusement—gambling—drew St. Louisans and tourists to the riverfront.

The recorded sounds of an old-fashioned calliope accompanied me as I made my way up the gangplank to the entrance. There a carnival barker handed out coupons for a free drink to passersby, tipping his straw bowler at an elderly woman ahead of me.

The flashing lights and clanging bells inside were designed, I knew, to up the excitement. The sounds of coins dropping into metal trays were accompanied by excited squeals of the women parked in front of the slot machines. Even the blank faces of the too-cool men barely scratching the top of the blackjack table with their cards felt familiar. My heart was racing and, damn, I loved it.

I pulled myself together and wandered through the different rooms looking for Noni. She was at the farthest table dealing blackjack. I knew I couldn't talk to her while she was working so I stopped at a nearby slot machine and bought a ten-dollar roll of quarters from a woman rolling a money cart up the aisle. I told myself to lose the money slowly, but I kept speeding up, hoping with each pull that I'd hit the big one.

An Elvis look-alike stepped up and straddled the stool next to me and gave me a quick glance, his slicked-back hair, sideburns, and pink-tinted glasses designed to appeal, I supposed. Getting no response from me, he hooked yellow-and-black snakeskin cowboy boots on the rungs of the stool and dropped a quarter in the slot. The clanging cacophony of coins spilling into the metal tray brought stares of envy from those around and a broad grin from Elvis. The ringing continued, alerting casino staff and security guards, who hurried over to the machine. Elvis sat back while red-jacketed ambassadors collected the coins in cloth money bags and uniformed guards escorted him and his winnings away.

I had gone through two more rolls of quarters when I spotted a balcony above Noni's table. I finished off the roll and headed for the stairway. I found a spot where I could look right down onto her table. She wore the standard uniform of black pants and white shirt and tie, but their simple lines only made her exotic beauty more apparent. Her hands moved surely and quickly as she dealt the cards, scooped them up, and stacked the chips with no wasted movements. She smiled at a customer who said something to her. Standing a few feet away, a man in a sport jacket and tie kept his eyes on her table, and occasionally looked up at me.

I watched as the dealer at the next table handed off her position to another dealer and heard her say she was taking a break. Noni did the same thing a few minutes later and I hurried down the stairs to try to catch her.

She looked surprised when she saw me. I asked if I could talk to her.

"It's against the rules to talk to the customers when I'm on break," she said, looking around. "What do you want anyway?"

"Can we go in here?" I asked, pointing to the ladies' room.

"I'm not supposed to. We have our own."

"Please. It's important."

"Make it quick."

She leaned against the sink and folded her arms across her chest.

"What can you tell me about Huey? Is there anyone who'd want to hurt him? Did he owe anybody big time?"

"Well, Huey always lived on the edge." She smiled.

"How much? Enough that someone would come after him?"

"The cops asked me that."

"What'd you tell them?"

"What could I tell them? I don't know."

"How about here? Do they let people get in debt here? No, I guess not with the limits."

"Oh, you mean the rule that says you can't lose more than $500 in two hours? Ha! That never stopped Huey. But, no, they don't let that happen. You can run up a credit card to the limit, a bunch of them if you want, but they don't cover anyone's gambling here." She turned as if to leave, then stopped. "Why are you here? You were his nurse, right? I thought Huey died from the cancer."

I hadn't thought of how to answer this question, which if I were a real investigator, I surely would have known.

"Listen, if you or anyone at that hospital did anything wrong. . . . I was a surgical tech in Texas before I moved up here. I know mistakes are made. That's it, isn't it? You think someone did something, don't you?" She faced me, hands on her hips. "Huey told me that he was afraid. If anyone did anything wrong, he told me, it would be someone at the hospital. But," she said, chewing the inside of her cheek. "I didn't believe him."

"Noni!" yelled a male voice. "What are you doing in there?"

"Just leaving," she told him.

I was still shaking when I got to my car. The encounter with Noni and the rush from gambling, just being in the casino, had left me feeling weak and scared. I started the car and backed out slowly over the bumpy bricks that still paved the riverfront. I drove around downtown until I found myself on a street with boarded-up buildings. I turned at the next corner and knew where to go next.

Hannah was surprised to see me. The girls were already in bed, Roger had gone to the men's meeting at church, and her three teenage boys were on a camping trip. She made some popcorn that we took out on the porch along with two Cokes. When we were settled in the wooden rocking chairs, she said, "Okay, what's up? There's something on your mind or you wouldn't have dropped in like this."

I took a few minutes to think, slowly rocking back and forth. Then it all poured out. How I was afraid Guardino's sons somehow knew that Bart hadn't resuscitated their father, that Huey's death wasn't from his cancer or an overdose of drugs and, finally, what I hadn't wanted to tell anyone.

"I felt like something had taken over my body and was controlling me. I just couldn't stop." I turned to her in the dark. "I wanted to stay in that casino and gamble until I turned numb. Every pull on the slot machine was a rush. When it didn't happen, I'd try again, each time thinking—no, knowing—I was going to win. A few times when some quarters fell in the tray, I just knew my luck had changed."

I heard her draw in her breath.

"Hannah, it's not winning. It's the anticipation. That's the rush. Just waiting, hoping, praying it will happen and, if it doesn't, wanting that rush again." A sob choked my voice.

Hannah reached across and took my hand in hers. "It's okay, Monika. You didn't stay. You left. You're okay now."

"I did, didn't I? I went in there, felt it, and still I left."

"That's all you can do. If you do have a gambling problem, just do what they say in AA—one day at a time."

"I've heard that."

"Just don't gamble for that one day. You can do that, can't you?"

"Heck, I don't think I ever want to be that scared again. I felt like the thing was controlling me and I couldn't do anything about it. I hated that feeling."

"That's good. Just remember it if you're tempted."

We rocked back and forth for a few moments, stirring a warm breeze. Cicadas' raucous voices got louder, then died down again. A car full of laughing teenagers passed by on the street. There was a taillight missing on their older model car.

"And if it ever happens again," she said softly. "Just do what you did tonight. Tell someone."

"You think I should go to Gamblers Anonymous?"

"Do you think you should?"

"I think I should just stay away from the boats. I haven't had any trouble otherwise. I just buy a lottery ticket now and then. That's all."

"You can sign up to have yourself barred from the casinos, you know. If you're still worried."

"No. I'm okay now." I handed her the popcorn bowl. "Thanks, Hannah, I think I'll go home. I'm beat."

She stood up to hug me.

"I don't know what I'd do without you," I told her, tears threatening.

"You don't have to find out. I'll always be here for you."

We patted each other on the back, and I mumbled a few more teary words. I felt better by the time I reached the corner. The top was down on Black Beauty and I laid my head back on the seat and let the warmth of the city envelop me. Mostly, I just felt lighter, as if a great weight had been lifted. Nothing could hurt me now.

Chapter 17

Thursday, 16 August, 0650 Hours

RUBY WAS WAITING for me when I came through the door the next morning. She handed me a stack of messages and left with a requisition for the lab. Serena, who had been standing at the corner of the desk, sidled up to me.

"I was wondering," Serena began, chewing on her lower lip.

"Yes," I said, impatient to get to work. Mr. Kleinfeldt was worse, Jessie'd said, and I'd need to talk to Jake about a DNR order.

"Do you know about getting a license to be a nurse?"

"Well, it's been a long time since I took boards. Aren't they preparing you for that at school?" I flipped open Kleinfeldt's chart.

"It's not about the exam. It's about the application for a license. We have to turn it in at school next week."

"I wish I could be more helpful, Serena," I said as I scanned Kleinfeldt's latest lab results, "but I can't. Why don't you ask one of your instructors?" Another EEG had been ordered on Kleinfeldt for today; maybe the brain scan would confirm the inevitable.

"I can't talk to them."

I shut Kleinfeldt's chart. "Why not? That's what they're there for, isn't it?"

Tears clouded her eyes.

I took her arm and gently led her into the conference room. "Now. What's this all about?" I asked after shutting the door.

"Do you have to tell the truth?" she asked, wiping her eyes with stubby fingers.

I didn't know what questions were on the application these days. All I remembered from mine was that it asked if you'd ever been convicted of a felony. We'd had one student who'd asked if a speeding ticket counted. It hadn't.

"Could you go to jail if you didn't tell them everything?" Serena asked.

"You need to answer the questions honestly. I don't think you have to volunteer anything that's not on the application. Does that help?" After she didn't respond I asked, "Are you in trouble, Serena?" I asked.

She pushed back her chair. "Right. Thanks." She gave me a quick smile as she scooted out the door.

Quirky though she was, Serena had the natural talent for nursing. She caught on quickly, seemed to enjoy learning, and had a genuine warmth for patients that I'd seen too seldom lately. How she'd do when she had to carry a full patient load after she graduated, I didn't know. But she had a good start. And I hoped she didn't have something in her short life that would prevent her from getting a license to practice nursing.

"SLOW DAY?" I asked Wanda, stopping by her office on my way back from lunch. She had a large textbook open on her desk and was eating a cheese sandwich.

"Trying to get a little studying done while it's quiet. Pull up a chair and take a break."

"I've got a question for you. An anesthesia question."

"I'll try. It's my first year, though."

"Succinylcholine. What do you know about it?"

"It's a neuroblocker we use routinely in surgery. We give it along with the anesthesia to put them to sleep. It paralyzes the muscles."

"All of them?"

"Well, sure. You don't want someone's arm to snap up and punch the surgeon in the eye, do you?" she added, chuckling.

"Is that what would happen?"

"I'm exaggerating. But they're not specific to any one muscle group. It's all or none. Why?"

"I'm trying to figure out how it works."

"That's why we have to intubate them and ventilate them mechanically. The respiratory muscles are paralyzed, too."

"What happens when the surgery's over?"

"We reverse it—using an antagonist—and the patient has his muscles back."

"Like we give Narcan for an overdose of narcotics."

"Exactly."

"And if you didn't give the antagonist? The patient wouldn't be able to breathe, right?"

"Right, again," she said. "Do you remember that advanced critical care course we took? Remember the guy with a heart transplant?"

"Oh, yes, the one with the hole in his chest."

"They had to leave the chest cavity open until the swelling went down so they paralyzed him with pavulon, I think, that's another paralytic agent used sometimes. He was on a vent to keep him breathing. Didn't you think it was really strange to look into his chest and see the heart pumping?"

"And keeping out infection was a challenge, I remember."

"Yes and that should remind you how neuroblockers work."

"Is succinylcholine controlled?" Controlled substances, also called scheduled drugs, are those under the jurisdiction of the Drug Enforcement Agency.

"It doesn't need to be. No one would use it to get high."

"So where is it kept? Is it at least locked up somewhere?"

"Sure. It's in the med room behind the supply room on the second floor. Right outside surgery. All the anesthesia meds are locked up in there." She tossed her sandwich wrapper in the trash can. "Why do you want to know all this, Monika? You thinking about anesthesia school? I'll tell you, it's the way up. Lots more money. Better hours. And . . ." she stopped and smiled, "the patients don't argue with you."

I hesitated. Wanda was a vital cog, I imagined, in the gossip machine. Finally, I explained. "Just that a patient had a respiratory arrest and they can't seem to find out why he died. Someone suggested succinylcholine, but I can't imagine how he could have received any."

"Who was the patient?"

"You wouldn't know him."

"You know, Monika, sometimes we just don't know why someone dies. Especially when they're terminal. Maybe they just give up."

"I know. I've seen people die who shouldn't have. And some live who we didn't expect to make it. We all know patients who struggle to stay alive until that something they are waiting to happen, happens."

"Like a son graduates or a grandchild is born."

"Exactly."

"Monika, let it go. Don't you have enough to do without getting all worked up about someone who's not your patient anymore?"

"I just can't, Wanda. I have to find out how it happened."

"Suit yourself." She turned back to her book.

TWO MEN WERE positioning a large vending machine against the wall when I entered the supply room. They grunted as first one, then the other, shoved his side a fraction farther. Finally, they stepped back.

The machine held a stack of scrubs—pants on the bottom, tops up above. A panel on the right indicated the choice of sizes. Color wasn't a choice. They were all puke green.

"Want to try it out?" the heavier of the two men asked me.

I came closer. Four dollars each. "Sorry. No money."

The men began moving the scrubs from a linen cart into the cabinet.

A surgical tech came in and grabbed a scrub top off the shelf the men were emptying.

"That's the last one you get for free," the hefty man told her.

"What?"

"See that." He pointed to the newly-installed machine. "From now on, you gotta buy them."

She glanced at the machine and then looked at me. "Can you believe this? Charging us for scrubs now!"

"Too many of them walked out of here," the man told her.

She stood there a moment, then reached over and grabbed a handful of tops and pants and hurried away.

The men shook their heads.

I went through the connecting door to the medication room Wanda had told me about. A floor-to-ceiling cabinet ran the length of the opposite wall. Rows of medications, in packets, jars and vials were visible through the glass doors. It was under lock and key all right. The key protruded from the lock.

Chapter 18

THURSDAY, 16 AUGUST, 1432 HOURS

"I'M HERE TO TALK about Huey Castle," I began, settling myself in Father Rudolf's small office next to the chapel.

"I wish he could have seen those detectives. I think it would have put his mind at ease." Rudolf fingered the multicolored paperweight on his desk, rubbing its polished finish as I went on.

"That's what I want to know about. What was it he was going to tell them? He told you, didn't he?"

Rudolf jiggled around in his seat. "I don't know if I should say."

I stayed quiet. I wasn't under any illusion that he'd just blurt it out.

"It wasn't a confession, if that's what you're thinking. But it was confidential," he said finally.

"And now he's dead."

"He was worried about that."

"About dying?"

"He said he was afraid he'd stop breathing and you wouldn't resuscitate him."

"He told us that, too, but I assured him that we would do everything to keep him alive although I did try to talk him into signing an advance directive."

"So you tried everything you possibly could to save him?"

"We did it all."

"Perhaps it was his fear of dying that made him so anxious that you might not revive him."

"Be that as it may, I'm here to ask you about what he wanted to tell Harding."

"I don't understand, Monika. How could what he wanted to talk to the police about have anything to do with his dying?"

"That's what I'm trying to find out."

"Did someone slip him some booze? That might mix with the drugs, couldn't it?"

"His blood alcohol was negative and narcotics high but not lethal. But now the medical examiner has labeled his death suspicious and one of my nurses is under suspicion."

"Oh, my," he said, his hands flying to his face. "I've been away. I didn't know."

I shifted forward. "What he was going say to the police? You know, don't you?"

"I promised, Monika."

"Let me ask you this. What do you think Huey would want you to do? Help find out how he died, or keep quiet because you'd promised not to tell anyone?" I'd said everything I could think of to convince Rudolf to tell me. Now it was up to him.

He shined the paperweight with the back of his sleeve. "All right," he said at last. "It won't make that much difference because he told me very little." He shifted in his seat. "And I can't imagine it having anything to do with his death. No one would bother killing him. They didn't need to. All they had to do was wait a little while. They wouldn't take the risk."

"So what'd he tell you?" I asked, getting antsy as he digressed.

"He knew something about a murder twenty years ago."

"Knew something? Like who did it?"

Rudolf shook his head. "He didn't say."

"Did you ask him?"

"He said that the less I knew, the better. I told him I knew a police detective and I'd bring him to see Huey. I knew we didn't have much time." He leaned back and his chair creaked. "Life wasn't easy for him. You know how he lost his arm, don't you?"

"I assumed it was a war injury."

"He threw himself on top of a land mine to save his buddies."

I caught my breath.

"He got a Purple Heart for it. But when he got home from Vietnam it was the time of the protests. There were no war heroes, then. Here he was, permanently wounded, and they couldn't even fit him for a normal-looking prosthesis because too much of his arm was gone. That's why he had that hook. He couldn't get a job—no rights for the disabled then. He got into drinking pretty heavy, did some gambling, and then he ran afoul of the law, as they say."

"He told us he was a pick-pocket, by profession."

"That was Huey. Everything was a joke to him."

HER PLACE WASN'T easy to find in the dwindling light. I'd gone home for supper and to feed Cat and by the time I'd changed into shorts and a T-shirt and figured out what I wanted to do, the light was fading. The temperature was still in the 90's and we could expect more of the same tomorrow, the weather station had predicted.

I found a parking spot in front of her building. As I stepped out of the car I noticed the red glow of a cigarette near the porch.

"Uh, am I taking your parking spot?" I asked the shadow seated on the top step.

"That's okay," she answered with a heavy European accent.

"I won't be long, I promise," I told her.

She scooted over so I could pass her on the steps, and she resumed her contemplation.

Inside, the building smelled like grease, onions, and cabbage but it wasn't unpleasant, just strange. I found CASTLE printed on a tag on the mailbox. Number 2A.

Mavis let me in with a sigh and waved toward a worn sofa under the front window. Paperback novels—their telltale covers displaying ripped bodices and long gazes—covered end tables and a coffee table and spilled into piles on the floor. A film of fine gray dust coated the tops.

Mavis' hair had been cut and sported the telltale brown of a home color kit. She wore a man's shirt—originally white but now a dishwater gray—with the sleeves rolled up and the top button missing, blue-and-white polka-dot boxer shorts and neon-pink flip-flops. She sat down in an overstuffed chair at right angles to the sofa, pushed on the arms and fell back to a reclining position. She asked me what I wanted.

"It's about Huey."

"That sonofabitch!" The recliner popped back up. "That asshole! He cheated me. All those years I worked when he couldn't. Or didn't. And now this." She pulled a pack of cigarettes out of her pocket and lit one with a kitchen match. She blew out the smoke with force. "I hope he rots in hell."

When I didn't say anything, she went on. "That bastard cashed in his life insurance, that's what he did. A long time ago. And I went right on supporting him, thinking at least someday I'd have enough to quit working." She stubbed the newly-lit cigarette out on a paper plate dribbled with watermelon juice and seeds. The cigarette sizzled for a moment and went out.

"I'm sorry to hear that."

"You're sorry! I hope that little twerp. . . ." She choked back a sob. "Oh, what am I saying? I loved the little bastard. He just couldn't stay away from the casinos. Or the women." She sniffed. "I just don't know what I'm going to do now."

She pulled a tissue out of her pocket and blew her nose. "At least I've got this building," she said, looking around. "It was my grandparents'. I grew up here in the apartment right below this one. 'Course it's changed now. Lots of foreigners. They don't bother me none. Gotta live somewheres, don't they? Better than where they came from. Bosnia, you know."

"I'm here to ask you about something."

She wiped her face and stowed the tissue between her leg and the chair arm. "What do you want to know?"

"It's about what Huey wanted to tell the police."

She studied me but didn't say anything.

"He knew something about a . . . a death." I let the words hang in the air.

"Why do you want to know? You think someone killed him? I thought the cancer got him, the little twerp."

"That was probably it," I said. "I'm just following up. I'm curious is all." If she thought there was something strange about a nurse following up about what a dead patient knew about a long ago death, she didn't say it.

"I guess it couldn't hurt now. He can't testify against anyone, and they can't hurt him." A sheen of tears clouded her eyes, and she pulled the used tissue back out and blew her nose, looking at the results before stuffing it back into the crack in the chair.

She seemed to gather her strength and gave me a small smile. "It was one night after he'd been drinking. Actually," she added with a slightly guilty look, "so had I. Anyway, he tells me about what he saw way back right after he got home from the war. He hadn't met me yet." Her chin went up in a proud gesture.

"He did a few things he shouldn't of back then. He couldn't get real work, what with his arm gone and all. So one day he's out at the airport, in the parking garage, and he spots a guy he knows—not a very nice guy—if you know what I mean. And Huey don't know him, just seen him around. Anyways, this guy's fooling around this black Caddy, and Huey's thinking the guy's getting ready to boost it. But he doesn't. A few minutes later the guy just walks off and gets in another car and drives away." She hesitated. "The next day Huey hears that a mobster was blown up in the airport parking garage. The bomb was in a black Cadillac, although there wasn't much left of it. Or him."

"My god."

"Uh uh. Huey's been scared ever since. He couldn't go to the police. And he couldn't tell anyone—he hated that he had told me—because word might get back to the mob. He's kept quiet all these years and now he wants—wanted—to do the right thing."

"Who was it?"

Mavis shook her head. "He passed out that night before he told me, or maybe I did. Maybe he told me but I don't remember. It don't matter 'cause he never would say. The less I knew, the better, he said." She pulled the tissue out again and wiped her nose. "I can't see how it could have anything to do with his death, though. That was a long time ago."

"You don't know who it was?"

"That's all I know." She jumped up. "Wanna see him?"

"Huh?"

She crossed the room to a small table where photos were clustered in frames around a large, painted jar. A small American flag stood in a wood base next to the jar. She showed me a photo of Huey in olive-green Army fatigues, his arms—both of them—were draped around two guys dressed the same. He was squinting into the sun and smiling the wide grin I'd come to know the last few weeks.

"He's a handsome devil, ain't he?" she asked, staring at the picture. She put it down and grabbed the jar. "You want to see him now?" she asked, taking off the lid and tipping the jar toward me. Ashes and a bit of white-gray pieces tumbled over inside.

"That's okay," I said, stepping back. "I'd rather remember him alive."

She reached into the jar and pulled out several laminated cards. She blew Huey dust off of them and showed them to me.

They were driver's licenses, all with different names, all with the same photo of Huey.

"Got them from some guy he used to run with when he was in the rackets. The numbers' rackets." She sighed and chucked the cards back in the jar.

"What guy?"

"Some guy with a long face. Hangs around down at the boats."

Dog.

She returned the jar to its place on the table and gave the top one last pat.

"Thanks for talking to me," I told her, heading toward the door.

"That's okay. It's good to talk about him."

"I liked him," I said, and I meant it.

"I know you guys took good care of my Huey. He liked the nurses, that's for sure."

"Are you sure you don't remember a name? The person Huey saw."

"I'm sorry. He said he didn't want me to get hurt. He loved me, he really did."

"I KNOW MORE than I did yesterday at this time," I told BJ when she joined me at Hauptmann's later. Don was working till midnight, she'd told me.

"Oh, yeah." She motioned to the bartender for a beer. "What about?"

BJ had changed into jeans and an oversized T promoting DARE, the Drug Abuse Resistance Education program sponsored by police departments across the country. Uncle Sam declared, "DARE NEEDS YOU!" on the front.

"Our little guy witnessed a murder."

The beer bottle stopped on its way to her mouth. "Who? What guy?"

"The one they think our nurse, Laura, killed."

"I heard they let her go. Don told me McNeil wanted to exhume the body."

"Ha!"

"What?"

"They couldn't have."

"Why not?"

"He's been cremated."

"You sure?"

"Saw the ashes myself."

"Yuk. How'd that happen?"

I told her about going to see Mavis.

"You really liked the guy, didn't you?"

I nodded.

"He'd been arrested a few times," she said. "Nothing too serious. And they never made anything stick."

"Like what?"

"He tried extortion."

"He did? Who? What happened?"

"Tried to blackmail a city alderman. Some guy lived in Soulard. Told the guy he knew what he did."

"Did he?"

"I doubt it, but the guy blinked. He had a girlfriend in Collinsville."

"That's nothing new, a politician with a girlfriend."

"He had a son with her."

"Uh oh."

"Yep. So the pol paid up." BJ laughed. "Probably would have again but an investigative reporter got wind of it and by the time the story broke, Castle's leverage was gone."

"How'd he know about the girlfriend?"

"Probably didn't. These guys try this all the time. Just tell a politician you know everything and they cave. They've all got something to hide."

"I'll tell you what he did see, though."

She took a swallow of beer and raised her eyebrows expectantly.

"Years ago he saw someone plant a bomb in a car that killed a guy."

"What?" Her beer came down hard on the soiled coaster in front of her.

"That's what the wife told me. And Father Rudolf said about the same thing."

"So it wasn't a confession?"

"But confidential, Father said. I went to see the wife and she told me the rest of the story."

"Who was it?"

"She didn't know. He'd only let it slip once while he was drunk. But it scared him, she said. Wouldn't talk about it ever again."

"But before he died, he wanted to tell."

"Seems like it."

"When was this? What he saw."

"I don't know. Twenty years ago, she said. In the airport parking garage."

She sat up straighter. "I remember that. I was in the academy and everyone was talking about it. A high-level mobster was killed. I don't think they ever caught the guy."

"So Huey's testimony would have helped."

"I guess they could get a deposition, but he couldn't have testified in court, could he? Didn't you say he wasn't going to leave the hospital?"

"No, but wouldn't it have helped the police to know who Huey saw?"

"Sure. And dying words count for a lot. People tend to tell the truth when they're about to meet their maker."

"BJ, what about the Guardino family? Could it have been any of them?"

"I suppose. But wasn't your patient about to die? Why bother?"

"Revenge maybe. Isn't the mob big on revenge?" I asked her. "As a lesson to others?"

"But they're not stupid. Why risk getting caught for killing a guy that'd be dead soon anyway? They are vindictive, though," she added, answering her own question.

"But if they had known that Huey had witnessed the bombing twenty years ago they had lots of time to kill him before last week. The Guardino father was in there at the same time as Huey. The family might have seen Huey."

"But how would they know Huey knew about the bombing?"

"I guess they wouldn't unless he'd told someone else."

She toyed with some peanuts in the bowl in front of us. "Just because they're in the hospital at the same time doesn't mean they're connected."

I giggled.

"What's so funny?"

"Connected. The mob—connected. Get it?" I added, giving her a punch to the arm.

"Funny," she said, deadpan. "Maybe someone got into ICU. I know how easy that was a few months ago."

"Things have changed since then. That hallway around the rooms is locked up now and everyone has to wear their ID badge at all times. We're checking every person we see in ICU. We caught some guy the other day wandering around, dragging an oxygen tank."

I nibbled on some peanuts BJ had dumped onto a napkin for us to share.

"Someone who works there then. Could they have killed him some other way? A pillow over his head? Shut off his oxygen?"

"Huey was conscious. He could breathe without the oxygen, just not very well. And he would have raised hell if anyone had tried to attack him. He was a fighter, I'll give him that."

"Okay," she began, holding her hand up. "One, who wanted him dead?" She folded her index finger down. "Two, how'd they do it?" The next finger came down. "And, three, why? He'd be dead anyway soon." She sat back, a satisfied look on her face.

"He had a girlfriend."

"I thought you said he was married."

I gave her a knowing look.

She slapped her forehead. "Where's my brain? Bad guys don't take their marriage vows seriously, do they?" she asked, rhetorically.

I told her about Noni and Mavis and how they'd narrowly missed running into each other on several occasions.

"You think either one of them killed him?"

"The girlfriend said she'd been a surgical tech, and we let her into ICU anytime as long as Mavis wasn't there. But why would she want to kill him?"

"Money? He have any?"

I explained how he'd cashed in his life insurance policy but had failed to tell his wife.

"So the wife might have found out and killed him out of spite. Or maybe she just killed him to get the cash she thought she'd get from the policy."

"I can't see her doing anything to hasten his death. She knew he was dying and just wanted him to be comfortable. She was really crazy about the guy, foibles and all."

"Just because someone was killed in your place before doesn't mean there's anything wrong with this death, regardless of the ME's pronouncement. It's been over a week and the police haven't found a thing."

"What about what Dog told the cops, about Huey being afraid someone might hurt him? And Father Rudolf said Huey told him the same thing. I just think that it's too much of a coincidence that a mobster dies in the same hospital, the same ICU, at the same time as a guy who might know something about another mobster."

"Cops don't like coincidences," she admitted.

And," I said, "right before he was to talk to the police about a crime."

"You don't know that what Huey knew had anything to do with Guardino. Maybe it worked the other way. Maybe Huey killed Guardino."

"Huey could hardly sit up and breathe at the same time. No way he could have made it to Guardino's room."

"You learn any more about Guardino? Weren't they running tests on him, too?"

"Everything checked out. No opiates in his blood. He'd been comatose and not in pain, so he hadn't needed any."

"I'd guess not if he was unconscious."

"People can be unconscious but still experience pain."

"Really? So how would you know? They send you a mental message?" she said, chuckling.

I looked up at her reflection in the mirror opposite us. "You can tell. Their pressure goes up, they're restless, signs like that."

"Hey," she said. "I've got an idea. I know a guy who used to work undercover, assigned to the mob. He's retired now, but I could get you his number if you want to call him. That way you could talk about it and put it behind you."

"Would he talk to me?"

"Probably. Those retired guys love to talk about the old days. Why don't you ask him? It's worth a shot anyway." When I nodded, she pulled her cell phone off her belt, turned away as she talked, and jotted a number on her palm. She read it back to me. "Tear that up when you're done," she said, nodding toward the scrap of napkin I'd written the number on. "His number's unlisted, but I have a friend in records," she explained. She spit on her hand and rubbed it on her jeans, obliterating the private number.

BLACK BEAUTY SPUTTERED a few times when I started her up until the engine caught. I gunned it to keep the engine from dying when I stopped at the first light. A '69 Cadillac DeVille, black, she'd been my dad's and I tried to keep her in top shape just as he had. But she needed a tune-up and that, like most of my other chores, had been ignored recently. Maybe BJ was right; I should just forget about Huey's death and Guardino's, for that matter, and take care of my own business.

Still, my brain kept churning.

Even though the police had released Laura, she was still a suspect, Tim's brother had told me. They just didn't have enough evidence yet to keep her. I couldn't imagine that Laura, or any other nurse, would actually harm a patient. Her chart notes indicated that she hadn't done anything for him except give him morphine and hang his IV bag, which had come up from the pharmacy designated specifically for him. What was it about the bag, though? Something niggled at my brain. I thought back. I'd used one of the ports on his IV line for his drugs after he'd coded, and a morphine syringe had been locked inside the PCA port.

A car behind me honked, and I jerked forward just as the green light turned yellow.

Why was Serena so concerned about her application for a nursing license? What had she done that she thought might make her ineligible to practice nursing? She'd said she found Huey creepy but maybe she wanted to avoid him because he knew something about her past and had threatened to reveal it. That seemed pretty far-fetched.

If anyone, Lisa seemed the most likely possibility. Lisa had worked on the unit last week and then our drugs had gone missing. And she'd tested positive for narcotics. She could have taken the morphine and substituted something in its place. But that would be extremely difficult to do. No one had reported a package that looked like it had been tampered with and that's something we'd notice immediately. And, besides, what would motivate her to kill Huey?

I could only think that someone must have gotten in, like they had before, in spite of our stepped-up security.

I swung past my street and turned onto the drive encircling the park. I found a parking place only a few doors from the Gunther's house. Sophie sent me out back to the gazebo, "Where Max goes to smoke his smelly cigars," she said.

The Gunther's German shepherd, Siegfried, lumbered up to greet me, nudging his nose under my hand until I had petted him sufficiently.

"He smells Cat, I imagine," I told Max, following the glow of his cigar up onto the platform. Max had built the gazebo himself, planning and measuring as carefully as he did his lab work. It was his refuge from the stress of the hospital, he'd told me.

My eyes adjusted to the night just enough so I could make out Max's bulky form. He laughed softly and asked me to join him.

We sat in quiet reverie for a few moments. Siegfried settled himself at my feet, laying his nose across my open-toed sandals. His breath felt warm on my toes.

"I don't like to beg," I said finally, getting ready to do just that. "But I'm here to ask you to reconsider."

"Reconsider what?" Max asked, unable to keep the sigh out of his voice. "I haven't heard about your test yet, if that's what you're wondering. Don't worry. I'm sure it was those poppy seeds."

"It's about that patient. Huey Castle. I think you should run that test for succinylcholine."

He reached down and patted his leg, signaling Siegfried to move over to him. "I told you it's too expensive." Siegfried's tail thumped on the floor as Max scratched behind the dog's ears.

"I went up to the med room on the second floor. The one by surgery."

Max's cigar glowed red for a moment.

"The key was in the lock. Anyone could have opened it and taken out anything inside. Including succinylcholine."

"How do you think they got from the second floor cabinet into your patient?"

"First let's find out if they did."

The moon came out from behind a cloud, a sliver of light illuminating Max's face. He was frowning. "I think you're wrong about this, Monika. Succinylcholine isn't very stable in solution. It would have to be mixed shortly before it's given."

"How long before?"

"I don't know. More than a few minutes but probably less than an hour. I couldn't say for sure."

A cloud moved in front of the moon, and we sat quietly for a few minutes. Finally, Max sighed. "I made some calls. There is a private lab in St. Louis that does them."

I quelled my desire to shout, and let him take his time.

"The test is called high-performance liquid chromatography. The more common assay is gas chromatography/mass spectrometry. It's used to determine the presence of a variety of chemicals, including narcotics. In both assays, chemicals are extracted into a concentrate."

I could picture him lecturing to the medical students.

"If the substance being measured is unusually complex or volatile, liquid chromatography is used and the concentrate is subjected to high pressure rather than heated gas. It's very specific, sensitive, and reliable."

The decision was made. I sat back, my small smile of triumph hidden. "You still have a specimen?" I asked.

"It'll take a few days," he said, standing.

"That's okay. He's not going anywhere."

Chapter 19

FRIDAY 17 AUGUST, 0845 HOURS

TONY VINCENTE LIVED in the Hill section of South St. Louis, the area that still housed many Italian-Americans in St. Ambrose parish. Neat bungalows, perfect lawns, and square-trimmed shrubbery made for a look-alike neighborhood. That was so no one would get "above himself" as Aunt Octavia was fond of saying.

The house was a white frame, shotgun house, so-called because if you stood at the front door you could shoot all the way through the house and out the back door. One room wide, the bedroom followed the living room and the kitchen was at the back. This arrangement eliminated hallways and so used every inch of space. With houses on either side within an arm's width away, it allowed the most light into the living room and kitchen and kept the bedroom relatively dark. Shotgun houses had been designed to fit on narrow, urban lots in residential neighborhoods in the early part of the twentieth century. Working class people, proud of their heritage whether it was Italian, Irish, or German, had kept them in good repair ever since.

A large American flag hung on one side of the front porch, capturing the morning heat in the narrow space. A metal porch chair had been recently painted kelly green, and the screen door sported newer mesh. The front door was open and I could hear water running in the kitchen. When it stopped, I knocked.

He came to the door wiping his hands on a dish towel, a pleasant, but not quite a welcoming, smile on his face. He wore a snug white T-shirt and well-washed jeans. He was a little on the small side as men go, but compact, as if he'd been packed tightly inside his skin.

I introduced myself and Mr. Vincente ushered me inside.

"I don't know what I can tell you," he said as we made our way through the house to the kitchen. He offered me lemonade and when I accepted, he pulled a tall glass out of the dish drainer beside the sink and filled it with lemonade that looked homemade. He added a sprig of mint that had been draining on a paper towel and motioned me toward the back door.

The postage-stamp back yard was as neatly trimmed as the front with zoysia grass leading to a vegetable garden along the back fence. Tomato plants, laden with late summer fruit, drooped from the weight, and two rows of corn guarded them, their tassels motionless in the muggy morning air.

"Like I told you on the phone," he said as we settled ourselves in wooden Adirondack chairs under a tree, "I've been retired for several years."

Adirondack chairs weren't the most comfortable for short people like me. The seats slanted backward at an angle so that my feet dangled a few inches above the ground.

He asked me about BJ's husband Don.

"He just got a promotion. He's a detective now."

"Good for him. He thinks like a detective. He's a good observer, pays attention to details, and he's curious if something doesn't seem right."

"That's what makes a good nurse, too."

"I never thought about that. How's his wife doing, by the way? She's a cop, too, isn't she?"

"BJ. She's a patrol officer in this area. She's the one who gave me your number. I really appreciate your willing to talk to me. I know you had a lot of experience."

He waved away my compliment.

"Do you hear anything about what's going on now?"

"I talk to a few of the guys from time to time."

"It's about a patient we had last week," I began, repeating what I had told him the evening before. "A few days earlier a Mr. Guardino died."

Mr. Vincente raised his eyebrows.

"Yeah, I know—BJ told me who he was. Anyway, the Guardino son was pretty upset." I rubbed my head automatically although the spot no longer hurt. "He shoved some of us around."

"You better stay away from those guys. They'd just as soon kill you as look at you."

"You knew them?"

Sun-browned skin crinkled around his blue eyes, and he scratched at the gray crew-cut on his head. "Yeah, I knew the older brother of the guy who died. He was the power then. But that damn lawyer got him off every time we nailed him."

"Silverman? I met him."

"You couldn't have met the Silverman I'm talking about. He's dead now. You must have met junior," he said, staring at me with a look that could nail a suspect to her chair. "Stay away from him. He's just like his dad, both of them shysters as bad as the criminals they represent. I never could understand it. How such a slimy guy could get the women," he said, shaking his head. "He has a wife and no end of other women hanging around just for a chance to be with him."

I squirmed in my seat, remembering how I'd felt when I met him.

He heaved a sigh. "But what does that have to do with this other man's death?"

"The patient wanted to talk to the police, but before they got there that day, he died. His name was Huey Castle. You know him?"

"Not offhand."

"He had one arm. Lost the other in Vietnam."

"Oh, yeah. He was small time, nothing too much. He hung around the edges of the mob, but I don't think they paid much attention to him. He wasn't a player, if that's what you want to know."

"Can you think of any reason the Guardinos . . ." I lowered my voice ". . . would want to get rid of him?"

"Why would they? He was dying anyway, you said. Those guys may not always be the sharpest, but they're not stupid. They're not going to take a chance when they don't need to."

He sat back and studied his garden as we sipped our lemonade. I was right; it was homemade. A slight breeze ruffled the tree above us, scattering a few yellowed leaves on the ground. Fall wasn't far away in spite of the day's heat.

"Mr. Vincente," I began.

"Call me Tony."

"Tony. Tell me about the mob. My friends said you worked that, uh, area . . . most of your career."

He scrubbed his face with work-roughened hands and looked off in his memory. "It's all different now. I don't know if we made a difference or if they changed. You know they came over from Sicily?"

I nodded.

"Prohibition gave them the big boost. Everyone wanted booze and they were glad to supply it." Leaning forward he added, "They didn't have to pay tax on something that was illegal. Or on the money they made. They couldn't have asked for a sweeter deal than the Nineteenth

Amendment." He chuckled softly and went on. "Here in St. Louis it wasn't quite as bad as say Chicago was bad, or Kansas City. But we had our fair share. Then Prohibition was repealed, but they had been used to all that money so they diversified." He smiled. "You know, like they tell you that about the stock market: diversify. And they did. Gambling, unions, politicians. They were all in bed together. Police even," he added with a grimace. "If you wanted to be a cop back then, you had to take payoffs or be run off. Or worse. Besides, being a cop didn't pay enough to risk your life or feed your family."

The sharp edges of wood were cutting into my legs. I wished I'd worn long pants instead of shorts. I pulled myself forward and perched on the edge of the seat so my feet would reach the ground.

"Unions, that's what they had," he said. "You probably know that."

"I've heard it, but what did they get from the unions?"

"Jobs. There were two hundred jobs in the Teamsters alone here in St. Louis. And the money, of course."

"They could make money off the unions?"

"It was the pension funds. They could launder money through them, but it also gave them a source of ready cash they could borrow at no interest."

"You knew some of them?" I asked.

"Yeah, I knew them. I wish I hadn't." He gazed into the middle distance. "I'll tell you a story," he began, "that might help you understand. But you can't repeat it." He turned toward me, his expression hard.

"I know about confidentiality. I'm a nurse."

"My partner and I went into a bar on the Southside one night. Inside were a bunch of mob big wigs, including Guardino—he was the older Guardino brother of your patient. Convicted murderers, felons, people of interest. They were all sitting around a table in the back, acting like they owned the place, which they probably did. Bar owners could lose their liquor license if they allowed convicted felons to gather in their place. We hassled them some and ended up citing the guy whose name was on the license. They had to close down for three, four days.

"Our intel later told us a contract had been put out on me. And my family. I had 24-hour protection. City, county, FBI all helped. I carried a shotgun inside my coat for more than a month. You can't imagine what it's like to walk around day after day, afraid, watching every moment, seeing shadows wherever you go, worrying about your kids and wife." He squinted into the sun, deepening the creases around his eyes. "We checked out where the contract came from. It was the Guardino brothers. They had hired a guy from Chicago for the hit.

"So one night we caught up with Guardino, took him down by the river and walked him out up to his waist. I stuck that shotgun in his mouth and told him if me or my family was hurt that every cop in the city would hunt him down and kill him." Tony grinned. "Know what he did?"

I shook my head.

"Defecated in his pants."

I sucked in my breath.

"We marched him back out and a little later our intel said the contract had been cancelled." Tony chuckled softly. "That ought to tell you a little bit about how it worked back then."

"But no longer."

"Nah. The older generation are all dead or dying—either from natural causes or otherwise—or in prison. In St. Louis at least. The younger ones who didn't become respectable business people are just thugs. People of interest might be watched if they come in from the outside. I heard there's some around right now."

"You mean mobsters?"

"Nah, just some muscle from Chicago. Union stuff, I heard."

I wiggled in my seat, wooden slats pressing against the backs of my legs. "Did you hear where? The nurses are trying to unionize at St. Teresa's."

He laughed. "I doubt they'd care about nurses. They're muscle for the heavy-duty laborers, steel-workers, for example."

"What do they do?"

"Intimidation, mostly. If a company threatens to use non-union workers, someone might call up a few of these guys to just hang around. They look menacing enough. They don't even have to do anything."

"Isn't that illegal?"

"It's not the union officials who do it. It's some of the workers trying to protect their jobs."

"Does it work?"

"Sometimes."

"But what the company's trying to do is illegal if they have a union contract, isn't it?"

"That's not new." He smiled at me as if I should know what he meant. "Crooks who wear suits and ties," he explained. "CEOs of big companies. Those are the bad guys today. They've stolen more money than the mob ever did. And gambling's legal. They call it gaming." He smiled to himself. "And the players, gamers." He turned to me. "I call them losers," he added with a chuckle.

I shifted on my seat, still smarting from my close call at the casino Wednesday night.

"And casino owners give their money to politicians legally," he said.

"What does that get them?"

"Access, mostly. When they go before the gaming commission, they want someone on their side. It's not illegal, every group and their brother gives to candidates they think will help them later. That's why they do it."

"I thought some of them were going bankrupt. Casinos."

"Probably a business decision."

"I heard they asked a judge to okay thirty thousand so they could donate to all three mayoral candidates' campaigns."

"I rest my case," he said, finishing his lemonade and perching forward, his arms flexed on the armrests.

"Everyone cheats, is that what you're saying?" I asked, knowing my time was about up.

"Pretty much. Whether it's legal or not is sometimes just a matter of who wrote the laws." He looked toward his garden. A hoe was propped against the garage.

"That's a nice garden you have," I told him, pushing myself up out of the chair.

"Hard to keep up," he said, with typical Southside self-deprecation.

"Looks like you do, though." Only a few weeds had pushed up between the rows, unlike my garden, I thought.

He shrugged, brushing off my compliment once again.

"And now you don't have to worry about the law."

"Nope. I took early retirement and enjoy myself. Haven't watched the news or read a newspaper since."

"I CAN'T TAKE her," Mrs. Bauer's daughter said, sitting down in a chair in the family waiting room. "I'm too busy and I travel for business," the woman, dressed expensively in business clothes, explained to me. She turned to her sister. "You'll have to do it."

The shorter woman—her last name was Whitaker—frowned. "I have three bedrooms and five kids," she said to me. "Where would I put her?" she asked, running a hand through her light-brown hair in need of a trim.

"Mrs. Sheldon—"

"Ms. Sheldon," the well-dressed woman corrected.

"Ms. Sheldon and Mrs. Whitaker, your mother's stroke was serious, but I think she'll have a good recovery. I suggest you consider placement for her at the Bethlehem Home."

"No, no!" Mrs. Whitaker said, her face flushing. "Never! I'll never put Mother in a nursing home!"

"I'm talking about their rehab unit." She started to say something but I continued. "It's for short stays—a few months at the most—and they have everything your mother will need to get back on her feet. Physical therapy, occupational therapy, and they'll get her up and moving every day."

Ms. Sheldon's face brightened. "That sounds like just what Mother needs."

"I don't know," her sister said, frowning. "What if she can't manage it and she doesn't get better or she goes down hill? What then?"

"Her prognosis is good," I told them. "Dr. Lord thinks she'll get back most of her functioning, if not all of it. From the other cases like hers I've seen, she should be able to go home to her own apartment after that."

"Don't they have assisted living there at Bethlehem?" Ms. Sheldon asked.

"They do. If she needed a bit more looking after, I imagine she could move into one of those apartments."

"That sounds good, Dorothy," Ms. Sheldon said to her sister, pulling keys out of her bag.

"Maybe," her sister said.

Ruby popped her head in the door. "They want you up in psych," she said. "ASAP."

I nodded.

"Roger that," she said, turning on her heel.

"I'll call our social worker," I said, standing, "and ask her to get you some information about it. If you come back tomorrow, you can talk to your mother about it."

LISA WAS SITTING in the chair next to Peggy's desk, shrunk down as if she was folded in on herself. She didn't look up when I arrived.

Peggy asked me to shut the door and, when I did, she nodded toward Lisa. "She wants help."

Lisa sniffed.

"She's agreed to go to treatment." Peggy smiled at Lisa's down-turned head, her hair mussed as if she had just woken up. "But there's just one problem."

I leaned against the door frame, not sure I wanted to hear what Peggy was going to ask of me.

"Judyth let her go, you know." When I didn't say anything, she went on. "That ended her health insurance."

"What about COBRA?" I asked. Federal law allows former employees to pay their insurance premiums themselves for eighteen months after ending employment. The law was designed to enable people to keep their insurance until they found another job with health benefits.

Peggy shook her head. "The hospital's self-insured."

"What? When did that happen?"

"Didn't you get the letter? About a month ago."

It was probably in the stack of mail piling up on my desk.

"It's no big deal for us," Peggy explained. "There's no co-pay if we get our care here and go to doctors on staff."

"So how does that help her?" I nodded toward Lisa who was rocking back and forth, her arms crossed over her abdomen.

"We have an agreement with Memorial for substance abuse treatment. But only current employees are eligible."

"I don't see how I—"

"Let me finish. We, uh, I, thought maybe you could talk to Judyth. Ask her to reinstate Lisa just so she can get treatment."

"Why don't you ask her? Or Lisa, you could yourself." Lisa moaned as I went on. "Judyth and I, we haven't exactly been pals," I said, turning back to Peggy. "I doubt I could do any good."

"I can't ask her," Peggy said. "She thinks I'm 'over-identifying' with Lisa because of my history. And she won't even talk to Lisa."

At that moment, Lisa doubled over and vomited. Undigested matter splashed on the tile floor and splattered my shoes. Peggy shoved a wastebasket toward Lisa but it was too late. Lisa wiped her mouth with the back of her hand as Peggy grabbed a wad of tissues and handed them to her, giving me some to wipe my shoes.

Lisa was swaying again as Peggy called housekeeping for a cleanup.

I opened the door for some air and tried to clean the mess off my shoes with tissues. And no gloves. I tossed the soaked wad in the trash can.

Lisa's chalk-white face was punctuated with red-rimmed eyes. "Can't you get me something?" she asked Peggy.

"No." She dropped another wad of tissues onto the vomitus on the floor, covering it partially. "You're not a patient here. No one's going to write you a script to get anything. But when you get to Memorial—there's a bed open there." She looked me. "They can take her today."

Lisa choked again and we braced for another episode but it was only a sob. Peggy put her arm around Lisa's shoulder and looked up at me, pleading.

"I don't know. . . ."

"Please, Monika. What have you got to lose?" She looked at Lisa with a small smile. "There's a lot to save."

"All right. I'll try—" I began.

"That's all we're asking."

In the restroom I washed my shoes with soapy paper towels and scrubbed my hands for a full five minutes, lathering twice, worrying about what Lisa's vomit might contain. An IV drug user, it was likely that she'd taken clean drugs from the hospital, but had she ever shared needles with a street user? What might she have picked up from those?

As I walked down the stairs to Judyth's office on the main floor, I came up with one argument to use. If Lisa was on the payroll, Judyth would have one more name to convince Joint Commission that we had enough staff. It wasn't much and I didn't know if Judyth would buy it.

She didn't.

She had a better argument. "If we hire her back, knowing she's been using drugs—and probably stealing them from us—and then someone gets hurt. . . ."

"No one would get hurt. She wouldn't even be working; she'd be in treatment."

"Then what?" Judyth asked, leaning back against the desk, her arms full of files.

"When she's released, she comes back to work."

She shook her head. "No way."

"You could fire her then."

"And get slapped with a discrimination suit? Addicts are a protected class. We have to make 'reasonable accommodations' for their disability," she said. "What kind of accommodations do we make for a nurse so she's not around drugs? In a hospital, for godsakes!" She pushed off from the desk. "Monika, I know you mean well, but please stay out of this." She waved a dismissive hand in my direction. "I have to see to our accreditation. They're giving their final report," she said, leading me out the door.

"I tried," I told Peggy her a few minutes later. She'd been waiting for me in my office.

Changing emotions played out across her face: sadness, dismay, frustration and, finally, anger. "She's dead then."

"What?"

Peggy shook her head. "There's no hope, Monika. If an addict doesn't get help, they're dead."

"Aren't you overdoing it a bit? Can't she go to AA or something? You could take her with you."

"She needs more help than that."

"Alcoholics do it."

"Drugs are tougher, and she's not strong enough."

"You mean she doesn't want to get off them."

"No. I mean they're just more powerful." She leaned forward. "You just don't know how it is, Monika. Once drugs have hold of you, they don't let go. Not without a fight, they don't."

"What about Bart? Can't he help?"

"He's pretty fed up with her."

"I'm not surprised," I said.

"She's threatened to kill herself."

"Yeah?" Another ploy to get sympathy, I thought, but didn't say.

"When there's no way out." Peggy looked away somewhere in her memory. "If you can't live without them, and you can't live if you keep taking them. . . ." Her voice trailed off.

"Look, you did it. Maybe she'll find some other way to get help."

"Yeah. Right," she said, standing. "And you're going to be six feet tall."

I WAS CHECKING the weekend schedule later when the phone rang. I picked it up cautiously, hoping it wasn't another staff member calling in too sick to work on the weekend.

At first I couldn't understand her.

"It's in the bag," Lisa repeated, slurring her words.

"What? What's 'in the bag?'"

"Don't you understand?" she asked. "It's in the bag." Her words slid off into nothing.

"You've taken something, Lisa. What was it?"

She mumbled something.

"I can't hear you!"

"It's for my back," she said. "Takes away the pain." She sounded far away.

"You'd better get some help, Lisa. Call Bart or Peggy."

"I'm right all right," she said, giggling.

"Call someone, will you? You shouldn't be there alone."

"All right," she said, enunciating each word.

She hung up.

I tried to reach Peggy, but she'd left for the day, and there was no answer at her home number. I called Lisa back but she didn't answer.

I sighed and went back to my work. Apparently Lisa had found some drugs after all, something in a bag. I still had two extra shifts to cover for the weekend. Tim had refused; he was working the union election the next two days and probably would have said no in any case. Jessie, without complaint, said she'd work both shifts.

Still thinking about Lisa, I stopped at Judyth's office on my way out. "I'm going by Lisa Milligan's and I could take her last paycheck if she didn't get it the other day," I told Norma.

"I have it right here." She sorted through some envelopes in her desk drawer and handed one to me. "You'll save me mailing it," she said with a smile.

BLACK BEAUTY STARTED right up and I slid out of the garage in record time since the rest of the day shift was long gone. Now I was caught in rush hour traffic, catching a red light at every corner, or so it seemed.

Stopped at a light at Hampton and Chippewa, I hunted around on the front seat for my phone, sticking my hand in the crack between the back and the seat. Where was that darn phone? I stretched to reach under the seat and a horn honked behind me. I jerked up, hitting my head on the steering wheel. The driver laid on his horn. I scooted through the intersection on the yellow, followed by a long line of drivers.

Where did I have it last? I slid into the right hand lane on Chippewa, cutting in front of a truck. The driver gave me an obscene gesture as he slammed on his brakes. My office, that's where it was. I'd kept trying to reach Lisa until I left, then I'd hurried out, anxious to get there now that I'd decided to check on her.

The sun played long shadows across the tiny yard in front of the house that Lisa and Bart shared in Dogtown, the South St. Louis neighborhood originally settled by Irish immigrants. The street was deserted but the steady beat of rock music punctuated the stillness. I pulled my scrub top loose from the seat where sweat had pasted it to the leather. A traffic copter whirled overhead, stirring a short-lived breeze.

I knocked several times with no response. Sweat trickled down my back.

A woman came out of the house next door and shook a dust mop over the side of her porch. "She's home," the woman said, propping herself up on the mop. "I saw her come in before he left."

I smiled and went back to knocking.

"Hear that music?" the woman asked. "Better knock louder."

"Thanks," I told her, hammering my fist against the door.

"She's always playing it loud when he's not home," she added, looking like she planned to stand there until Lisa came to the door.

We waited while the music continued to pound. Finally, the woman shrugged and went back inside.

I peeked through the picture window, cupping my hands around my face to block out the glare. Lisa was sprawled on the sofa, one arm hanging down to the floor, the other covering her eyes as if the light was too much for her.

"Lisa," I said, rapping on the glass with my knuckles.

She didn't move.

"Lisa. Wake up!" A hard knot of worry formed in my throat. "Lisa," I yelled. I beat on the window with my fist.

I tried the door. Locked.

I looked around for a hiding place for a key. No flower pots or statuary. Just a dented, rusty metal chair. I pulled it over to the door and climbed up, rocking on the unsteady chair. I felt along the ledge above the door. Nothing. Where would they hide a key? Several pieces of mail were peeking out of the box next to the door. I took the mail out and reached in the box, stretching on my toes to reach the bottom. There it was.

The screen door banged against my legs but I hesitated. What would I say if she was just sleeping? Or high? What if she called the cops? How would I explain breaking into her house?

I slipped the key in the lock and it turned easily. The door opened directly into the living room and the pounding music. Lisa hadn't moved. The air smelled musty, as if the house had been closed up all day. I shut off the CD player. The sudden quiet startled me and I stepped back quickly.

"Lisa," I said into the silence.

The constant drone of the air conditioner in a dining room window was the only sound.

I repeated her name as I took the few steps to her side.

Nothing.

My heart was pounding in my ears. I shook her shoulder gently. The arm slipped off her face and Lisa stared at me with unseeing eyes.

Chapter 20

FRIDAY, 17 AUGUST, 1734 HOURS

"YOU BROKE INTO the house?" the young officer asked me. He had checked Lisa's neck for a pulse and used his radio to call it in.

I'd stumbled around the living room until I had spotted a cordless phone on the floor and called the police. Then I couldn't get out of there fast enough, slamming the screen door against the porch railing, as waves of nausea rolled over me. I'd dropped my head between my knees and took some deep breaths to settle my stomach as a siren screamed in the distance, becoming louder as it approached the house.

"I saw her through the window," I said, following the officer back into the house. I tried not to look at Lisa but my eyes kept straying to her body. Her head had turned when the officer had pressed his fingers to her neck so that her eyes seemed to follow me even as I edged toward the door.

"She let you in?" he asked, a frown forming. BJ had told me that the last person to see someone alive was always the first suspect in a murder.

"Of course not," I said with more emphasis than I'd intended. "How could she? I found the key in the mailbox." I hurried on. "We work together. Worked, " I corrected. "St. Teresa's. We're both nurses." No point in mentioning her stealing drugs. Her death made that all too apparent.

"I guess that's where she got that," he said, motioning toward the syringe under the edge of the sofa, its needle pointed outward. Lisa's arm lay stretched toward the floor, her hand curled slightly as if reaching for something that had just rolled away. Lisa's red knit top was pulled up, revealing the navel ring I'd seen before. Tiny needle marks peppered the antecubal space inside her elbow, a slight bruising around it.

The officer answered a call on his radio, clipped it back on his belt, and told me to wait outside. I was glad to.

A white Crown Victoria pulled up, double-parked in front of the house, and a female officer dressed in street clothes stepped out. An ambulance drew up behind it and angled into an open slot. A paramedic jumped out and hurried up the steps with the cop.

I stayed out of their way.

"Everything okay?" asked a voice coming up the steps. The woman from next door.

An officer tried to block her view but she caught a glimpse inside. "Oh, my god," she said, listing to one side. Pink scalp showed through her thin white hair.

"She lives next door," I told him. "She's the one who told me that Lisa was home."

The officer grabbed her elbow and steered her back down the steps.

"Tell her to stay put, I'll be over to talk to her as soon as we finish here," said the detective who introduced herself as Deborah Rosan.

BJ sprinted up to the door. I had told the first officer that BJ was a friend of mine—this was in her district—and he'd passed the word along when he'd called it in. I followed her and the detective back in, steeling myself to treat this death like many others I'd seen, composed and detached.

BJ grabbed my arm and steered me back out. I sat in the rusty chair on the porch, but I couldn't keep from watching through the window. A police photographer had arrived along with two men with Crime Scene Unit stamped on the back of their shirts. One tugged on latex gloves and wiped sweat off his forehead with the back of his arm. He picked up the syringe and held it up to the light. He placed it in a paper bag, folded the top down and taped it shut, careful to avoid the exposed needle protruding from one end. He squatted on the floor, pulled out the cap from underneath the sofa and put it in another bag. The photographer moved around the body, clicking shots from various angles while the detective made notes.

Another CSU officer was sprinkling black powder on a table top. He twirled a brush on top and when he seemed satisfied with what he saw, he unrolled a length of plastic tape and pressed it down on the surface. He lifted it, studied the tape, and adhered it to a small, white index card. He moved on to another spot on the table.

So far no one had touched Lisa except the paramedic who had come and gone.

"How did you know the dead girl?" the detective asked me, coming out onto the porch. Detective Rosan was slightly taller than me and significantly heavier. She sat down on the concrete railing around the porch. Her cream-colored blouse strained to cover her ample bosom and a tight belt squeezed her tan pants closed.

The photographer came outside, took a few shots of the house from the sidewalk, and went back in.

I explained that I knew Lisa from the hospital, and Detective Rosan wanted to know why I had come here.

"She called me. She sounded drugged. I decided to bring over her paycheck and just check up on her. Her boyfriend's hardly ever home because he works full time and is going to school full time. He works for me. That's how I know her. Maybe if I'd gotten here sooner. . . . She'd just been fired."

"Oh?" she asked, looking up from her notebook. "You know why?"

I hesitated. "You'd better ask them."

"You don't know?"

"She didn't work for me. Talk to the chief nurse." I gave her Judyth's name and phone number.

"You got here when?" she asked.

The photographer stowed his equipment in a weathered bag and made his way around the cluster of people in the room, sketching a wave as he went down the steps.

Detective Rosan repeated her question.

"About five." I looked back inside.

The CSU officer continued on to other tables, collecting fingerprints. Another officer moved through the house. The refrigerator door opened and closed.

When were they going to do something with Lisa?

"If she was already dead when you got here, how'd you get in?" Rosan asked with a nod toward the door.

I told her about finding the key in the mailbox.

"What'd you do then?" She leaned back against the pillar and shielded her eyes from the sun that had dipped into the west.

"Uh, I checked to see if she had a pulse." My hand shook as I wiped sweat off my forehead.

"So you touched the body?"

"Yes." Was I a suspect?

BJ came out and stood off to the side.

"She wasn't breathing?"

"No," I answered.

"Then what?" Detective Rosan asked.

"I called 911."

"You touch anything else?"

I shook my head.

"What about the phone?"

I nodded.

"You don't have a cell phone?"

"I left it at work."

"You said the neighbor saw the vic?" Rosan nodded toward the house next door.

"Yes. And she knew Lisa was home because of the music."

"Music?" Rosan asked, glancing around.

"Loud music. I turned it off. The CD player on the floor."

"Bag that player," Rosan yelled over her shoulder to the officers inside.

A panel van pulled up, dislodging two men dressed in casual clothes. "Got one for us?" one of them asked. "Ready?"

"Any time," Rosan answered.

They returned with a gurney they'd pulled from the back, a limp black body bag on top. They rolled it to the steps, lifted it quickly onto the top sidewalk and then up the steps. Rosan followed them back in.

I stared through the window as they jockeyed the gurney into place next to the sofa and took positions at either end. "On the count of three," one said, gripping Lisa's shoulders. But before he had finished counting, the other man jerked Lisa's feet up, pulling her out of his partner's hands and sending Lisa's head banging onto the floor.

I caught my breath.

BJ touched my arm.

They got Lisa onto the gurney, zipped the body bag shut, and handed Detective Rosan a clipboard to sign. BJ held the screen door open while one man backed out, holding the gurney level. Footsteps pounded up behind us.

Bart let out a howl. He pushed the attendant aside and grabbed at the body bag, pulling the zipper open before anyone could stop him. He fell on top of Lisa with a sob.

BJ pulled him off. "You can't help her now," she said, her voice soothing.

I explained who Bart was to Rosan.

BJ led Bart to the far side of the porch and motioned for him to sit next to her on the concrete ledge. She faced him away from the door, but as the gurney bumped down the steps Bart looked around, his expression pained.

"What happened? Someone break in?" Bart asked, his voice choked.

"I think it was an overdose, Bart," I told him in the voice I use to tell families bad news about their loved ones.

Bart nodded and watched as the gurney disappeared into the van. He lowered his head to his hands and sobbed quietly.

"You say you came here because she called you," Rosan said to me. It sounded like a question. "What did she say?"

"She mumbled something like 'it's in the bag.'"

Bart looked up.

"What'd she mean by that?" Rosan asked.

"I have no idea. Just the hallucinations of someone drugged," I said. I gave Bart a small smile of apology. "It happens to patients sometimes when they're coming out of an anesthetic. It doesn't mean anything."

An officer came out and Rosan nodded toward Bart. The man took Bart's arm and led him into the house.

"We'll need your fingerprints," Rosan said to me.

"Why? Am I a suspect?"

"Just routine. We need to rule you out."

"Rule me out for what? She obviously killed herself."

"Looks that way," Rosan admitted.

"What about him?" BJ asked, nodding toward the inside where Bart was standing, looking lost in his own home.

"His prints will be everywhere, so we can usually rule those out without much trouble."

"Okay," I said with a sigh. "Go ahead, take my prints."

Rosan snorted. "You need to come into the station. We'll take you just as soon as we finish up here."

BJ interrupted. "Can't she come in later?"

Rosan frowned. "Standard operating procedure. I need to take you in."

"Look, she's not going to book," BJ told her. "She's a nurse at St. Teresa's, she lives in the neighborhood, and I've known her all my life."

I interjected into this conversation about me, "I'll come in first thing Monday morning. I promise."

"Well . . ." Rosan began.

"I guarantee she'll be there." BJ gave Rosan a long look.

"Okay." Rosan shrugged. "Seven a. m., Sharp," she said and turned on her heel and went inside.

I watched as she led Bart to a chair and spoke to him. He kept shaking his head as if he didn't believe what had happened.

Finally the police left and I followed BJ back inside. I offered to call someone for Bart.

"I'll be fine," he said, his voice flat.

"Can I call her parents for you?" I asked, hoping he'd decline.

He did.

"I knew it, I knew it," Bart said suddenly. "If she'd just stopped, dammit." He slammed his fist into his palm. "I tried and tried and she kept promising and then it'd happen again. She'd say she was in pain and. . . ." He broke off, choking. He sat down on the sofa and doubled over, moaning.

I sat down next to him and patted his shoulder. We stayed that way for a few moments until his sobs subsided. BJ had moved away and now stood looking out the door, shifting her weight back and forth.

Bart wiped his face with the backs of his hands, sniffed, and gave me a small smile of thanks. "How'd she get it?" he asked. "I knew she'd been fired so she couldn't have gotten it at the hospital." He looked around the room. "She must have had some hidden. Why me?" he said suddenly, standing. "What will I do now?" He threw up his hands and let them drop to his sides. "How could she do this to me?" he asked, pacing back and forth. "Damn her!" He stabbed the air with a fist. "How could she?"

He had gone from sad to mad in the time it took to take a breath.

"Don't act like you're blameless," I said when I could stand it no longer.

Bart's face darkened. "Get out!" he screamed. "Get out now!" He lunged forward, but BJ pulled me behind her with one arm, her other hand on her holster.

Bart looked at her face and stood still, jaws clenched, then his face sagged. "Just get out," he said turning away.

On the sidewalk outside, BJ shaded her eyes against the sun. "Seems like you were right to be worried about her." She looked back toward the house. "Why'd you come here anyway?"

"I knew she'd been on the unit the morning Huey died. It's possible she saw something or someone."

"And you think she'd tell you?" BJ asked. "You're not a cop, Monika. You don't know that people lie all the time about things they don't even need to. And in her state, believe me, you'd have gotten squat out of her."

Chapter 21

FRIDAY, 17 AUGUST, 2218 HOURS

I FELL ASLEEP on the couch with the TV still on. BJ had followed me home, watched me go inside, and waved goodbye before she went back on patrol. I had gathered Cat in my arms and hugged her until she wiggled away, then changed to shorts and my favorite T-shirt with "NURSING IS A WORK OF HEART" on the front, gathered what snacks I could find—potato chips, cheese crackers, some grapes beginning to go soft, and a big glass of milk—and plopped on the couch. I'd shared my makeshift dinner with Cat and settled down to watch an old movie, determinedly putting the vision of Lisa's body out of my mind.

Lisa had obviously needed help, but Bart seemed more worried about himself than about her and what she'd been going through. Besides, I'd told BJ, it was possible that he had supplied drugs for her, which might explain some of the missing narcotics. I'd seen him with some other drugs leftover from surgery, but those weren't narcotics, and Lisa wouldn't have wanted them. I'm going around in circles, I thought, turning back to Gregory Peck issuing orders to his World War II troops.

THUNDER WOKE ME up. The TV was off and everything was dark. I tried the lamp by the couch but it, too, was out. Outside, torrents of rain tore at the trees next door, sending leaves scattering. A few plastered themselves against the window. Streetlights were out so the whole neighborhood was without power. I started to gather my quilt and pillow to head to bed when the scene at Bart and Lisa's flashed back into my thoughts. I sat back down, thoughts tumbling over one another.

What had happened to Lisa? Had she felt so hopeless that she killed herself? She had stolen the drugs, I was sure, accounting for the shortages. Was her death an accident? A lot of addicts die that way, mistaking the dosage or forgetting they had already injected themselves. Mainlining directly into the vein—the ultimate high—allows no time for a mistake. And how did she get morphine or meperidine or fentanyl or whatever she took now that she wasn't working at St. T's? Maybe she'd turned to street drugs; heroin was the opiate of choice for those without access to safe medicines. I'd seen her in withdrawal in Peggy's office. She'd been begging for something to help her over it. By the time she called me, it was obvious she had found it.

Cat jumped up on my lap and began kneading the quilt. I slung her under my arm and we made off to the bedroom. The storm had dwindled to a steady rain. Good for sleeping, I thought, tucking Cat under the covers with me. For once, she didn't mind being my security blanket.

Chapter 22

Saturday, 18 August, 0530 Hours

THE RAIN HAD STOPPED and a lazy sun peeked through the leaves. The power was still out so I couldn't start laundry or cleaning. Still wearing my old, nursing-slogan T-shirt, I pulled on my gray gym shorts, dirt-stained from gardening a week ago, and I headed toward Carondelet Park. I decided to take the long route around the park—just over four miles—and try to shake off the past few days.

As always, the sight of the majestic homes surrounding the park lifted my spirits. I didn't know anyone who lived in any of the places that could rightly be called mansions. Built in the 1920s, they were designed to reflect the styles of that time in California, the builders hoping to bring a bit of Hollywood glamour to St. Louis. Each home was constructed with its own unique features.

One home on the corner was for sale, I'd heard, although for-sale signs were never allowed to deface the front yards circling the park. I came up to the house and stood for a moment, studying it. Neatly-trimmed shrubbery framed the windows and front porch, and the multicolored blooms of pastel impatiens plants peeked out under the evergreens. Graceful ivy clung to the brick, and matching pots of red geraniums, an American flag stuck in each pot, stood sentry on the porch.

A third-floor turret held one round window, its glass distorted with age. I was picturing Sleeping Beauty inside, awaiting Prince Charming, when Lisa's body came unbidden into my mind. I caught my breath and turned quickly, hurrying across the street toward the park. I turned onto the familiar walking path and watched a runner ahead with studied attention.

The rain had done little to cool down the heat. The air hung overhead like wet cotton, and an overcast sky promised more rain. Stepping over a downed tree, I tried to tell myself that all of my suspicions about Huey's death and now Lisa's were the result of my remembering the ICU death that actually did turn out to be murder only a few months before.

I passed under a tree where one limb hung precariously, sliced as neatly as if an axe had chopped it off. Lisa had killed herself, that much was clear. Whether it had been accidental or intentional, we probably would never know. Huey, however, should probably not have died so soon, and not in the way he had. Had something gone wrong? Had someone given him the wrong medication? Had it been an accident? Or, as the police seemed to think, had someone intentionally murdered him?

Water from an overhanging tree dripped onto my face and I swiped at it with my hand. As long as we were under this cloud of suspicion I would just have to keep trying to find out what had happened to Huey.

I stepped out from under the trees and onto the path that wound around the lake just as the sun emerged from the clouds. A wisp of steam rose from the water's surface, gathering in puffs of mist.

I squatted down and watched a mother duck trailed by her six ducklings. They swam silently over to me, their mouths working.

"Sorry boys and girls," I told them. "Nothing for you today."

A fish plopped nearby and the ducks chased after it.

I sat down on the grass and pulled my knees up, wrapping my arms around them. A man in a straw hat sat on a wooden pier that jutted out into the water opposite me, his fishing line hanging into the barely-moving water. I would have thought he was a life-like statue, like the ones that had graced St. Louis' public places a few years ago, had it not been for the occasional bob of his fishing pole.

Sunlight sparkled off the water, mirroring the trees behind me on its nearly-still surface. Only a fountain spraying jets of mist high into the air at the far end of the lake kept the water, already dark with the summer's sludge, undulating.

I dropped my chin to my knees and watched the sun play across the water, letting my worry drift along with the ripples. A whisper of a breeze stirred the water and lifted the mist until it dissipated in the air. The answer to why and how Huey died seemed just as elusive as the steam that had disappeared.

Back home, a blast of cool air greeted me when I opened the front door. The power was back on. Walking through the living room, I picked up yesterday's paper and the remains of my snack, then tossed the trash away and piled my dirty dishes in the sink.

By the time I came up from the basement after depositing the last load of laundry in the dryer, Lisa's death had intruded into my thoughts once again. If only Judyth had helped her, she would have been in treatment by now. Well, maybe, I admitted to myself. If she'd gone. And stayed.

While the kitchen floor dried, I unwrapped the morning paper, brought in the mail, picked up the overnight mail envelope tucked between the screen and front doors, and settled in my favorite easy chair. The chair had been my dad's, and after he and Mom had both died, I'd had it recovered in a cheerful red-and-blue plaid that never failed to comfort me. The Saturday paper spouted the usual miserable stories about bombings, threatened wars, and auto accidents. BJ had told me they didn't call them accidents any more. Human or mechanical errors caused what were now called "crashes."

In the mail was a letter from the Missouri State Board of Nursing with my license that I had been late in renewing. I put it aside to take to the hospital on Monday. Human Resources had to have the original to copy for the files. That was the law, the accreditor had reminded us.

The overnight mail envelope had slipped down between the seat cushion and the side of the chair. Heavy cellophane tape covered the tear-off strip so I carried it into the kitchen and, using a sharp knife, sliced it open. I reached inside and pulled my hand out with a yelp.

I'd stabbed my finger on an uncapped needle.

Chapter 23

Saturday, 18 August, 1035 Hours

Rushing to the sink, I ran my hand under hot water, scrubbing my finger with soap and milking it toward the tip. This was a nurse's worst fear: a needle stick. HIV or hepatitis, both life-threatening. Holding my finger up to the light, I examined my finger carefully. The skin was intact.

The phone rang.

"I was just going to call you," I told BJ.

"You were? Want to have lunch? Or are you too busy with your compulsive cleaning?" She laughed.

"Can you come over?"

"Trouble?"

A lump formed in my throat. She must have heard something in my voice.

"I'll be right there."

I poured myself some iced tea, put Cat on my lap, and stroked her comforting fur until BJ arrived.

When the doorbell rang I jumped up, spilling Cat unceremoniously on the floor.

"I thought maybe I'd get a siren," I said, smiling faintly.

"It's that serious?"

I nodded.

"Tell me," she said as I led her to the kitchen. I motioned her into a chair and then showed her the envelope, with the needle protruding out of it.

"Who's it from?" She turned the envelope over, using a ballpoint pen she'd pulled from her pocket. "No return address."

I looked at my finger, still pink but without a puncture wound, thank god.

BJ reached across the table and patted my arm. "Calm down, sweetie, this is just why they did this—to frighten you."

"It worked."

"Someone's trying to scare you," BJ said.

"What for?"

"Well, you have been asking a lot of questions about Huey Castle's death."

"So you think the murderer—if Huey was murdered—did this?"

"You don't know anything about it, though, do you?"

"I wish I did but, no, I'm no closer to finding out what happened to him than when I started."

"What about the nurse who died yesterday? Maybe she sent it."

"And then killed herself? That doesn't make sense, BJ."

"No, I guess not."

"She was trying to tell me something though."

"Oh, that business about a bag?" BJ asked.

"Maybe she was referring to this envelope."

"What about the boyfriend? He was pretty mad at you last night."

"That was grief talking. I see it all the time. And I know from experience that he gets pretty excited about things. Overly so, in my estimation."

BJ examined the envelope, back and front. "This wasn't mailed."

"What?"

"No postal stamp, nothing."

"Then how'd it get here?"

"Did you notice anyone strange around this morning?"

"Oh, my god, BJ, you mean they brought it right up to my door?" I wrapped my arms around myself.

"It's okay now. They're gone. What about those union people?" she asked after a few moments. "I heard there are some muscle, hired muscle, in town. People who skirt around the edges of the law use guys like them to intimidate folks."

I tried to talk but my voice came out in a squeak. "The Guardinos," I said at last. "Maybe they're the ones who gave Lisa bad drugs, or something worse."

"Huh? Why would they do that?"

"To get back at Bart?" I suggested.

"I suppose, but they'd be more likely to run someone down on the street—something direct like that. And it'd probably be Bart they'd kill, not his girlfriend. Unless she happened to get in the way. And besides, how could they know about Bart?"

I pointed to the envelope. "Could they have sent me this?"

"Nah, that'd be way too subtle for them. They do something, they want you to know it's them," she said. "Anything else in here?" she asked, pulling on a pair of latex gloves.

"Only an empty syringe and needle," I said. The syringe had been fastened to the inside of the envelope with masking tape so that the needle tip poked up along the top. The needle looked like it was about a 21 gauge, one-and-a-half inches long, straight, and sharp. It looked undamaged. Maybe never used.

She turned the envelope upside down and a folded slip of paper fell out. The words were hand-printed in heavy black marker "STOP," it said. "OR YOU'RE NEXT."

I slumped in my chair.

BJ got up and came around the table to me. She wrapped her arm around my shoulders and hugged me to her. "Well, he accomplished what he wanted." She gave me a reassuring squeeze. "Might be fingerprints on it, the syringe—although they're probably too smudged—or on the envelope," she said, sitting back down. BJ pulled a notebook out of her pocket, noted the time, and asked me a few more questions.

"Do you really think you can find out who did this?"

"If he's ever been arrested, I can. And if we get some usable prints." Touching only the edge of the envelope, she picked it up and dropped it in the brown paper grocery bag I gave her.

"I'll write this up right away and get this over to the lab this afternoon. And I'll alert the guys on patrol. They'll be driving by often. You be sure to call 911 if you see anyone around. Okay?" She gave me a quick hug. "And keep your doors locked."

She was gone.

The house felt empty.

Housework forgotten, I stretched out on my bed.

The next thing I knew, Cat was meowing in my ear and parading back and forth on my bed. I swatted her off to the floor and rolled over to check the time.

Yikes! I was scheduled for the two to four o'clock shift to help monitor the union voting; it was one-thirty now.

I jumped up, untangling the quilt on the way to the bathroom. I splashed water on my face, pulled on some clean scrubs, ran my fingers through my tangled curls and dashed out the door.

A CLUSTER OF nurses were gathered by the side entrance to the hospital. Even from a distance I could see an argument in progress. I swung around the demonstrators and pulled into the garage, bracing myself for what was to come.

Several nurses handed out literature while others stood around chatting, placards reading, "THINK OF OUR PATIENTS—VOTE UNION," drooped on their shoulders. The line of nurses waiting to vote stretched around the corner. They squished themselves up close to the building to garner what little bit of shade there was. Most carried water bottles or soda cans, intermittently fanning themselves with copies of the handouts they'd been given. One woman poured water over her head and shook it vigorously, cooling her laughing colleagues.

Lucille, the former head nurse turned union activist, barked at the nurse I'd seen her with in the gift shop. "Traitor," Lucille screamed, shoving her colleague forward with crossed arms. Lucille towered over the woman who stumbled backward.

"I changed my mind, that's all," the woman said, pushing back.

"Yeah, I bet," sneered Lucille. "What'd they offer you? More money? Better hours?" She gave the woman another shove.

"Nothing. Honest. I just thought about it and don't think it's the best way. We've got to give a little, that's all."

"Give!" Lucille screamed. "We gotta give, she says," Lucille yelled to the crowd who by now had grown silent. Turning back to her former colleague, she said, "That's what nurses have been doing since Florence's time. Don't you think it's about time we *get*?"

A rent-a-cop swaggered over to them as I scooted inside. Tim gave me a nod, but no smile. Just as well. If we had to share the next two hours, there was no reason to get into an argument ourselves.

As the nurses entered, they signed in at the polling table, handed over their eligibility slips, were checked off on the master list, and received a ballot. Similar to the city voting a few days ago, they took the ballot to a booth opposite the polling table, and when they had finished voting, they dropped their ballots into the locked box manned by a security officer. Tim, representing the union, and I, for management, were there to monitor the process. We stood behind the polling table but we were not supposed to talk to anyone or to interfere unless a problem emerged.

Who could have put that package in my door? Did any other manager get a booby-trapped delivery today? If that had happened, surely the word would be spreading through the grapevine and someone would have said something to me by now. Could it have anything to do with the union fight? Other than Tim and possibly, Laura, I hadn't argued with anyone about it.

A rumbling from the back of the line brought me back to the present. A woman pushed around the group clustered by the door. "I got this in the mail," she said, thrusting her voting notice in front of the polling staff.

"You have to wait your turn," the union representative working the table said.

"I'm not waiting. I want to know why I got this."

"What's the problem?" I asked, moving up behind the table at the same time as Tim did.

This time an administrator spoke. "You can't vote; you're not on the list."

"I don't want to vote; I don't even work here anymore. What I want to know is, why did I get this?"

"Why are you here?" I asked. "Why didn't you just toss it out?"

She waved it in front of me. "See. This number here." She pointed to a machine-inked four-digit number in the right hand corner. "It must be numbered for a reason, and I thought you should know about it. Maybe something fishy is going on, or else somebody's really unorganized. I just wanted to help." With that, she turned and marched out, those in line pressing back against the door frame to let her pass.

The administrator initialed the notice. She handed it to the union representative who added her initials and put it in a box on the floor.

Tim walked out with me when our shift was over. We were both quiet until we reached our cars. I turned to him. "Whatever happens, Tim, I just want you to know, I hope we can still work together."

He popped the lock on his Xterra and stood looking at it. The bruise on his face was a smudge of gray. He'd recently had his hair cut; a narrow light strip showed above his tan.

"Soon it'll be over," I went on. "And regardless, I'll abide by the rules and work with the union."

"If we get a union," he said. He opened the door.

The latest polls had the union and the hospital tied.

"You hear about her latest stunt? Judyth's," Tim said. "Yesterday after the surveyors left she called a meeting of RNs, no managers."

"So?"

"On work time. That's not allowed by the NLRB." The National Labor Relations Board. "We can't meet on work time and neither can the hospital."

"Did you go?"

"At the last minute, she cancelled it. I won't quit," Tim said, sliding into his Xterra. "How would I pay for this?" he added, patting the door frame. He squealed around the corner and down the ramp.

I didn't know if he meant he wouldn't quit fighting or wouldn't quit his job. I hoped the latter.

I decided to go back into the hospital. Paperwork had been piling up all week, and I had a phone call I needed to make.

Peggy stood at the information desk using the phone. She hung up with a sour look as I approached.

"Something wrong?"

"My car. It won't start."

"Can I help?"

"Thanks, but no. My brother's on his way."

"Peggy, I have to tell you about Lisa."

"I already know." She stared out the entrance, unseeing. "Didn't I tell you?" She left, her slow steps echoing down the eerily-silent hall.

Suddenly I was exhausted. But there was one thing I wanted to check before I left.

I wanted to see if someone could get in or out of ICU without walking through the main doors. The hallway that circled around the rooms of intensive care, originally intended for fire safety, also allowed family members entry to patients' rooms without going through the central part of the unit. Such a design kept them from getting in our way, especially now, when we were always in a hurry. But after the previous murder, administration had decided the doors should be kept locked from both sides.

Most of the doors in the hospital shut automatically in case of fire, in order to prevent a blaze from spreading. But only the ICU doors were locked. If fire broke out in ICU and we couldn't escape through the main doors, we and our patients would be trapped inside. I had argued with Judyth, but it hadn't changed her mind. They had to decide what was the greater risk, and administration had opted to keep strangers out and us locked in. But maybe they'd changed their mind for some cost-cutting reason. We were all so busy we'd never notice if a door had been unlocked, inadvertently or not.

After checking with Jessie that everything was quiet in ICU, I stepped into our one empty room and made my way to the fire door. It was locked. I went back out of the unit and around to the outside and checked all the doors. Locked. No one could have entered ICU this way.

Chapter 24

Saturday, 18 August, 1745

I DECIDED TO keep my appointment at the spa. Actually I had forgotten I'd scheduled it until I got home and listened to the message reminding me. My staff had bought me the gift certificate for my birthday in July, and Serena kept asking me if I'd gone yet. Finally, I had set it up several weeks ago, and then forgotten about it.

By the time I found the salon in far West County—I didn't know Olive Boulevard became Clarkson Road out west—I was frazzled enough to be glad I was about to have a massage.

The receptionist offered me some herbal tea while I waited. I was alone in the reception area, which was momentarily quiet. Yellow roses spilled out of a vase, releasing a faint floral scent. I sipped my tea, let my eyes soften, and took some long, slow breaths.

The receptionist called my name and the masseuse, whose name tag read "Jan," led me into a room with a sheet-covered table, told me to undress and lie face down with the sheet over me while she waited outside.

Waiting for her return, I let myself relax. A side table held a cluster of votive candles, a trickling table-top waterfall, and a collection of lotions and oils. New Age music played in the background. I had almost drifted off to sleep when she came back in.

Jan asked if I was comfortable and if anything in particular bothered me. I quelled the urge to tell her—I was certain she didn't want to know my real troubles—and pointed to my neck and shoulders.

She warmed some aromatic oils in her hands, and I took a deep breath, letting the scent surround me. She pressed and pulled with sure, strong strokes, and I felt myself relaxing into the movement she made of my body. Suddenly, I had an overwhelming urge to cry. Feelings rushed over me in waves and sadness leaked out in my tears. She stopped, gave me some tissues and said she'd be back in a few minutes.

By the time she returned, I felt more peaceful than I had in days. I gave into her soothing ministrations, my body relaxed, and I floated somewhere warm and comforting. She whispered for me to turn over, and I settled back into my reverie as she rotated my ankles, pressing hard on the balls of my feet.

Then it hit me. I jerked my leg free but Jan pressed it back down and continued massaging up my leg. I knew what Lisa had meant. I tried to relax again but my mind was reeling. Jan seemed to take forever, massaging each arm in turn and moving to my head. Her fingers dug into my scalp and I felt as if I were pinned to the table like a butterfly on a mat.

What to do? How could I find out for sure?

Jan slid her hands down to my neck, squeezing taut muscles with practiced precision. Positioning her fingers at the base of my skull, she pulled my neck into alignment. My vertebrae clicked into place with a gentle pop, the pieces in my mind tumbling into position as perfectly as my spine.

The room was quiet; she was gone. I sat up quickly, feeling dizzy, forgetting she had told me to raise up slowly. I sat still for a moment, then dressed and hurried out. I knew what I had to do.

Chapter 25

Sunday, 19 August, 0556

IT WAS ALMOST six when I pulled up in front of Bart's house and parked in the shade of a tree. The sun had poked through the leaves of the overhanging branches and a gentle breeze sent droplets of dew plopping onto the hood of my car. I sat for a few moments while Black Beauty's engine cooled down and I screwed up my courage. Bart had insisted on working last night, Jessie had told me. He said he'd rather keep busy. I knew I had until 7:30, at least, and probably longer until he had finished charting and drove home.

A woman dressed in a halter, shorts and clogs walked a miniature white poodle down the street away from me, and a man came out in his boxer shorts and bare feet to grab the Sunday paper off his lawn before hurrying back inside.

I got out of the car cautiously and tried to shut the door without making noise, but it wouldn't catch. I pulled it open and slammed it, cringing at the noise it made. But no one came out to see what it was. Just act normal, I told myself. A small giggle bubbled up but I swallowed it. I needed to keep my wits about me. It wasn't every day that I broke into someone's house. I had found the key in my lab coat pocket this morning and that had cinched it.

Lisa had used a syringe to take the drug. That much I knew because it had been laying on the floor beside her. And she would have drawn it up from a vial, a vial that had been nowhere in sight when I'd found her! That's what I had realized on the massage table. It had been years since I'd seen morphine in a vial instead of a Tubex. When Lisa had said, "It's in the bag," she must have meant her drugs but, if so, where was the vial she'd used? And where did she get it?

Inside, the house was silent. And empty. A fine dusting of black fingerprint powder covered most surfaces. I peeked out the front window just to be sure no one had noticed me, but only a lone bicycle rider pedaled by.

I started in the living room, sliding the sofa out from the wall and reaching along the baseboard. Nothing there. Then I went from chair to chair, moving each one aside, searching under and around them, and replacing them in the same spot so that the dents in the carpet lined up with the legs. I reached around the legs of the three side tables in the room but I found only some dust balls caught in the fold of the carpet.

The dining room was next but there was nothing in it except some packed boxes and a stack of books. No bag and no vial anywhere.

In the only bedroom a stack of uniform scrubs rested on a cedar chest and on the dresser were a few odds and ends that looked like the detritus from someone's pocket or purse, and a woman's wallet. I hesitated a moment. The vial wasn't in the wallet, that much was certain. I decided to take a quick peek inside. It was disappointingly ordinary, containing not much more than a driver's license and nursing licenses.

I sifted through the mail sitting on the dresser. There was a letter to Lisa from the Missouri State Board of Nursing congratulating her on receiving her license to practice nursing in Missouri. The rest was junk mail advertising continuing education programs for nurses, already-approved credit cards, and an introductory subscription to a local magazine.

I checked my watch. I had been in the house for almost thirty minutes. And I hadn't checked the bathroom or kitchen yet.

Neither the medicine cabinet nor the linen closet contained anything stronger than aspirin. Only a few dishes, some mismatched silverware, and two battered aluminum pans were in the kitchen cabinets. Some packaged food was stored in the pantry along with a few cans of soup and a six-pack of Diet Coke. The milk in the refrigerator looked fresh but it was the only food that did; a ripe banana was a squishy brown and a cut lemon had grown mold.

What could she have done with the vial? She had to have drawn up the syringe from some container and it had to be somewhere.

I went back through the house looking for wastebaskets. There were only two. The one in the bathroom held a crumpled tissue but it wasn't hiding anything. A fresh plastic bag was in the trash can in the kitchen. I pulled it out and dumped the can upside down. Nothing.

I took one last look around the house, nervous shivers creeping up my neck as I realized I'd been inside for nearly an hour. Bart would be home from work any time now. I locked the door behind me, scurried out the door, and down the sidewalk toward my car.

"Hello there!"

I jerked around. Bart's neighbor stood on her front porch holding on a broom.

"Is he doing okay?" she asked, giving each step a swipe with her broom as she came down the stairs. "I haven't seen him since last night. Poor thing. He looked a mess then." She shook her head. "She was so young. I can't imagine why she'd—"

"I think he's doing as well as can be expected," I said when I'd gathered my wits about me. "I'm sorry, I'm in a hurry." My hand shook as I unlocked the car door. I gave her a quick wave as I pulled away.

Chapter 26

SUNDAY, 19 AUGUST, 0726 HOURS

"MY GOD, GIRL, what'd you think you were doing?" BJ asked. "What if he'd come home?"

We'd met at Uncle Bob's Pancake House after I'd awakened her.

"Bart was at work. And," I said, "I still had the key."

"What if someone saw you and called the cops?"

"I didn't think about that," I replied.

"You sure didn't," BJ said, as a waitress dropped off our menus and hurried away.

BJ squinted at me. "Just what do you think Rosan would have thought then?" When I didn't answer she went on. "That you had something to hide, at the least, or that you'd killed the girl—or driven her to it—at the worst. What were you thinking?" she asked, slapping her menu on the table. "And I put myself on the line for you!"

Two women at the next table looked over at us.

I leaned forward and spoke softly. "BJ, I'm sorry, I just didn't think."

BJ's eyes held their fix on me, and I knew how suspects felt when she had them in her sights. "You're just lucky I didn't let Rosan take you down to headquarters in a cop car. You know what that's like?"

Mute, I shook my head.

"You'd have been locked in the back in the cage. It'd give you a taste of what jail is like."

"Someone did see me," I admitted. "Bart's neighbor, the one I met last night."

BJ laid her menu aside and considered me. Finally she said, "You're lucky she knew who you were. Who did you think you were, some hotshot detective?"

"Remember when you'd told me about a crime scene? How thorough they are? What all they look for?"

"Like that made you an investigator. Cops go to school to learn how to do it and then they work with experienced officers, sometimes for years."

"I figured out she meant her drugs were in the bag when she called me. If that was so, where was the bag? Or the vial of morphine? She had to draw it up from something. Where was it? If she had killed herself, wouldn't the vial still be there?"

"Why do you care where it is or what she took? What difference does it make now?"

"I'm worried about where she got it. She'd been fired so she didn't have access to drugs at the hospital."

"Unless the boyfriend got it for her," BJ said.

"I don't think he would. From what she'd said he was mad about her using, and we saw how angry he could get. I don't see him getting her drugs."

"But what's your point? Why does it matter to you where she got the stuff?"

I chewed my lip. "To tell the truth, BJ, I'm worried that someone else on the staff got it for her. Stole it, maybe."

"Whoa, there, kiddo. That's a different story. Then you've got somebody dealing drugs. Now we're talking prison time, heavy time."

"That's why I have to find out."

The waitress came back for our orders. BJ ordered French toast, and I chose scrambled eggs and a blueberry muffin.

"How do you know the cops don't have it?"

"I didn't see them take it."

"But you were outside. You couldn't see everything with all the people milling around in there."

"What if they missed it?"

"Cops don't miss something like that. A woman overdoses and they're going to look for a container of some kind. The first place they'd check would be the garbage," BJ said as the waitress returned to pour coffee for both of us, leaving a warming pot on the table.

"I don't see her putting it in the trash before shooting up."

BJ shoved the coffee pot aside and said, "I'll tell you what. If it will make you feel any better, I'll check with headquarters to see if they bagged anything like that. If they did, I'm sure it's been analyzed—or will be soon."

"It was just. . . . They were so nonchalant Friday night, so sure it was suicide."

"Look. The girl killed herself. Maybe on purpose, maybe she didn't mean to. We got too many others that leave no doubt they were murdered. One they're working on right now—man stabbed in the back—he sure as hell didn't do that to himself."

The waitress refilled our water glasses and hurried away.

"Just what'd you think you'd find? What *did* you find?" she asked.

I didn't answer.

"Of course you didn't. What if you had found something? We couldn't have used it, and you'd have been charged with B and E—breaking and entering," she explained, "and you could be charged with theft if you took anything."

"I left everything just as I found it."

"Along with your fingerprints."

I pulled myself up. "I wore gloves. I brought them from the hospital."

"How about footprints? Fibers from your clothes? Dust off your shoes? A strand of hair?"

"Oh."

"Well, don't worry. It's not a crime scene or they wouldn't have let Bart stay there," she admitted.

"I found her wallet."

"I hope to god you left it there."

"I did.

"And?"

"A few bucks, Kentucky driver's license, two nursing licenses."

"Two?"

"Nurses have to have a license for every state they work in."

"So you found diddly," she said, summing up my investigative career.

Chapter 27

Sunday, 19 August, 2245 Hours

THIS TIME I thought ahead. If Lisa had taken her drug from the hospital, she would have tossed it in the trash.

After BJ's lecture about breaking into Bart's house, I'd run some long-delayed errands, then gone home to watch the ballgame. I had fallen asleep on the sofa by the third inning, only waking up in time to hear the commentators rehash the highlights. I couldn't stop thinking about the vial, though, and I had decided to try one more time to find it.

It was nearly eleven when I parked on a side street across from the alley that ran behind Bart's house. The city of St. Louis places dumpsters in the alleys about every three houses apart. I figured Bart would've thrown his trash in one of the two that were closest to his house. I had waited until after he would have left for work; I didn't want to run into him tossing garbage at the last moment.

I pulled a full plastic bag from my trunk and made my way up the alley. Street lights illuminated the narrow passageway. Ambient sounds of traffic were muffled in the hot, still air. A dog barked somewhere ahead and a mother shooed a couple of young children inside as I passed. The next yard smelled of freshly-mowed grass. A whippoorwill complained and then quieted. The first dumpster was bulging with bags, debris strung out over the edge; it reeked of rotting meat, greasy food wrappers, and dog poop. I almost turned back.

Then I did what nurses always do when faced with bad odors—I breathed through my mouth—and pulled on latex gloves. I yanked out a white bag about the size of the one I'd seen in Bart's kitchen, untied it, and clicked on the penlight I'd brought. Milk cartons, soda cans, egg shells, and a jumble of chicken bones, but no medicine vial. The next bag was stuck under the lid but I brought it down with a jerk, its contents spilling out on my head. I jumped back, scraping potato peelings and coffee grounds off my T-shirt. Tomato sauce plastered my nose and I wiped it off with a slightly-soiled paper towel and then sorted through the mess on the ground with a stick. Thinking a vial could have rolled away, I clicked on my flashlight and searched along the fence where grass was tangled in the chain link.

A light flashed on above me and I was caught in the proverbial spotlight. Had I been thinking clearly, I'd have done just what I did: stay just where I was, crouched down behind the fence. As it was, I stayed there because I was too paralyzed to move.

"Anyone there?" yelled a man I could see through the web of aluminum and weeds. He waited. My legs began to cramp and sweat rolled down under my arms. Something scurried behind me and I almost jumped up. Finally the door shut but the light stayed on. I looked around, didn't see anyone, and slowly rose to a standing position, my knees creaking loudly. Casually, I walked down the alley. When I got to the next dumpster, I raised the lid and tossed my own bag of trash over the edge, hearing the soft plop as it landed. I peeled back my gloves and tossed them in on top of the trash. I strolled to the end of the street, saying a prayer that Black Beauty wouldn't fail me tonight. She didn't.

Even though I hadn't found the vial, at least the bag of dope from Huey's girlfriend was gone. It had gone into the dumpster behind Bart's, buried appropriately in grass clippings.

Chapter 28

Monday, 20 August, 0627 Hours

Judyth smiled as she greeted the management staff straggling through the door. She'd called the meeting for 6:30—before our shift began—and ordered us not to clock in until afterward, an action that was surely illegal. More than that, now I'd have to take vacation time to double back to the main police station downtown to have my fingerprints taken when I could have done it on my way in.

"I know everyone wants to know what Joint Commission said." Judyth looked around to be sure she had our attention. "We have another six months. Not the best report. They were impressed by how much we'd done in such a short time. Especially with all the new hires I've added."

Someone asked if they'd be back.

"No. We just have to submit a written report in another six months with an update on our staffing. If that is satisfactory, we're approved for the full four years," Judyth explained.

Another manager asked about the union vote. It was being tallied today, she told us. We'd have the results tomorrow.

I hurried out to my car for the drive down to police headquarters at Clark and Fourth streets. After several laps around the block without finding a parking spot, I gave in, pulled into a lot, and paid the four dollars.

The building was old but it had a solidness about it that reflected the city's longevity and its permanence. I made my way up the steps with more than a little trepidation. An officer at the information desk told me the fingerprint section was upstairs on the fifth floor. I joined a group waiting for the elevator. After my excursions into what BJ had called "breaking and entering," and with my drug test results still unknown, the last thing I wanted was to have my fingerprints on file somewhere. But BJ had bet her job on my coming in this morning. Now, thanks to Judyth, I was late.

The officer behind the mesh-laced glass window told me to have a seat until they called me. The room was furnished with blond, 60s-era furniture that looked as if it had been there since then. A coffee table in front of a settee was scarred from cigarette burns and coffee cups; several names and messages had been carved into the wood. The room smelled of stale smoke, Pine-sol, and sweat.

Two women sat next to each other on pink plastic chairs to the side of the settee. I chose a straight-back chair opposite them and picked up a well-thumbed garden magazine. It was dated last year.

One of the woman, who looked about thirty but was probably younger, stared at the floor, her shoulders slumped forward and her hands gripped together between her legs. The other woman—she looked more like a teenager than an adult—bounced a baby boy on her lap and attempted unsuccessfully to occupy him with a set a keys. The baby squirmed around on his mother's lap until she finally let him down on the floor, when he promptly crawled toward the door. With a heavy sigh, she grabbed him up and put him back on her lap. She dug through a torn diaper bag while the baby tried to pull on her hair. She shook her hair loose and plopped a bottle in the baby's mouth. His sucking was the only sound in the room.

The officer knocked on the glass. "Hursch," he yelled through the opening.

The older woman stood and shuffled over to the window. The officer said something to her and motioned her to a door that he then buzzed her through.

The baby had finished his bottle and lay back on his mother's arm, his eyes drooping shut.

"Cute baby," I said to her.

She gave me a shy smile, her hair dropping forward as she ducked her head.

Another officer came in and leaned into the opening in the window.

"How's it going?" he asked his colleague behind the glass.

"The usual," was the answer. "Lots of perps. None of them did a thing."

They both laughed.

"I tell you about my daughter?" the officer asked, raising his voice and speaking to the room.

His co-worker said something I couldn't hear.

"I told that boyfriend of hers he better not forget I'm a cop," he said with a laugh, checking to see if we'd heard him.

I studied my magazine until he had left.

"You here for somebody?" the young mother asked me.

"I just need to have my fingerprints taken." I looked at the clock on the wall. I had been sitting here for twenty minutes. Damn. They wanted me down here early and now they were keeping me waiting. I needed to get back to work. I tossed the magazine on the table. "You?" I asked the girl.

She frowned. "For my boyfriend. To bail him out." She shifted the baby on her arm. His eyes fluttered for a moment but he didn't wake up. "Again," she added.

"Everhardt," the officer yelled.

The process didn't take long. BJ had told me that the police department didn't use ink to take fingerprints. Instead they use a computer program called Lifescan. After they've been arrested, suspects put their hands flat on the horizontal screen and it records their fingerprints.

"Not in this situation," the female officer said after I'd asked her about it. "We only use it for perpetrators. Too expensive to use for people who need their prints taken for work or, like in your case, to rule you out at a crime scene," she said as she rolled my fingers, one at a time, on an ink pad and transferred the print onto a card identified for each finger and thumb. When she had finished she handed me a jar of goop and assured me it would take the ink off. Still, I stopped in the restroom and scrubbed my hands as if I were prepping for surgery.

BACK IN MY office I sat staring at the sixty-two unanswered e-mail messages and the mountain of mail overflowing the inbox on my desk.

"You busy?" Serena asked, poking her head around the corner.

"Come on in." I told her, clicking my computer to standby.

She plopped down in the chair next to my desk. "Can I ask you something if you promise not to tell anyone? Not anyone."

"I can't do that, Serena. Not if it's something I have to pass on."

"What would that be?" She played with a tuft of straw-like hair, newly-dyed a darker red.

"If someone's in danger, for example." I squinted at her. "Do you know something about Huey's death?"

"No. No. Nothing like that. It's personal."

"You'll have to trust me if you want to tell me. If I think I have to tell someone, I will."

She seemed to make up her mind. "You know I asked you about the license, nursing license."

"Go on."

"I don't know if you know this, but the FBI does a background check on everyone applying for a license. We have to be fingerprinted and everything."

I held my hands still on my lap, pressing curled fingers into my legs. "Really." I said, finally. "They didn't used to."

"They do now. It asks if you've ever been arrested."

"I think they want to know if you've ever been convicted."

"That's what they used to ask. Now you have to say if you've even been arrested."

I waited, dreading what probably was coming.

"I was only fifteen," she began, her hands twisting a tattered tissue in her lap. "I didn't know he had pot on him. But they didn't believe me."

"What happened?"

"Nothing, really. They told Mom to keep me away from him." A quick, cute smile. "You want to ask me if I did it, too?" When I didn't answer, she went on. "I tried it once but it just brought me down. I didn't like the feeling."

"What's this about, Serena? How can I help you?"

"The application. For my license." She turned away and swallowed. "And then the drugs here went missing."

"But you can't access the cabinet where the drugs are kept, so you wouldn't be a suspect. Besides, we know who did that."

"You do? Who?"

"That's not the point. I don't think the state board cares about what you did when you were fifteen. You weren't convicted of anything."

"They ask if you've been *arrested*, Monika. And I was." She bit her lip.

"But didn't they let you go?"

"Uh huh."

"Besides, you were a juvenile. I don't think that counts."

"It doesn't say that. Monika, I don't know what to do. I really want to be a

nurse. . . ."

"I doubt this will keep you from getting a license."

"What happens if I don't tell them about it? Will they find out?"

"You can't lie on something like this. You'd be in a lot worse trouble if they found out later."

"I can't see how they'd find out. Juvenile records are sealed. No one can get them, my lawyer said."

"Serena, you're going to have a long career in nursing. You don't want to do anything to jeopardize that." I smiled at her. "You're going to be an excellent nurse. You never know what might happen later."

"Umm." She didn't look convinced.

"You know what would be the worst of it?"

She looked at me expectantly.

"You'd have it hanging over you all your career. You'd always be worried about someone finding out."

"I hadn't thought of that."

"Tell you what. I know someone at the state board. Why don't I call and ask her about it?"

"No, no, don't tell!" She jumped up. "Please!"

"I won't tell her who. I'll just ask her what happens if someone who was never convicted admits to having been arrested and lists it on the application. Is that okay?"

"All right. Just don't tell her my name. Please," she begged with a quick look back as she went out the door.

"She probably won't have a problem," Karla began, answering my question about Serena. "But I don't speak for the board, you know." Karla and I had gone to nursing school together, and I'd found her decision to leave clinical practice to work in a state office puzzling.

"Of course she has to tell the truth," Karla went on. "Then she'll have to attach a letter explaining her answer. That's all in the instructions," Karla said, sounding as if she'd given these directions many times. "Then the board will decide whether or not it's been resolved, and whether or not they want to grant her a license."

"And when they see it's ancient history and she was never convicted, then she's in the clear?"

"Mostly. They'll keep the letter on file. In case something happens in the future."

So it would hang over her forever, after all.

"How's things with you, Monika? Still running ICU at St. T's?"

"Umm," I said. "Maybe you can tell me what to do about this, if it's something I should report."

"About the nursing student?" she asked.

"No," I said. "About another matter."

I told her about Bart not doing a full code on Mr. Guardino.

"That sounds like an in-house discipline issue, but you'd better report it anyway."

"He's in grad school and I'd hate to lose him."

"He'd probably just receive a reprimand, depending on what the investigators find out."

"So there has to be an investigation?"

"It might be done by mail. In any case, I recommend that you report it."

"My boss doesn't want to."

"He doesn't have any choice."

"She. The chief nurse."

"Uh oh."

"What?"

"It's her license, too. Yours and hers. A violation of the nurse practice act, Missouri statute 335.066. If you don't report and something else happens, you're both in trouble. And the hospital's certification with the state is in jeopardy, too."

"That sounds a little excessive. The patient wasn't expected to survive."

"Well, that's my recommendation."

"Okay," I said with a sigh. "What do I do to report him?"

"You make a formal complaint."

"Will this do? Can I tell you?"

"It has to be in writing. I'd do it right away, if I were you. Who is it?"

I gave her Bart's name.

"That name doesn't ring a bell. But that's not surprising. There are more than twenty-five thousand nurses in Missouri."

I hung up, sorry that I had told her about Bart, especially now right after Lisa's death.

The phone rang.

"They've got it," BJ said, "that container you were looking for." Traffic sounded in the background.

"Lisa's?"

A horn honked and BJ mumbled something under her breath. "Yeah," she said finally. "It was labeled 'morphine.' They're testing it to make sure."

"What about fingerprints? Are they checking to see whose prints are on the vial?"

"That's routine in suspected suicides."

Tires squealed.

"Son of a bitch!" BJ blurted out. Then she said, "Sorry, someone just cut me off. Hold on." Her siren screamed and I jerked the phone away from my ear.

A few minutes later she was back.

"Okay," she said, "I got him. I have to go write up this cowboy."

So Lisa had found a vial of morphine. BJ had hung up before I could ask her more about it. Did it have a DEA number on it? Had it come from St. T's?

The phone rang again.

"Your test came back," Max said with studied calmness.

"Test?"

"Drug test."

"And?"

"Just what I thought. You're fine. You're in the clear. It was a false positive."

"With everything else that's been going on, I had forgotten about it. Speaking of that, what about the test for succinylcholine? Have you heard from the lab?"

"They should be done by now. I'll give them a call. But I wouldn't worry, Monika, it's unlikely they'll find anything."

"Max, do you know if we carry vials of morphine, rather than Tubex, anywhere in the hospital?"

"Sure. I think they have some in the ER, and they use it in surgery all the time when they need to draw up extra large doses and need it in a hurry."

"GIVE ME THAT name again. The nurse you told me about," Karla asked when she reached me later.

I told her.

"He's not licensed."

"Of course he is. He's in graduate school, he works here, he's got to be."

"I don't know about the other states, but he's not licensed in Missouri."

"He came here from Kentucky. I'm sure he has a license there. It's where he went to school. Maybe just doesn't have a Missouri one yet."

"I checked the pending applications; it's not there. He hasn't applied for a license. It doesn't matter what he has from any other state. If he's not licensed in Missouri, he's not licensed."

"Karla, that makes no sense. Doesn't everyone take the same exam, regardless of what state they're in?"

"According to the Missouri Nurse Practice Act," she began, sounding more and more like a bureaucrat, "a valid Missouri license is required in order to practice nursing in this state. No excuses."

"Does this complicate the complaint? Should I include it in my report?"

"No use sending a letter now. We can't investigate a nurse who isn't licensed. But, you'd better call your supervisor and your nurse had better get his application in ASAP. You're all violating the law if he's working without a license," she said, a note of satisfaction in her voice.

Why didn't Bart have a nursing license in Missouri? Applying for a license in Missouri when you had a license in another state was relatively simple. And easy to put off when you're busy. I knew about that. I'd neglected to renew my own license—required every two years—until the last minute. Now I was a week past due delivering it to human resources.

INSTEAD OF LUNCH, I had another errand to run. Cat had been lethargic ever since she'd coughed up the plant last week, and the lunch hour was the only time the veterinarian could fit us in. Thankfully, he found nothing wrong with Cat that time wouldn't resolve so I'd dropped her off at home and hurried back again to try to find a parking spot in the garage now crowded with visitors' vehicles. The roof had a few places left and I slid into one of them. I was hurrying toward the elevator when I spotted Noni getting out of her car.

"What are you doing here?" I asked her when she caught up with me.

"I was coming to see you," she said. "About, uh, something I left for Huey."

Uh oh.

"I gave it to the clerk," she said, "the woman at the desk. It was in a bag."

"Huh?"

"It was in a bag," she repeated. Black hair swung loosely around her face.

"What was?"

She looked around and, seeing there was no one nearby, she said, "The joints, marijuana. Do you have it?"

"We got rid of it." I punched the down elevator button.

"You threw it out?"

"Listen, you shouldn't have brought that in here in the first place."

"I know. It's just that I wanted to make him comfortable. He couldn't get any booze and . . . I guess I wasn't thinking very clearly."

"Well, you put me, us, in a difficult position, leaving an illegal substance on the premises."

"I'm sorry," she said, stopping when we reached the elevators. "I wanted to talk to you privately anyway. I've thought a lot about what you said when you came to the Ambassador. I wanted to make sure Huey had died from the cancer." She dabbed at her eyes, careful not to smear her mascara.

I wanted to reassure her, but I couldn't. Not only did we not know why Huey died or if anyone caused his death, I wouldn't be able to say anything even if I knew. She wasn't his next of kin and, with the more-stringent privacy regulations now in force, I couldn't tell her anything.

The elevator doors opened and I stepped inside. "I'm sorry about Huey," I told her. "I really am. I liked him," I added as the door slid shut.

As I walked through the basement tunnel back to the hospital, thoughts twirled in my head. Lisa had said something was "in a bag." Did she know about the pot Noni had left with Ruby? I shook my head to clear it. That makes no sense, I thought, more confused than ever.

"HOPE THIS WON'T take long," Joyce in human resources said, nodding at the clock. "I have to leave for a doctor's appointment."

"Here's my license and I have a question." I'd stopped at her office on my way back to the unit.

She studied my license. "Late, aren't you?" she said as she levered herself up and walked over to the copy machine.

"I checked on one of my nurses," I said, following her. "The state board said he doesn't have a Missouri license. Can you see what you have in your files?"

"Just 'cause someone don't have a license in the file don't mean they don't have one," she said, peering at me above reading glasses. "Just that they forgot to bring it in."

"It's illegal for him to be working here if he doesn't have one."

She handed my license back to me and headed over to a row of filing cabinets along one wall.

"Don't you have them on a computer file?"

She pulled one long drawer out. "Not these, just their employment records. These are copies just like yours."

"But couldn't you scan them in?"

"And just where would I get the money to do that?" she asked, not expecting an answer.

"Mickelson, Bart," she read from a folder she'd pulled out. "Here's a copy of a Kentucky license and a note from the day he was hired that he would apply for a Missouri one immediately."

In earlier times, we would have required the license first—that was the law—but as needy as we were for nurses, I wasn't surprised Judyth had hired him without waiting for the license.

"That's funny," she said.

"What is?"

She went back to her desk and searched through a stack of files. "They asked me to pull this one. She's the one killed herself." She spread a file open on her desk, putting Bart's beside it. "I thought the number looked familiar."

The numbers of Lisa's and Bart's Kentucky licenses were the same except for the last digit. Lisa's ended in a three and Bart's in an eight.

"Probably because their names are so close: Milligan and Mickelson. I'll give him a call right away," she said, closing both files.

All states had reciprocal agreements with each other. Bart only had to fill out the application and pay the fee, and he could have done that immediately. Obviously Judyth hadn't stalled his hire date in order to wait until he had a Missouri license, regardless of what Karla had said about requirements and regulations. But why hadn't he come in with a Missouri license yet? It had been six months.

I HAD STOWED my bag in my desk drawer, locked it and dropped the keys in my lab coat pocket when the phone rang.

"Good, you're back," Max said.

"I'm so far behind—"

"I thought you'd want to know about Mr. Castle."

"Yes?"

"They did find succinylcholine in his blood," Max said, his voice quiet, steady. "Enough to kill him."

My voice caught in my throat.

"What happens next?" I asked finally.

"I call the ME and administration, of course. Someone will contact the police. You were right after all."

"I didn't want to be right. I wanted you to tell me you didn't find anything."

"Believe me, I wish I could."

How could Huey get succinylcholine, a drug that we seldom used in ICU? Where had it come from?

I called Max back. "How did he get it? In his IV line?"

Max laughed.

"I'm glad you can laugh," I snapped.

"Sorry, Monika. I was just picturing him if he got a straight shot of succinylcholine. Every muscle would contract and he'd pop right up. My guess is somehow it got in his IV bag. It had to be a slow infusion or someone would have noticed what was happening to him."

"So what did happen?"

"He had respiratory paralysis, then severe hypoxia set in."

"So," I said, "he suffocated to death."

"Yes."

I let out a breath that I didn't know I'd been holding.

"How much time would it take?"

"Hmm. With his fatty liver, the muscle paralysis would be prolonged, but I couldn't say how long it would be until he couldn't breathe at all."

"Would he be aware of what was happening?"

"I'm sure of it. Not an easy death, that's for certain."

"But wait, didn't you say succinylcholine is unstable in solution? Huey had a TPN bag hanging, a high concentration of glucose, wouldn't that affect the potency? Wouldn't it break down pretty quickly?"

"Not right away, it wouldn't, and I think it would hold up okay. They use a variety of mixtures in surgery and it still works. You say he had a central line?"

"In the jugular."

"Well, in that case, it'd go pretty quickly. I assume the bag's gone."

"It went out the day he died."

"Anyway, we're out of it now. I've started the legal machinery. They'll be taking over. Let them find out what happened."

I sat staring at the phone and listening to a dial tone.

Someone had deliberately tampered with Huey's IV bag, adding a lethal drug intended to kill him. I couldn't seem to take it all in. Who would do that? And why?

Laura?

Laura had been traumatized after a patient of hers died a few months ago. She'd been hospitalized in the psych ward for a week afterward, but she had been conscientious since she'd come back to work. I felt certain that Laura did not have any reason to kill Huey. She did have the opportunity, though. She'd been caring for Huey that morning, albeit only for a short while. She'd given him morphine—that the ME had confirmed from the first blood test—and hung his IV bag, which apparently contained succinylcholine. So she had the opportunity but no motive. Someone had put it in the bag, though. But who?

Someone knocked on my office door.

"Laura," I said.

She burst into tears.

"Come into my office," I told her, taking her arm.

After I had her settled, a tissue box at the ready, she began. "You can't imagine how awful it is. Locked up like a, a. . . ." She stopped to blow her nose. "I was so scared. I was afraid I'd never get out!" She clasped her trembling hands tightly in her lap.

I pulled the trash can over for her used tissues.

"They might arrest me again, Tim's brother said. Just because they don't have enough to charge me doesn't mean they won't. What am I going to do?" Her normally pale face was flushed. "I'm a nurse, not some criminal. I was only doing my job." She pulled a thin white sweater tightly around her body.

The phone rang but I let my voice mail pick up.

"You know I didn't kill him, don't you, Monika?" she asked, looking at me with tear-filled eyes.

"There's a problem," I said.

She started to interrupt, but I held up my hand.

"They found succinylcholine in Huey's blood. Max says he got it in the IV bag."

"Oh, my god, no!" Her hand shook as she reached up and wiped her hand across her face as if to erase what she'd just heard. "I didn't do it, Monika, you've got to believe me! I wouldn't even know where it's kept, or what to do with it."

"Laura, I'm not accusing you. I'm just telling you what was found. Let's think of how it could have happened."

She nodded and looked up at me, her vision clearing.

"Now, when did you get the bag? Did it look like it had been tampered with in any way?"

"Okay, let me think." She closed her eyes, hands pressed to her cheeks. "First, I checked on Huey. His BP was high and he complained of pain. His morphine syringe was empty so I went in the med room and signed out the morphine.

"That's when I saw the bag," she said, looking up. "It was laying on the counter. Maybe the pharmacy was late in sending it up, or Bart was in a hurry. I checked it carefully. Huey's name was on it, I remember that specifically because it was the only one there. I carried it back out with the morphine. Huey's bag was nearly empty so I changed it. Bart had signed off that he'd flushed the port, and I just assumed he hadn't had time to change the bag."

She sat back in the chair and her arms dropped to her lap. "How could this have happened, Monika? Are you sure they didn't make a mistake in the lab? It just doesn't make sense."

"It happened, though, and Max is certain the results are correct."

"Well, I know I didn't do anything wrong," she said, pushing her chin into the air. "So when can I come back to work?"

"Hmm. That's a problem right now. Judyth has put you on administrative leave until all of this is straightened out."

"What am I supposed to do for money? I've got rent due, school loans. . . ."

"You'll still get your salary, don't worry about that. And I'm sure it won't be long. I hope not, I need you!" I added, smiling. "Why don't you go home and get some rest, and I'm sure this will all be over soon."

"I am tired," she admitted. "I just came in to get some things out of my locker."

After she left I got up, went back out to the unit, waved off Ruby's question, and grabbed a Coke out of the refrigerator in the conference room. Back in my office, I locked the door, pulled out the bottom drawer of my desk, and propped my feet on it. The tab on the can gave a reassuring hiss as I folded it back on itself. I took a long drink and let the fizzy bubbles work their way into my brain.

Even though she seemed to be the most likely suspect, I just couldn't see Laura killing Huey. She lacked the initiative and the cunning to do anything so devious. She had enough trouble just following her patients' care plans. How could she devise and carry out a scheme that demanded such resourcefulness and nerve? No, I just didn't see her doing it.

Had it not been for Ruby's insistence that she kept Lisa out of the med room, I would have suspected Lisa, although what her motive could have been I couldn't imagine.

Noni had been a surgical tech, she'd told me. She most likely knew what succinylcholine was and what it would do. But how would she know where it was kept? Even if she found it, how could she get into the unit without being seen? And the most important question, why would she want to kill him?

Then it must have been someone on the staff. That seemed the only logical conclusion. Even if they had never worked in surgery, everyone had been to the adjacent supply room for scrubs, and anyone could see the med cabinet with its key in the lock. It must have been someone who knew what succinylcholine would do. And someone who would have had a reason to want Huey dead.

Tim and Jessie had known Huey when he'd been hospitalized a few months ago when he'd hemorrhaged in a parking lot close to St. T's. I couldn't see any connection between Huey and either of them. They were both experienced, competent nurses. By no stretch of the imagination could I think that Tim would harm a patient just because he was fighting with administration. He just wanted better care for patients and better treatment for nurses. Who could argue with that?

Serena's questions about the licensure application troubled me, but only because I was worried about her being eligible to sit for the exam, not because I thought she'd killed Huey. Her brush with the law had been when she was a juvenile; I didn't think she was the criminal type. And she, like Tim and the others, didn't know Huey and wouldn't have any reason to harm him.

I tossed the empty can in the trash and stretched my arms up over my head. I grabbed an elbow and pulled it across my back, doing the same with the other one. My neck still felt tight so I swung my head around in half circles.

Something was wiggling around the edges of my mind but I couldn't get to it. Something I could almost remember.

I closed my eyes, letting my arms drop into my lap. I took a breath and let my mind drift. Maybe if I didn't try. . . .

I rolled my shoulders several times and the vertebrae in my neck shifted.

The bag! Now I remembered what it was about Huey's bag that had kept troubling me! The foil covering on one of the ports on his IV line had been removed and its stopper had been discolored, which wouldn't have been unusual if the bag had been in use for some time. But it had been a *new* bag. The foil covering should have been intact, keeping the stopper sterile.

That's where the succinylcholine had been injected, purposely, to end Huey's life in a most painful way.

Only one person could have done it.

Bart.

Bart had access to all kinds of paralytic agents in the OR, including succinylcholine, commonly used. It would have been easy for him to pocket a vial and then mix it into Huey's IV bag right before the end of his shift. He must have left the bag on the counter for Laura to hang. That way, in the unlikely event that anyone would test Huey's blood for succinylcholine and discover its presence, Laura would be the most obvious suspect, especially because she had abandoned a former patient and she was still on probation with the state licensing board.

And Lisa had been there. She had seen him do it! That's what she'd been trying to tell me!

I dialed BJ's cell phone. Her voice mail picked up.

"BJ, listen. I'm at the hospital. I know what happened! Bart did it! I don't know why, but it was Bart. I need you to—"

"Your time is up," a robotic operator on BJ's phone intoned.

"Damn." I slammed the phone down.

I looked up. Bart stood outside my door. A smile spread slowly across his face. He walked away and I dialed BJ again. Her cell phone voice mail picked up. I left a message: "It's Monika! I need you!" Then I called the station. "I need to talk to BJ Nieswander, now. It's an emergency."

"Okay, ma'am, just a minute please."

I waited while "Meet me in St. Louis" played in the background. I stood up and stretched the phone out, trying to see if Bart was still outside my office. Finally a voice came on the phone. "Hello, this is Officer Nieswander—"

"BJ," I said, "listen—"

But her voice kept going, it was her voice mail at the station. I pressed "O" and got a recording. "Just a minute and we'll connect you to the operator." I waited, the phone clamped to my ear until a voice answered, "This is the St. Louis City Police Department. All operators are busy now, but if you'll wait on the line, the next available operator will take your call."

"Damn!" I slammed the phone down and promptly picked it back up. I punched in the number again. This time the operator answered, and I asked her to page BJ.

Ruby stuck her head in the door. "Phone for you," she said, but I waved her off. The line clicked and BJ's voice mail came on again. I hung up and dialed her cell. Her voice mail picked up again and I left another message, "Call me!"

Panic fluttered up from my stomach into my chest, but I pushed it down. I had to think what to do. Would anyone in our security office do anything? They probably wouldn't believe me and even if they did, I doubted they'd stop Bart. I had to find BJ.

I grabbed my bag, tossed my cell phone and keys into it, and dashed out. The strap of my bag caught in the door as I slammed it shut. The door locked automatically. Shit! The strap was tangled in the door, the bag hanging on the outside. I took a breath. I squashed my fingers together and squeezed them between the door knob and the opening to my bag, which in my hurry I had not zipped shut. I could just snag the key ring. I wiggled it out, unlocked the door, and pulled the strap free.

Ruby called out to me but I ignored her. I heard my name over the paging system, but all I could think about was how I had to get to the police station and tell BJ. Or Rosan. I should have called her, but I wanted to get out of there and away from Bart. Who knew what he was capable of doing.

I didn't wait for the elevator but ran down the four floors to the lobby entrance where I stopped to take a breath. I pulled my phone out and tried BJ again. This time the automated voice told me I couldn't leave a message because BJ's voice mailbox was full.

I took the stairs down to the basement tunnel that snaked under the street to the garage. I reached the door just as it opened. Bart stepped aside and waved me through.

I tried to catch my breath.

Bart smiled, his handsome face calm and collected. "So you found out, didn't you?" he asked. He stood with his legs spread, hands in his lab coat pockets.

I turned back with a quick move, but Bart grabbed my arm. "I was afraid you'd figure it out somehow." Bart whipped a syringe out of his lab coat pocket, put the needle cap in his mouth, pulled the syringe away from his face with practiced skill, and spit the cap out. It bounced away on the tile floor.

"Put that thing away," I demanded, trying to sound stern. But the quiver in my voice betrayed me. "Or I'll call security," I added with more force.

With a lunge Bart shoved me back and slammed my head against the wall. Waves of dizziness washed over me. When my vision cleared, Bart had his arm across my chest, pinning me to the wall. My arms flapped uselessly as I struggled to get free.

Where was everyone? Why didn't someone come along?

"Ever since I got here, you've been out to get me. What's the matter, don't you like men?" He snickered. "Want to know what's in this?" Bart asked, his voice sly.

I felt a tiny prick on my neck.

"Succinylcholine."

My knees buckled.

Bart jerked me back up and shoved me into the wall.

The drug wouldn't kill me immediately unless he hit an artery. I'd be paralyzed and awake until the drug reached my respiratory muscles.

Then I would no longer be able to take in even a single breath. It would be a while before I'd lose consciousness.

I stood completely still, barely breathing.

"You told the cops what Lisa said about the bag. They thought it was just another junkie off in la-la land."

I took a cautious breath and very deliberately pushed my fear away.

"But you put it together. Who was it you told on the phone?" He pushed his arm into my neck.

I gagged.

"What'd Huey do to you?" I choked out.

"Him," he said with a small shrug. "He threatened to tell Guardino's family that I killed him. It wasn't true, but we made a deal anyway. He wanted more drugs so I played along for a while. But after I learned who the Guardinos were. . . . Well, let's just say he got his drugs all right. And now he's silent." Bart shoved his face close to mine.

I had to keep him talking; someone was bound to come along soon.

"Where do you want it, bitch? In your neck, straight into the carotid? No, that'd be too quick. How about your butt?" He twisted me around by my shoulders and shoved my face against the wall, the tile cold on my cheek.

The door at the other end of the tunnel swished open. I heard hard-soled shoes striding purposely toward us. Bart glanced toward the sound and his arm loosened slightly on my back. I twisted out of his grasp, stumbling as I turned. But I righted myself and ran toward the footsteps. Bart was close behind me, his rubber soles squishing. I rounded a curve and slammed into Pete, the night guard. His eyes on Bart, Pete pushed me aside. I fell against the wall and sprawled on the floor.

I sat still, once more holding my breath.

Pete unsnapped his holster and placed his large black hand on the butt of his gun.

Bart looked around like a rabbit caught in the cross-hairs.

"You better give me that." Pete's voice was calm but carried a threat.

A siren screamed in the distance.

Bart looked at the syringe as if he didn't know where it had come from. I thought he was going to drop it, but instead he plunged it into his own groin, going deep; he must have hit the femoral artery. His body arched back, arms flung out as he slammed to the floor, spasms twitched his arms and legs, and he banged his head on the concrete. Then he lay still, staring at the ceiling.

Chapter 29

Wednesday, 22 August, 1830 Hours

I slept most of the next day. Judyth called in the late afternoon to tell me that they'd inventoried the OR supply cabinet, which was supposed to be done weekly when new supplies were ordered. Because the staff had been constantly in a rush they had just looked to see what need restocking and ordered that. A complete inventory hadn't been done in months. Several vials of succinylcholine were missing. Also, Joyce in human resources had become suspicious after I talked to her about Bart, Judyth said, and had called the Kentucky Board of Nursing. Bart had never been licensed in Kentucky. And the nurses' votes had been tallied: the union had been defeated, but the count was so close that investigators had been called in for a recount.

It had taken several hours after Bart's death to finish with the hospital administrators and city police. BJ had been among the first to arrive, followed by the crime-scene investigators, police photographer, several other officers, and Detective Rosan. Several administrators had come and gone, Judyth had not been among them. Detective Rosan had taken my statement, and Bart's body had been sent to the morgue. BJ had driven me home in her police car.

When the phone rang again, I was awake, watching the sun play across the ceiling of my bedroom and willing myself to get up. BJ offered to take me to pick up Black Beauty, still in the hospital garage, and drop her at the service station for her needed tune-up. I'd showered the night before, trying to get the stench of hospital and Bart out of my nostrils, and dropped into bed exhausted, but I needed another scrubbing after tossing in sweat-soaked sheets most of the day. I grabbed shorts and T-shirt, shook out my curls, and tossed a helping of Purina Cat Chow in Cat's dish right before BJ honked.

Black Beauty had survived the night away from home, and we dropped her off at the service station. She was his favorite patient Harry, the owner, had often reminded me. I rode with BJ to the Shakes and Steak near my house. I'd walk home from there, I'd told her.

"So he never was a nurse," BJ said when we were seated. A waitress hurried over to take our orders. We had taken the last table, and two groups of customers were waiting at the entrance. I ordered a double steakburger with cheese, fries, and a chocolate shake. BJ had chili and a large Coke.

"He did go to nursing school, though," I said, "but he never graduated."

The waitress returned with BJ's Coke.

"The hospital got a fax from the university, Judyth told me. Seems he flunked out—the critical care course to be specific."

"How'd he do it?" BJ asked, tearing off the wrapper and waving her straw in the air. "How'd he get a license if he didn't have one?" She stabbed the straw into her Coke and drank deeply, stifling a belch.

The waitress brought our food, asking if we needed anything else before she hurried away.

"He somehow copied his girlfriend's license very professionally and put his name on it. I saw a copy in the file. His and Lisa's were just one number different. Hers ended in a three and he must have closed up the loops to make his an eight," I said, squirting ketchup on my French fries. "Apparently they didn't make him provide the original like I had to do. He probably told them he'd misplaced it. He was pretty persuasive when he wanted something." I nibbled on a French fry. "I suspected there was something wrong, maybe an investigation in Kentucky, but I never figured he didn't have a license at all."

"How'd he get into grad school? Didn't they find out he hadn't graduated?" BJ crumbled Saltines on her chili and took a cautious bite. "Hot," she said, fanning her mouth. She downed a quick drink of Coke.

"Judyth told me about that, too. Seems they let him start classes before his transcript arrived." I opened the steakburger and checked: onion, mustard, and pickle, just the way I ordered it. "I think they need students as badly as we need nurses."

"And the hospital took him on with just the Kentucky license, I suppose." BJ blew on a spoonful of chili. "The *fake* Kentucky license," she added.

"That was Judyth's doing. She'd signed the authorization; I saw it in the file."

"His prints were on your package. I just got the news a few hours ago."

"They were?"

"Guess he thought that'd scare you off." BJ tasted her chili.

"Joyce in human resources must have told him I'd been in."

I'd forgotten to turn my cell phone off when we got to the restaurant, and it rang. "Nobody has this number except my staff," I told BJ before I answered it.

When I didn't say anything for a moment, BJ stared at me, her expression questioning.

"Uh, uh," I said. "No, no, I don't, uh, think so." I straightened up. "No, that's not a good idea," I added, my voice firmer. I clicked off.

"Who was that?" BJ asked, smiling.

I shoved my phone down into my bag.

"Hey, I never saw you blush before," she said with a laugh.

"I'm not blushing." I fanned myself with my hand. "It's just hot in here."

"Yeah, right. So, what gives? Who's your mystery caller?"

"Just some lawyer."

"And?"

"Guardino's lawyer."

"What'd he want?" She leaned back and crossed her arms. "I'm waiting."

"Never mind."

My phone rang again. I grabbed it and punched the talk button. "Don't you understand I'm not—"

"Hold on there a minute," Ruby said. "You're gonna' want to know this."

"Sorry, Ruby."

"I'll tell you if you can be quiet a minute."

"Get to the point," I said, my voice drawing stares nearby. I turned away toward the window and lowered my voice. "Why are you calling?"

"She fired. Miss Nose-up-in-the-air."

"Who? What are you talking about?"

"Your Ms. Lancelot. Ms. Judyth Lancelot. I told you about her. Right from the start I knew she was no good. Didn't I tell you?"

"Why'd they fire her?"

"De-verted, is what they say."

"Diverted? What? Drugs? Patients?"

"Money. She took money," she said with a self-satisfied smack.

"Huh?"

"What don't you understand about M-O-N—"

"What money? From where?"

"Here, of course."

"I know, but how?"

"You know all those checks coming in that didn't belong here? Peoples who quit?"

"She took them?"

"She did and she didn't."

"What does that mean?"

BJ put her finger to her lips.

I took my phone outside. "How did she do it?" I asked Ruby.

She told me.

"So she didn't steal any money?"

"De-verted, like I told you. Just the same, they fired her ass."

I went back inside. My food was cold but I didn't care. I'd missed breakfast and lunch. I waved off BJ's questions while I ate, thinking about what Ruby had said. I scarfed the last of my steakburger into my mouth and wiped my hands on a paper napkin.

I told BJ what Judyth had done. "She just didn't do the paperwork to terminate the staff who'd quit. When their checks came in, she kept them so we'd look good when the accreditors arrived. It looked like we had more nurses than we did."

"Think they'll charge her?" BJ asked, brushing cracker crumbs off the front of her T-shirt.

"I doubt it. She didn't cash them, and the hospital wouldn't want the publicity." I slurped the bottom of my shake cup, opened the lid and let the dregs slide down into my mouth. "You'd think they'd have figured it out sooner when those checks weren't cashed, but Ruby said the finance office was short on staff, too."

"So you'll be getting a new boss."

"Maybe. Some hospitals are cutting the chief nurse job."

"How can they do that? Who's in charge of the nurses?"

"They just assign the nursing staff to another administrator, someone who only looks at the bottom line and knows nothing about clinical care."

"Think that will happen at St. T's?" she asked.

"Bound to."

"But you'll stay, won't you? You wouldn't leave St. Teresa's?"

I was spared from answering when the waitress brought our checks and asked if we needed anything else. The crowd at the door had grown.

While we waited in line to pay, I mentioned Huey.

"Pretty stupid to threaten someone who's taking care of you." BJ pulled bills and change out of her pocket. "Once a con, always a con, I guess."

"Bart didn't even have to be there," I said once we were outside. "All he had to do was mix the succinylcholine in the bag and leave. He diverted all suspicion onto Laura that way."

A cop car, idling at the light, suddenly turned on his siren and scooted around the corner in a swirl of flashing lights.

I asked BJ if she knew anything else about Lisa's death. When she'd called earlier she had told me that the cops were looking into Lisa's death now that her boyfriend was known to have committed one murder already.

"She died from the same drug as Castle."

"So he killed her, too," I said, staring out into the street.

"It had traces of suck-see—however you pronounce that—in it."

"So he substituted succinylcholine for her morphine, and ensured her silence as well. She saw him put the drug in Huey's bag, and it makes sense that she didn't want to report her boyfriend. In the end, though, her conscience won out." A whisper of breeze lifted my hair.

"And it cost her," BJ said.

"Her life," I added.

BJ swung into her cruiser and rolled down the window.

I leaned in. "I told you, didn't I?"

The engine purred. "Told me what?"

"A nurse couldn't have done it."

Photo by Pamela Mougin

Eleanor Sullivan was a young widow with five children whose ages ranged from school age to infant when she embarked on a career in nursing.

Entering college and finishing graduate school was a challenge for a young working mother, but Eleanor persevered and became Dean of a major university school of nursing, president of an international nursing organization, author of five award winning textbooks and forty scientific articles.

And now Eleanor has turned her hand to writing mysteries. Deadly Diversion is the second book in a new series about Monika Everhardt and her friend B.J. who were introduced in Twice Dead.

Visit Eleanor's website at www.eleanorsullivan.com

Printed in the United States
106786LV00004B/96/A

9 781591 330769